SHRINKING

A NOVEL BY JACK MCDERMOTT

Peerage Press

First Published in the United States of America by Peerage Press 2016

Peerage Press 46 Hatchville Road , East Falmouth, Cape Cod Ma. 02536

Copyright (c) Jack McDermott 2016

ISBN-13

Softcover: 978-0692403716

This a work of fiction. All names, characters, places, and incidents are used fictitiously, and are products of the author's imagination. Any coincidences and resemblances to actual facts or persons are unintended.

Printed in the United States of America by Create Space an Amazon company

PART One

Sedona Arizona

1

It came out of nowhere.

Two quick seconds, that's all it took. An eye blinked and their disparate paths collided. He should have seen it coming, everyone else did. Just a split in time, two seconds, that he'd relive everyday of his life. One thousand and one, one thousand and two, Bang!

The hairline fracture in their marriage had been visible for months, but Archie, fearing the worst, didn't dare acknowledge its existence. He had hoped it was just a temporary phase, that it would somehow repair itself. So per usual the workaholic's attention remained focused on his practice. He chose to dedicate his waking hours to helping others cope.

But as anyone could have predicted, the fracture had ruptured. Burst wide open beyond repair when he learned the outrageous news that she'd been cheating on him with several of his patients and worse, that her loose lips had broadcast their secrets once she was through with them. It was a seismic rupture. He cracked..she didn't.

The always in control Archimedes Moon wasn't prepared for the shock. He was immobilized.

Ironic, because it was Archie who had counseled others that character was built on how well we handled these major unexpected events in our lives that were often accompanied by great pain. Those sudden occurrences that either chiseled out our strengths or exposed our flaws. Yet now that he was put to the ultimate test, the advice he had so easily dispensed to others he found near impossible to prescribe for himself. For several days he wallowed in self-pity and did what he did best, analyzed the situation ad nauseam.

But in due time when it had at last sunk in that Marlie didn't love him anymore and never would again, a determined Archie managed to salvage some semblance of backbone. The semi-coward snapped out of his *poor me* coma and emerged rebellious, ready to make a stand.

She had created the cataclysmic rift and this time he vowed he'd create the aftershocks not wait for them. He'd deliver, not receive the next blow. Closure was his ultimate cure. Her defiance had backed him into a corner. His dignity had been trampled. His practice ruined, ruined by her selfishness and promiscuity. He needed to grow some balls for once in his life. He couldn't let her continue without paying the ultimate penalty. He wanted his unbearable hurt to backfire on her its evil source. For his own mental survival it was imperative that he act now, tonight.

2

Archie continued his midnight prowl outside their rustic cabin, he'd been waiting almost an hour for the right moment to strike. His legs felt heavy, his hamstrings burnt with tightness. The pitch darkness and frosty November temperatures amplified his discomfort. He was cold, but at least the adrenaline, the rage and the alcohol circulated some warmth within.

Neither the adulterous young Marlie, nor her middle aged companion had seen Archie stalk them to their, no longer secret, rendezvous along Oak Creek. And although Archie hadn't gotten a good look at his rival to know who he was for certain, did it really matter which one of her lovers she was nailing? The important thing was that he now saw for certain with his own eyes, not through the vision of all those hurtful rumors, what he had known in his heart to be true for some time, that there was no room left in her world for him.

Even though he was clueless as to the cabin's layout, he had managed to locate the bedroom, *Marlie's stage.* It was inevitable that the cheaters would end up there and where they would be the most vulnerable. He would trap the wicked spider in the very web that she'd spun. Archie would wait for them to come to him.

"I can't believe it will end this way. She's given me no choice."

He drank a large gulp and the hard liquor traveled unimpeded through his pipes and burned in his empty stomach.

While he lurked his mind wrestled with the uncertainty that he could pull this off and that he could handle the aftermath when he would have to barter his own unused freedom for a life behind bars. He had the weapon, the question was did he have the guts to use it?

No, no, he had a plan damn it and he would carry it out. The serial cheat had stolen what remained of his miserable life. He felt naked, he didn't have another layer of skin to shed. Archie wanted an eye for an eye. "I'm so tired playing the fool."

Pissed, he downed another long swig.

"Our love has been my illusion. She's destroyed me for what? Because I'm a responsible bore dedicated to my work, a nice honest guy and she a decadent night owl? Because I've loved her too much? Are those grounds for obliteration? She called me a friggin' recluse cuz I wouldn't socialize with all those phonies, was that it? Why's my torture such a turn on to her?"

Pools of self-pity welled in his eyes. "They'll be mourned as the sacrificial victims, but society has it all wrong. The emptiness I feel inside, the humiliation and embarrassment I've endured for so long, I'm the asshole ensnared in loneliness' trap. I have no options. I've done no wrong won't they see that it's self-defense? I'm not the predator, I'm the prey."

He downed the last remains of Scotch and managed, with some effort, to steady the empty bottle on top of a medium sized rock. This was by far the most alcohol he'd ever imbibed.

He wobbled over to the woodpile and relieved himself for the third time that night.

After another few minutes Archie succumbed to his discomfort. Their station wagon doors weren't locked so he decided to slip in on the driver's side to get warm. Once seated behind the wheel he leaned over to his right and opened the glovebox. He wanted to know who the hell she was there with. He fumbled through the messy contents but couldn't find the registration. Next he opened the center console, turned down the visors and even reached underneath his seat, but found nothing. There was an open compartment on the side door to his left and when he felt around in it he removed a large, blank note pad. He set the pad down on the passenger seat. He belched, and could taste the hot liquor rise in his throat.

Archie spotted a small cosmetic bag lying on the passenger side floor and he was so drunk that he almost fell over the console stretching to retrieve it. He knew it was Marlie's. He put the red plastic bag on his lap, combed through it for a second and took out one of her lipsticks. He picked up the notepad from the passenger seat, turned the tube to extend the red stick and wrote in large capital letters on the yellow paper. He returned the lipstick to its plastic bag and threw the bag back onto the floor. He ripped off the top piece of paper and when he put the pad back into the side door compartment he could feel that something else was at the bottom. He managed to get hold of it and bring it out. It was a small metal tool kit which contained a screwdriver, a pair of pliers and a couple of crescent wrenches.

It was then that a great idea sprung into his drunken head. He reached down to his left and popped open the car's hood, and exited the vehicle. It was jet black outside so he removed his iPhone from his jacket pocket and, although it took him a while, he was able to locate and turn on the phone's flashlight. He went around to the front of the vehicle, paper in hand.

Five minutes later Archie went back up to the cabin where he would remain motionless for quite awhile. He just stared adrift in his angry stupor. He waffled. He still loved her. His biggest regret was that he wasn't enough for her.

Soon an intra-cranial conversation began. "If I'd paid more attention to her would it have been any different? In hindsight maybe I could've stopped her? Fuck hindsight! All that hindsight teaches are should haves and I told you sos. It's overrated. I knew what she was up to but chose to look the other way.

"Shit, I don't know what fucking end's up. I came here to scare the hell out of them and now I'm coming up with these crazy murder plans. I'm so full of shit. Anyway, whatever I do I know that this unbearable hurt has to be stopped right now. I can't take another..."

Just then Archie was jolted back into the *pain of now* when a sharp beam of light exited the bedroom windows that he faced, and like a disco strobe it flickered on the tree branches that were being whiplashed by the mighty wind. It was a beacon, it commanded him into action.

Archie had been shocked by her betrayals and wanted to return the favor. He was irrational, he hurt real bad. Tonight he hated them all: the phonies and their unsolicited opinions; the braggers and selfie-promoters; the cheaters; the greedy; the racists; the grifters; the cold-hearted; just about everyone, two-timer Marlie in particular.

It's hard to imagine that this exemplary man of good, this trusted and compassionate man who had dedicated most of his thirty-seven years to enhancing the lives of others, and at his own expense, was about to break character and do the unthinkable.

The alcohol had unleashed the courage and the insanity that the vengeful act required. Could he do it? He was hammered and ready to embark on his uncharted mission.

3

Archie crept up to the understated cabin, and for the first time in his life he envied those who believed in the afterlife. "Marlie's so young and vibrant, so passionate, I hope for her sake there's more to come."

He could hear Marlie's coquettish giggles as her lover chased her around the room. Vexed, Archie clutched his bowie knife and tiptoed up to the window on his left. "I can do this."

He angled his head to one side and was able to get a fair view of the room, even though the sheer curtains were pulled. He peered in and hoped that he was wrong.

His mind shouted, "Gideon schizo Grann! How could she do it with that little runt? Maybe I should tell her about his split personalities so she'd at least know which loser she was screwing. The phony bastard changed his name from Gregor Gregoryev for his shitty little radio career. The chameleon would say or do anything to make himself look good. He changes more than Zelig."

Archie watched Marlie dance around the room and perform a slow erotic striptease while Gideon salivated. She took off her shoes and skirt and tossed them, with perfect femininity, onto the wooden floor.

"Real original," Archie fumed.

Gideon's eyes were riveted on Marlie and at one point when he tried to remove his socks and pants, he tripped over himself and fell backwards onto the mattress. He extended his arms and longed for her to join him.

But Marlie ignored him. Instead she tied her long ash blond hair into a perfect bun atop her head and hopped onto the bed. She stood with her legs straddled over him and in the slowest motion she unbuttoned her silk blouse and licked her curvy pink lips. She was the queen of foreplay.

Archie had an ideal view of her from behind and began to get aroused at the site of Marlie's incredible tight, young body, which had been kept from his embraces far too long. He watched her sway in a seductive rhythm as she reached behind herself and undid her black laced bra. She fondled with her perfect breasts and gave a sensuous moan as she pulled on her large nipples while lover boy lie mesmerized on his back, his underwear lifted by his hardened tent pole.

Marlie knelt down, ripped off his white boxers and leaned her mouth over his erection. Gideon was about to explode.

The erotic scene awoke the voyeur's dormant libido. Archie's knife slipped from his grasp and clanged on the near frozen earth. He unzipped his pants and reached inside to join in the ménage à trois. He kept his eyes affixed on her splendid physique as he vigorously stroked himself. In but a few second his eyes crossed and went out of focus, as an earthquake rumbled throughout his entire body bringing him to a welcome, yet unfamiliar climax.

Archie would be the only one of the threesome to reach euphoria that night.

Fatigued, Archie leaned his left arm up against the cabin wall and couldn't stop panting. It sounded so loud to him in fact that he feared the cheaters would detect his presence. But soon his breathing normalized and he was able to recoup his anger. He zipped up his pants and looked into the bedroom once again and loathed what he saw. Marlie now faced in his direction and appeared to be in total ecstasy. She was on top of Gideon with her head thrown back as she yelled out for more.

Archie was crazed. He turned away from the window, bent down and retrieved his heavy knife and wiped it clean on his flannel shirt. "Showtime!"

But when he stood back up again, unbeknownst to him, his shadowy figure had been cast upon the cabin window and it caught Marlie's attention. She gasped and stopped their copulation in mid stroke. She didn't scream, she was way too cool under pressure. Instead she whispered to Gideon that she saw someone outside.

Gideon didn't want to go soft. "It's just the wind blowing the trees around sweet cakes, nothing else." He put his hands back on her hips and begged her to finish him off.

But to his displeasure, like a talented gymnast dismounting a balance beam, Marlie swung off of him and stuck a perfect landing on the cold wooden floor. She grabbed her blouse and held it up in front of her breasts, as if it were some sort of armor.

"Well, come on Grann. Get over to the window and see who's out there. You don't expect me to do it do ya? I swear I saw a man's silhouette move past. It's way too creepy Gideon. Chase him the hell out of here!" she commanded.

Archie meanwhile had gone up to the window on his left to resume his position. He looked in but couldn't see either of them. He felt cold and struggled with his gloved hands to button up his jacket. The wind was howling and he couldn't hear his own voice, let alone theirs inside. Distracted, he hadn't noticed that Marlie's suspicions had been aroused.

"What the hell do you want me to do?" Gideon said.

"You're the man for Christ's sake you figure it out. Grab that poker next to the fireplace," she pointed to the small hearth to the left of the bed.

He moaned his disapproval, but slipped on his pants and in his bare feet hurried over to the fireplace. He picked up the iron weapon while Marlie retreated toward the bathroom door.

The two of them were so silent that for the first time Gideon was scared. It was now official, he'd gone limp, even with the dose of Cialis swimming through his veins.

Gideon looked at both windows that were four feet apart and decided to approach the one on his left. He looked over his shoulder seeking Marlie's encouragement but she was annoyed with this display of weakness and waved the back of her hands to shoo the little man into action.

Gideon edged along the wall up to the window and took a deep breath. With the poker in his right hand raised above his shoulder, with his left hand he took hold of the white lace curtain. He looked back at Marlie and again he sought her approval as he lip-synced, "Ready?"

His heart pounded as he counted to three in his head and then yanked the curtain open with one swift motion. No one there. Thank God! Except for his own reflection. Relief.

Gideon smiled and swaggered over to the next window. He was much more calm and confident, certain that what Marlie thought she saw was just a figment of her imagination. He mimicked a matador with his bull-teasing red cape as he took hold of the curtain, bowed to Marlie, and snatched it open.

To his immediate horror, and to Archie's as well, for a split second they both stood frozen, face to face. It was a surreal moment for the inebriated Gideon when he saw the bizarre collage of the peeper's vague outline; his own image; the room's behind him as well, and the movement of the bent trees, all intertwined in a single reflection. Gideon's knee-jerk reaction was to drop the iron poker onto the floor and throw a halfhearted punch at the baseball capped peeper on the other side of the glass. His fist rebounded off the triple paned window and Marlie screamed.

Meanwhile, Archie panicked and flung his large knife into the wood pile. He bent down and lifted the heavy object that he had put on the ground next their station wagon, and as he attempted to flee the scene, he tripped over a gasoline can which splashed fuel onto his right pant leg. He ran as fast as he could into the dense woods, back to where he hoped he'd parked his truck. "Wimp!" he berated himself.

Inside the cabin Gideon rushed to get his shirt and shoes on and picked up the poker off of the floor before he went outside to have a look around. He told Marlie to lock the door behind him and to not let anyone in until he returned. He told her to call 9-1-1 but they agreed it was a bad idea, because it could blow their cover. Besides, Marlie reminded him that neither of them had cell reception up there in the woods anyway.. AT&T.

She tossed him the thin metal flashlight that stood tall on the fireplace mantle and he flipped on the outside flood light and left out the front door. She was alone.

Unnerved, Marlie rushed through the cabin and closed all the curtains and tested all the windows and doors to make sure they too were secure. Then she went back into the bedroom and after she had put on her clothes, she returned to the great room. She snatched an iron shovel from its fireplace holder, held it with both hands in front of her chest and stood rigid on the hearth. Her eyes darted back and forth across the room as she looked at all the possible entry points for any sign of the intruder.

A few minutes later, when Gideon banged on the front door, it put her in a momentary shock. She remained still until she could discern that it was in fact him. She unlatched the door.

"Well?" Marlie asked.

"Nada," Gideon answered. "I checked around with this piece of shit flashlight, didn't see squat."

"Let's get packed and get the hell out of here Grann. They all return to the scene of the crime and I don't plan on stickin' around for act two," Marlie demanded.

Gideon set the poker and flashlight down on the hearth and said, "Don't worry Mar, I scared him off. Whomever it was is miles from here by now. Anyway, we'll be much safer staying put here than driving around on dark mountain roads with all those wild drunken teenagers out and about."

Marlie disagreed. "There's no way in hell that I'll take a chance with some stoned out teenager wandering around on some crazy initiation dare. Get packed and take me home."

"You can't go home, what will you tell your husband? You're supposed to be with your aunt in Tucson until Monday, remember? Even he'll be suspicious if you come home at one in the morning on the same night that you left. We have to come up with a better plan. Besides, my *ball and chain* thinks I'm in Utah," Gideon reminded her.

"Whatever. But let's get in your car and figure it out. I won't stay here another damn minute I swear," Marlie said.

It took them a few minutes to gather their stuff, put out the fire and lock up. Gideon snatched the flashlight and they scurried outside.

The crisp November air was at its' coldest, so Marlie hurried to get inside the car and Gideon went around to the back of the station wagon, opened the rear door and threw in their suitcases.

When he sat behind the wheel Gideon propositioned, "How about if we drive up to Flag and find a motel, or a nice quiet pull off where we can finish what we started?"

"Let's just go dammit," she said.

He turned the key in the ignition but the engine didn't start.

"Shit! Now what? Let's get the hell out of here Gideon," Marlie said, frustrated that the Volvo wouldn't start, and afraid that they were easy targets, that someone was watching them.

He had pumped the gas pedal and turned the key on and off enough times to realize that they were in a load of trouble. The only sound they heard was the clicking of the starter. The battery was dead. He reached down, grabbed the release and popped open the hood. He got out of the car and went around to the front to have a look.

Marlie wasn't too optimistic that he'd be able to get the engine to turn over because she knew Gideon didn't have a *Mr. Fixit* bone in his body. When it came to repairs, his idea was to call in his brother-in-law, provide the cold beers, and stay out of the way.

Gideon lifted the hood and shone the flashlight to the where the battery was housed. But the damn battery was gone! In its place a ripped eight by eleven piece of yellow lined paper was attached to the connectors. He yanked the paper from its moorings and held it up to the dim flashlight. He trembled when he read the capitalized letters that were printed in bold red lipstick, "MARLIE IS A VERY BAD GIRL."

"Shit, Shit, Shit!" he yelled as he kicked the front bumper and slammed the hood with such force that the sound reverberated throughout the night for a few eerie seconds. He crumpled up the note and wasn't sure what to do with it at first, but then threw it in a nearby topless metal garbage can. Gideon ran around to Marlie's side of the vehicle.

The power windows didn't work so he waited for her to open the door.

"The battery's been removed. It's not there," Gideon told her. "What? Why didn't you lock the car you dipshit?" she said.

"Who the hell thinks your battery is gonna get pinched? We have to call the cops," he answered.

"No cell signal up here remember? What'll we do?" she asked .

Tense, he said, "Be quiet for a minute will ya. Let me think this through."

He felt it best to protect her and not share the note, as they both were already awash in fear and he didn't need to compound their anxiety. He thought, "What's this game and who's behind it. Must be her husband. But how in the hell does Archie know?"

"Well then give me the damn cabin key and let's get back inside. We'll be much safer in there than sitting like ducks in this Swedish shooting gallery," Marlie said.

Gideon handed her the key and went around to the rear of the Volvo to retrieve their bags. Marlie held the cabin door open for him and stood on her tip toes looking behind him for any sinister signs, while he carried their luggage into the cabin.

They remained silent for a long while.

"So what's your plan Clouseau? I'm not feeling all that safe with your silence ya know," she said.

"I can't figure it out Mar. Peep in on us is one thing, but take the battery? I should have another look around to see if maybe he tossed it nearby?"

"What time is it Gideon?" Marlie asked, as she put a log in the fireplace.

He looked at his watch and said, "Almost one twenty."

"You won't be able to see shit out there with that pathetic flashlight. Besides, it'd be too dangerous for you. You don't have a clue about this area. There's a deep creek and muddy banks. It'll be light out around six thirty so let's hunker down here until then. It's two against one if the asshole should return," she reasoned, as she placed a wad of paper under the logs and lit a long stick match.

He thought, "I sure as hell hope there's no one else with him. She thinks it's some kid on a prank, maybe I should tell her about the note."

Marlie was a lot more calm than he and said, "You know, when I was a drunken, know-it-all teen, we used to pull some awful stunts on people too. I remember at dawn one time I opened up a neighbor's car, put the shift in neutral and my friend and I pushed it down the steep hill. We watched all excited as it careened off of a bunch of parked cars and crashed into a telephone pole near the intersection. Total destruction!

"Why's vandalism such a turn on to young ones? Why's it such a rush to damage someone else's property or cause a terrible inconvenience, just for kicks?" Marlie asked.

He didn't answer Marlie, he was too preoccupied calculating whether her husband was still out there and if he intended to scare the shit out of them, or worse? He knew Archie Moon somewhat, but Archie knew him like a book. Gideon had been Archie's patient for over two years and it was at Archie's office where he was first introduced to Marlie. That's where she met most of her lovers it turned out. They had an immediate connection but didn't act on their sexual attraction until a few months ago.

Gideon thought, "There's no way that the oblivious Archimedes Moon could know that we're together. No way. He's far too busy with all his Sedona crazies, he hasn't time or energy for anyone else, even for Marlie, the fool. No wonder she cheats on him.

"No, the more I think about it the more certain I am that it couldn't be Archie out there tonight. He's in bed by nine o'clock for Christ's sake. Besides he's a man of the mind. If he were on to us he'd challenge us right on the spot, he's not shy. It's his business to confront people all day long. Pranking isn't in his DNA.

"Then who the fuck knows Marlie's here? Another boy toy? Shit I don't know what the fuck gives. Why'd I ever get involved with her?"

"Well?" Marlie asked, still awaiting his response.

"Oh. Um. Yeah vandalism is senseless. You're right Mar," he answered.

"Look, I agree that it's best that we wait 'til sunup, then I can walk down to the road and hitch a ride back into town and get a new battery. Or maybe I could have a service guy come back with me to see what else might need attention," Gideon said.

"Good luck on a Sunday in bustling Sedona," she said.

"Shit you're right. Don't fret, I'll figure something out. In the meantime why don't you try to get a little sleep. I'll stand watch," Gideon told her.

"If you're the one headed into town in the morning you'll need some zzz's not me. I'm way too keyed up," Marlie said.

Gideon went silent. He knew there was no way he'd be able to nod off. The stalker had scared the sleep from his eyes.

4

Gideon had lain awake all night, his paranoia had kept him alert. So when the first of dawn's light filtered into the cabin he got out of bed and started pacing around the room, anxious to put the plan in play, the one that he had formulated in the stillness of the morn.

At one point he stood at the foot of the bed and admired Marlie's voluptuous figure as she slept underneath the white sheets. How peaceful and innocent she looked. He couldn't get up the gumption to disturb her, so instead, to burn off his fidgety energy, he decided to step outdoors, get some fresh air, and have another look around.

Outside, the cold air attacked his senses with an immediate welcome shock that cleared the cobwebs from his sleep deprived brain. He was a bit hungover as he walked to his car, opened the driver's side door and reached down and pulled the hood latch. He walked around to the front, lifted the bonnet, but no miracle.

Next he walked the perimeter of the cabin and looked down at the ground for any clues to the prior night's intrusion. But the earth was so firm that it didn't showcase any foot prints. He scanned the immediate area. "You never know what you might find, maybe even my car battery?" he thought.

He turned his attention to the cabin itself and made certain that all the windows and doors were locked. Once he was satisfied that nothing had been tampered with, he wandered off to inspect the woods on either side of the cabin. At some point he followed a serpentine path that led a short distance to Oak Creek.

Gideon sat down on a large gray rock to admire the remnants of the Fall foliage on display across the water. He became captivated by the meditative sounds of the babbling stream. But his mind couldn't relax for very long before it once again turned over the strange occurrence of last night's disturbance.

He surveyed the area, and to his left, several hundred yards away, he caught sight of a house camouflaged in the woods, the smoke from its chimney gave away its disguise. He had an urge to rush over and ask the occupants if they had seen or heard any trouble last night, but because of the hour he didn't feel he should. So after a few more peaceful minutes he got up and hurried back to the cabin to check on Marlie.

When he neared the cabin he spotted an empty bottle of Scotch on a rock near the woodpile. He examined it for a second and deduced that since Archie wasn't a drinker, the peeper had to have been someone else. He gave the bottle a hefty toss into the woods.

Gideon trotted up the steps and unlocked the front door. He walked straight into the bedroom but she wasn't there. His blood boiled and he yelled out her name, "Marlie, Marlie!"

She threw open the bathroom door and to his relief, and pleasure, Marlie stood naked to perfection. She was aggravated, "I'm right here. What's the panic?"

He went over to embrace her but she pulled away, she didn't want to get him too excited. He was such a *horn ball*, and she was in no mood, not after she'd had such a poor night's sleep. She asked, "Where were you?"

After Gideon had told her she asked him to put on a pot of coffee. She went into the bedroom and dressed.

When they were both seated at the round wooden kitchen table, with warm mugs in front of them, they rehashed what had happened last night. It was clear to Gideon that Marlie had pretty much written it off as a fluke prank by some high school kid.

After they had exhausted the subject Gideon relayed his plan for the day. He would jog down to the main road and flag a ride into town. He'd buy a new battery, or if that wasn't possible, he'd rent a car at the Mobile station. He was pretty sure they were an Avis affiliate. It shouldn't take him more than an hour and a half, two hours, tops.

Marlie corrected him." It's seven on a Sunday. Most places don't open 'til ten, or worse 'til noon. This is the off season ya know. And this is no bustling city were talking about for Christ's sake. Do you have AAA? If you could get somewhere where there's a cell signal you could call them. They'd bring you a battery."

"No, I don't. You're right, businesses aren't open yet. Any ideas?" Gideon asked.

After some thought she said, "Why don't I give you my keys and you can drive my car back here? Then we can go up to Flag and buy a battery for your piece of shit."

Marlie had parked her Boxter in a motel lot in West Sedona where she had supposedly taken the airport shuttle bus to Sky Harbor Airport in Phoenix and flown to Tucson to visit her aunt. But in fact Gideon had picked her up there for their weekend soiree.

"Great idea. Do you want to come with me then?" he said.

"Shit no. It'll be hard enough for one of us to hitch a ride. I'll be fine here I'm sure. You said it was nice down by the creek so maybe I'll take my book and chill there for a while," she said.

Gideon felt confident that the intruder wouldn't be bold enough to return in daylight, so he didn't give another thought to Marlie's safety. He was out the door twenty minutes later. He jogged down the pine needle covered driveway and onto the dirt road that led to the main road, Alt Rte 89.

Marlie had bundled up and stepped outside to wave goodbye to Gideon. With her coffee mug still warm in her hands she sat down on the top step and looked around at the private, woodsy area.

She had acted nonchalant to Gideon because she didn't want to get him distracted. But truth was she was very concerned about what had happened and what might be the peeper's motive. "Did he need a battery for his broken-down car and just happened to look in on us? Was this some sort of stunt for initiation into a gang? Or was it just a plain, good ole, scare the shit out of 'em prank?" She never once considered that it could have been her husband.

Marlie spaced out for a while as she sipped the coffee and stared at Gideon's useless vehicle.

However, at some point her musing was interrupted when she heard the leaves rustle nearby. She began to shiver and experience that same sensation that had come over her the night before, that someone was watching her. She jumped to her feet and set the mug down on the railing. With great caution, and against better judgment, she tiptoed in the direction of the sound.

To her surprise, and his, up from the ground where he lie in a tiny ball behind a bush next to the woodpile, a small figure leapt to his feet. He sped off in the opposite direction from Marlie, in the direction of the creek.

"Stop! Wait, don't worry I won't hurt you," she shouted after the little person, whom, as she had gotten a bit closer to him, she recognized to be a young boy.

But the kid sprinted away from her and when he had reached the creek he scampered left and, with impressive agility, negotiated the jagged rocks and boulders that made up the creek's uneven shore. He dashed along his route as if he were on a flat paved road.

When Marlie reached the creek's edge and saw the difficult path that the boy had navigated she decided it best to give up the chase. She stood and watched him as he disappeared into the woods headed toward the other cottage that she could see hidden by the trees.

She looked around for another few seconds and sat down on a large boulder that basked in the sun (the same one that Gideon had sat on earlier). She looked back at the hidden cottage and hoped that the little young one would feel safe enough to come back and pay her a visit.

Her wish somewhat came true, because, not more than three minutes later, headed in her direction, she spotted a giant of a man who was dragging the little boy along by his ear.

Marlie stood up (her animal instincts prompted her to be on guard) and awaited their arrival.

When they were a few yards away from her she could see the absolute terror broadcast in the child's dark brown eyes and the brutality written all over the man's face.

The lumberjack spoke, "This here boy been botherin' ya mam?" He tugged harder on the boy's ear and in an upward motion which lifted him up onto his tip toes. The kid winced but seemed determined not to announce his pain, because he didn't even make a peep.

"No. Not at all. I scared him when I spotted him behind the bush. I called for him to stop but he ran off instead." Like the boy, she too tried to show the man no sign of fear.

"Can't hear a bomb drop. He's stone deaf. Bin so all his nine years. Don't talk neither. Runs on his mamma's side a the family," the man said.

"Oh! I'm so sorry. I...", Marlie said.

"Why you'd be sorry? He's my kid, an he ain't too bad a one neither. Well mos a the time.

"You rentin' that fairy boy's shack over there are ya'?"

She nodded. She didn't care to be in his presence much longer.

He stretched his suspender forward with his free hand and said, "Sit back down, I don't bite."

He let go of the boy's ear and leaned his foot on a boulder just five feet away from her.

She followed his mild order and on the edge of the rock she sat down once again in the sunlight. She looked radiant.

"Awful quiet upin these parts this time a year. Ain't used ta seein' nobody but ourselves. Yuse a writer or somethin' gettin' away for some sort a meditation?"

"No. My husband's friend gave us his cabin for the weekend. It's our anniversary," she lied. She was defensive as she considered whether this disgusting man could have been the peeper.

She ventured, "You say no one comes up here this time of year. What about all of those drunken high school kids and their parties?"

"Oh I don't think a them as people. No man. They're jus wild animals if ya know what I mean."

The boy drifted off to skip stones across the creek.

The big man stroked his unkempt beard and said, "My Pappy usta say the teenager is the mos dangerous animal on earth. Yup. They don't need no rhyme o' reason, no motive. They jus do some crazy stuff jus fer laughs." He grinned, and she felt comfortable enough to smile back.

"Did you see any of those.. dangerous animals out and about late last night by any chance?" she asked.

"Honey I'm a workin' man an I gotta take care a my deaf mute here an his two l'il sisters. Wife died in childbirth with the las one, three years ago next Sundee. My plate's all full. If I'm up pass ten a'clock that's late. Them dang teens don't start their carousin' until much later than that. An even so, they knowed better than ta bother me and mine. Why'd ya ask? They hassle yuse folks last night?"

She thought for a moment whether it was wise to relay the night's event, then decided it couldn't do any harm to tell him some of the details. "Maybe he'll be able to shed some light on it. Or, if he's the sicko, perhaps I can get him to tip his hand."

"Well as a matter of fact we did get quite a scare last night from a peeper," Marlie said.

She proceeded to tell him, and the little boy, who had come back and stood next to his father and concentrated on reading her lips, most of what had transpired.

The man remained attentive and when she had ended her story with the fact that the car battery had been removed he chimed in. "Don't sound like no kids ta me. No mam. Whoever took the battery musta wanted ya ta remain right where yuse was at fur some reason. Musta bin plannin' on comin' back ya ask me. Sounds ta me like it's yur husbin or yur friend's wife that's not too happy with ya bein' here and all." He didn't buy her version that she was here with her husband, he knew better.

"But whoever the lucky duck was that saw ya naked an all musta knowed somethin'. Heck I wish I'd a knowed ya was puttin' on a titty show las night. I'd a come runnin' an paid good money ta see it!"

As he smiled with his mouth opened wide she saw his horrid mossy green teeth, and the several dark holes where others once resided. Marlie felt a rush of adrenaline. She got defensive. She hadn't anticipated this sudden lecherous turn in the conversation.

In her best scorned act she said, "How dare you! We thought we were in the privacy of our own space."

"Sorry. I meant no harm mam. Jus that I ain't bin with a woman since Mary died, so I'm a little excited I guess. Now don't go gettin' yurself or yur boyfriend all hot 'n bothered about my stupid words. Ya jus get back ta yur cabin an wait fur him. I saw him leave down the path a while ago. I'll keep a good eye on yur place an have the boy here do the same. If that son a bitch peepin' Tom dares come back we'll take care a him for ya. No doubt about it.

"An please be so kind ta let me know when the next show is so's I can get my rest, make some popcorn, an come sit in the front row."

He said, "Sorry. Relax I'm jus joshin' ya. I'm such a tease."

He offered to take her to town and get a battery, or to tow the car for a price. She thanked him but said that her husband had it under control.

"I kin go down ta 89 an give yur fella a lift ta town if ya wish, 'cause chances are he's got his thumb up his ass waitin' fur some fool ta pick him up. Could be waitin' all day in these parts on a Sundee."

"That's very thoughtful of you, but I'm sure that he's already made it to town," she said.

What she didn't tell him was that she would feel a whole lot safer if he stayed and watched over her here. She didn't want to be left alone.

"Aw right mam. Yur choice," he told her.

"Please, call me Marlie."

"Yes um, Marlie. This here's my boy *L'il Bull*. I'm just called plain ole *Bull*, but the fellas at work call me *Full a Bull*."

Marlie enjoyed a good laugh, her first since the peeper had showed up.

She told him she had to get back to the cabin and said goodbye. She offered her hand to the little boy but he blushed and latched on to his father's pant leg and buried his head deep into his daddy's side.

As she walked away Bull un-velcroed his son from his leg and signed to him to wave goodbye to the pretty lady.

After she disappeared from view the big man tickled the boy under his arm pit, lifted him up over his broad shoulder like a sack of potatoes, laughed, and headed for home.

Meanwhile, Marlie entered the cabin with caution and felt weird to be all alone in the silence. She knew that she had been down by the creek for quite a while and was pissed that she'd left the doors open. Could he have returned? She became fearful and stopped to listen for any sign of trouble. She figured the odds were with her that the kid wouldn't dare show up in broad daylight, and anyway, she felt confident that she could hold her own against a teenager if he did reappear.

She tiptoed from room to room and all seemed fine as far as she could tell. So she walked over to the front door and bolted it. But when she walked over to kitchen door to do the same she was stopped in her tracks, startled when she saw the massive six foot seven inch frame of Big Bull who stood in the doorway. His shadow covered the width of the room. Marlie was frightened stiff. She felt helpless. It was him all along!

Bull said, "Didn't mean ta scare ya mam, I mean Marlie. I jus got ta thinkin' that it weren't very neighberly a me ta let ya come back ta yer shack alone an all. So I came by ta check on ya ta make sure you was cool, an that that sneaky guy didn't come back ta do more peepin' on ya, ur worse."

Marlie was speechless.

"Ya want me ta stay a while with ya fur some company?" he said with a Cheshire cat grin.

"No. No thanks. I'm fine. You surprised me."

She gathered herself somewhat. "That was very thoughtful of you to come by and check on me. I must admit that I was a little bit edgy when I first came back and realized that I'd left the doors open. But I've checked all around and everything's in order."

Then she lied, just in case. "My husband called a moment ago and said he's on his way back so there's no need for you to wait here with me. I'm sure your three little children need their daddy."

"Well that'd be a first! No one gets cell service upin these parts. Ya sure is lucky Marlie," he said. His wink told her that he knew she had lied.

"Well I'll be gettin' goin' then. I'm sure my house's upside down by now. An don't worry Marlie, me an the boy will be watchin' ya with binoculars from our house. He's real good at stayin' concentratin' on stuff. Hey ain't that a kick? We'll be peepin' on ya too. Jus from a longer distance than that fella did las night. Jus joshin'. Yur welcome ta come by my digs if ya want ta. Jus give us a holler. Take care Marlie."

Big Bull trudged down the steps while Marlie stood in the window and watched him until she was certain that he had walked all the way back to his cabin..

It took her a few more minutes to calm down as she considered what had just happened. She came to the conclusion that Bull's intentions were good. But she reminded herself to remain on guard all the same.

Hungry, Marlie went into the kitchen and made herself a hearty bacon and eggs breakfast. She seemed much more at ease. She felt protected, knowing that the giant next door had her back.

Or did?

5

Big Bull was right, Gideon was unable, as of yet, to secure a ride into town. However, per hitch hiking's unwritten rule, he had continued to walk in the direction of his destination, so when he looked at his watch and saw that it was seven fifty-five he was at least a mile closer to Sedona. No big consolation though, he still had a few more miles to go.

Another half hour passed and he had counted four vehicles that had sped by, and not one had even tapped on their brakes to consider giving him a ride. He thought he would've been to Sedona and back by now.

Frustrated and cranky from lack of sleep, Gideon decided he needed to do something drastic. So without considering the danger that he might cause himself and others he sat himself down on Route 89, smack in the middle of the south bound lane. That would be sure to stop the next vehicle, hopefully before it turned him into a buzzard's pancake.

It didn't take long for his dangerous tactic to work, because just five minutes later the operator of a small red pickup truck, which was barreling down the mountain road at a very fast clip, was shocked to see Gideon sitting *Ghandi-like* on the road up ahead. The driver tried to make sense of the absurd scene as he panicked and stomped on the brake pedal with both feet. His reaction caused the truck to swerve left and right, and to lay rubber for at least five yards as it came to a screeching halt just a few feet from Gideon. The once pristine mountain air had become filled with the pungent smell of burnt Michelins.

The trucker raised his hands over his head and Gideon could read his pissed-off lips, "What the fuck, asshole!"

Gideon struggled to unlock his legs and get to his feet. He brushed himself off and hurried over to the pickup. The driver stretched out across the passenger seat and threw open the door to be able to hear what Gideon had to say, before he smacked him upside the head.

Gideon apologized and rattled off a litany of his incredible problems, and begged the young man to take him to town.

The trucker waved for him to come on board. "Jesus Christ man you coulda been road kill."

"Thanks man. I can't tell you what a relief it is to get off of my feet. I've been out here for almost two hours," Gideon said.

The driver corrected him. "Yur feet? Looks like you was on yur ass ta me."

The driver reeked of liquor, which complimented the distinct aroma of marijuana that permeated the truck's cabin. He was a muscular guy in his late twenties at most and wore the typical blue jean jacket and flannel shirt uniform of his tribe. His baseball cap hid any evidence of hair, and why he wore dark sunglasses on this cloudy day only he could answer. Gideon became concerned because the man looked like he'd been up all night too, so the drive into town might prove to be an adventurous one.

The young man asked, and Gideon answered, several questions about what had happened last night. But Gideon never mentioned Marlie by name.

The driver asked, "So you have no idea who it was? Weird. Weird. I know that area pretty good. I think I know which cabin yur talkin' about. My pop an I built the fireplace there an in the next two homes ta the south. He's a mason an I'm his apprentice. No one goes there this time a year though. Most places are boarded up."

"You're right. That's why my wife and I chose it. You know, to get away for a little peace and quiet," Gideon fibbed.

"So where's yur wife now?" the driver asked. "Ya didn't leave her all alone up there did ya?"

"The owner lives next door and he and his mate asked her over for breakfast," Gideon said.

It was obvious to the young guy that Gideon was bullshitting him because his voice and tone had changed when he gave his phony answer. That prompted the trucker to take a harder look at his passenger and not the road. "Sure as shit its Gideon Grann the radio jerk!" he yelled in his head.

He was suspicious. "First I find this guy sittin' Muslim-like in the middle a the goddamn road, then he starts tellin' this crazy story full a lies."

He thought that maybe this so called celebrity had killed his wife or whatever, and had left her back in the woods. He was about to remove his pistol from beneath his seat but decided he'd first see where this might lead. By the looks of little Grann there wasn't much to fear. "Lady killers and child molesters pick on the weak people. They're scared stiff a tough guys like me," he thought.

"How's yur radio gig doin'?" He showed Grann that he recognized him.

"Damn," Gideon thought. Then answered, "We're fine. So fine in fact, that they promoted me to prime time at eight a.m. 'til ten starting next month. You a fan, what'd you say your name was?"

"Never said it 'til now. Names Andy, an hell no I don't listen ta yur show. Don't know what yur discussin' half the fuckin' time. All ya do is act all intellectual an make fun a people. Good ordinary people that don't agree with yur crap."

The two hungover occupants drove in silence the rest of the trip. Gideon felt uneasy since Andy had acted so feisty but if the driver wanted quiet he wouldn't argue with him, the lift to town was all that mattered.

The remainder of the ride proved uneventful and when they had reached West Sedona Andy pulled into the motel lot and dropped Gideon off near the front entrance, so he could use the restroom.

"Thank you so much Andy. How can I repay you?" Gideon asked.

"Don't bother about it man. I was headin' this way anyhoo," Andy said.

As he circled out of the parking lot, Andy spotted the license plate *MarLuv* on the white Boxter that was parked way off in the corner. He stopped his truck." Hell, that's Marlie Stone's car aint it?" Wonder what she's doin' here?"...

Despite their agreed plan that they could drive her car to Flagstaff and get his car battery there, Gideon was bent on finding one in town. So he went to a couple of gas stations and asked if they carried one for his particular Volvo wagon. They did not. The Shell station attendant however suggested that he drive over to the Walmart in Cottonwood. But since it was about nine o'clock he'd have to wait for another hour for them to open.

Gideon didn't give it a second thought and headed west out of town to Cottonwood. He pulled into the empty Walmart parking lot and waited for it to open. He reclined the driver's seat as far back as possible and, although he fought the onslaught, he fell into a deep sleep.

Much later he awakened from his nightmare reenactment of the prior night's trouble when he heard the loud sound of a car's horn. Startled, he looked out the windows and saw that the lot was quite full. He glanced at his watch, it was almost ten thirty. "Fuck!"

He darted into the store and looked for the automotive section, but there was none. They don't sell car batteries at Walmart. A clerk told him to go to the Auto Zone on Highway 89 back in Sedona, and that it had been open since eight a.m.!

He jumped back into her car and was irate. "Why didn't that asshole Shell guy, *The Answer Fucking Man,* tell me about AutoZone? I'd have been back to Oak Creek by now, the mother fucker."

Another twenty minutes passed before he was in the Auto Zone store. By the time he got served, figured out which one hundred and twenty dollar lifetime battery to purchase and paid for it, he wasn't back behind the wheel until eleven twenty and he still had another twenty five, thirty minute drive back to the cabin. "She'll be rip roaring pissed," he knew, as he sped the Porsche north on Route 89.

Meanwhile, Marlie had worked herself into a frenzy. She paced back and forth and screamed aloud, "Where the hell is he? Did he run into some sort of trouble? I hope the fool remembers that he's supposed to be in Utah and isn't prancing around in public. He's so goddam addicted to praise. He needs everyone to recognize him. Pathetic.

"Gideon Grann get your ass back here this instant!" she shouted to the deaf walls.

"Shit. I've got to get rid of this guy he's nothing but trouble. There's always a dark cloud hanging over his thick, greasy head."

As if on cue, outside the November sky had turned an inky black, and she noticed that tiny rain droplets had begun to attach themselves to the cabin windows. She thought how unusual it was because it hadn't rained there for months. She went throughout the cabin and turned on several lights. She stoked the fire, grabbed a magazine from the rack next to the sofa, and sat down. A moment later the clouds opened up with a torrential downpour.

About twenty more minutes passed and the rain had not subsided, in fact it had gotten heavier. It was then that she heard the faint, but distinctive sound of her Boxter's engine as it neared. "About fucking time."

She got up off of the couch and looked out the window. When she saw where he had parked she wondered why the jerk had stopped so faraway from the cabin? "Grann you asshole," she said aloud, "we've got to carry all this damn luggage you dipstick. Park closer."

Gideon had parked the car fifty feet away because he saw that the area up near the cabin was very muddy. With the way their luck was running he knew that it was a sure bet that the Boxter would get stuck.

He got out of the roadster and pulled his jacket up over his head, in order to protect the heavy battery that he now carried under his other arm. The rain soaked him through and through as he slipped and slid his way up toward the cabin.

Marlie flung the front door open to let him in and put both her hands on her hips in disgust when she saw what he was carrying. She was livid. "No wonder you've been gone so long. Why'd you buy the battery in Sedona you retard?"

He cowered as he walked up the stairs and past her into the cabin. After she slammed the door behind him she told him to change his clothes and to take her the hell away from there in her car. "We can come back for your shitty little Volvo later."

He felt guilty, so he put up no resistance and followed her orders.

Meanwhile, the sounds of rolling thunder and lightning were deafening, their power rattled the cabin walls. The storm was directly overhead.

When Gideon came out of the bathroom Marlie told him that there was no need to rush because they would have to sit tight a while, and let the worst of the storm pass. Neither of them knew that its intensity was predicted to last another hour or more.

Marlie made Gideon sit down on the couch and then, as if she were scolding a little school boy slumped in his chair, she unleashed all her pent up anger and fear. Why hadn't he listened to her? Why was he so damn stubborn and selfish? And why had he left her alone for so long?

Gideon acted sheepish and paid close attention to her. He was either too tired or too scared to defend himself.

But soon to his rescue the cabin was lit up by a frightening bolt of lightening, that was followed by a violent clap of thunder. Marlie's rant stopped in mid-sentence. Lucky for Gideon, Mother Nature's wrath had put an exclamation point to her anger and saved him from further castration. They both went silent for quite some time, as Marlie steamed and Gideon repented.

After a while, since she had taken it all out on him and had gotten it off of her chest, a more calm and compassionate Marlie went into the kitchen to whip up a surprise for Gideon. She prepared a nice breakfast of bacon and eggs. "Come and get it. Truce", she said.

The odd pair remained quiet while he ate and both enjoyed the tranquil drumbeats that the sheets of rain tapped upon the cabin's tin roof. Their tensions had eased.

When he had finished eating, Gideon rinsed off his plate and flirt-ed, "Hey Mar, before I take a little snooze care to roll around in the hay for a bit?" She agreed.

As they dropped their guards and retreated to the bedroom there was no way for them to know that the storm's soothing rhythm had lulled them into a false sense of security. Because, in a very short time, before they'd ever again step foot outside the rustic cabin, a vicious and vengeful human tempest, unlike any they'd ever known, was about to rain absolute bedlam upon them.

PART TWO

Cape Cod
Ten Months Later

1

T ourists..

Thousands flocked to the beaches of this tiny seaside community and every week their footprints were washed away and replaced by a new wave of sun worshipers to come ashore. *Controlled turnover,* innkeeper Martha Nickerson Lawrence called it. This lucrative cycle was so vital to the local economy, and to her bank account, that she was more than willing to put up with its disruptive side effects of rude behavior, higher prices, long waiting lines and bumper to bumper traffic.

"I don't know how you can stand these strangers and their constant invasions Martha," her brother whined. "It's almost October for heaven's sake and unlike you, everyone else in this town has become apoplectic at the mere mention of the word tourist. At this point we just want them to show us their taillights and go home. Give us our lives back!"

"Why has tourist become such a dirty word Calvert? Where on earth would we be without them? Indeed I recognize the toll that these intrusions have exacted on everyone, but even so, I cannot fathom what all the fuss is about. If I had my way summer would be endless, the more tourists the merrier. I am in no hurry for Autumn's vibrant leaves to fall and the cold colorless winter that will follow," Martha said.

Martha gathered herself and with much trepidation she changed the conversation to the subject that they'd been avoiding up until now, the real reason why she had phoned her brother in the first place: the tragic death of little Carrie Baker. They were both devastated by the news and were awkward in expressing their disbelief and heartfelt sorrow to one another. Martha ended their short, uneasy discussion when she told her younger brother, "I have written a sympathy note to the Baker family and I will see to it that you get it in the morning, so that you can sign it as well. Goodnight Calvert."

She hung up the kitchen phone and in sort of a mini-trance she shuffled across the room and plopped down in her favorite upholstered arm chair in front of the stone fire place. She felt low, which was very unusual for Martha, her moods seldom swung. She sat staring at the dying embers, she couldn't get Carrie's drowning out of her mind.

Meanwhile, outside Martha's magnificent Inn, the cold moon, full and bright, spotlighted its beam on the man who stood at the base of its wide wooden steps. The contrast of the stark white Victorian masterpiece and the man and his dark overstretched shadow, created a surreal scene that appeared more befitting a stage set than a sleepy village backdrop.

The man seemed moved by the moon's powerful presence. He faced it with his chin raised and his eyes closed as if he were concentrating on soaking up a lunar tan. A moment or so later, when he opened his eyes, he said aloud to the earth's natural satellite, "Thanks Father Moon for guiding me here."

Back inside, as was her habit, Martha reached for the remote control and turned on the late-night news for company and for a distraction from her present melancholy. Big mistake. She became even more dejected because CNN bombarded her with crisis after crisis in Syria, Iran, ISIS, Iraq, on and on.

"Get hold of yourself Martha!" she chastised. "I live in one of the most desirable places on the edge of North America, lapped by the great Atlantic Ocean, and I have to be drawn into all the hatred and strife that is exploding in a desert halfway around the world? I should say not. I will not let them effect me. Why should I care about those heathens if they cannot sort things out themselves? I have my civilized guests to attend to."

She was about to turn off the flat screen when another story shouted for her attention. An unarmed black teen had been gun downed by a white cop, an all too common occurrence it seemed. Although she often sided with the authorities, these constant, senseless murders made her question who the real thugs were. "He was just a child for heaven's sake", she said. "Why on earth are they trained to shoot to kill?"

She feared for all the good policemen who would now be the targets of the community's wrath thanks to a few rogue colleagues. She watched the riot squad, clad in their over-the-top military gear, teargas the protesters and it made her anxious. "My God! I cannot tell the difference between that dreadful Middle East and rural America. The world is unraveling. It is the sixties all over again."

Martha pointed the remote at the Sony and the screen went black.

It was eleven forty-five and her inner clock prompted her to get up from her chair and walk over to her well-appointed bathroom to begin her cleansing ritual, which would last fifteen minutes, no more, no less. Once she had completed her hygienic tasks she made certain that every item she had used was put back in its proper place before she turned out the lights. That included aligning the stripes on the wash cloth with the stripes on the towel that it lied upon. Martha was a very meticulous woman.

But when she exited the bathroom to head for bed her routine was upended by the doorbell's loud ring. It startled her as it pierced the stillness of midnight. "Who on earth could be calling at this late hour?"

Martha didn't hesitate, she dashed straight toward the entrance as fast as her seventy-six-year-old legs would take her, afraid that if it rang again her guests would be disturbed. As she sped through the living room she glimpsed at a landscape painting that had tilted off center. It annoyed her that she didn't have time to stop to straighten it. She panted as she reached the front door, and although rushed, she dared to take another precious few seconds to touch up her hair and straighten her housecoat. She was in the present, the Baker girl's death had been relegated to the depths of her mind.

She peered through the stained glass door but the wavy design distorted the figure of the man who stood on the porch. She gathered her thoughts, took a short breath, pressed the intercom button and said, "How may I help you sir?"

Martha couldn't understand his muffled response so she instructed, "Please hold down the button on the white box above the doorbell and speak into it."

"I would like a room please," he put his mouth too close to the speaker and semi-shouted.

She considered for a brief second if she should let the man in, then threw caution to the wind and hurried to open the door before his voice blasted through the speaker once again.

Martha didn't get a good look at the tourist at first because his tall dark silhouette eclipsed the porch light behind him, it produced a halo effect. "Come in please, come in," she whispered, as she motioned for him to be quick.

After Martha had locked the door behind him and turned off the neon *Vacancy* sign, she excused herself to the traveler and hurried over to the living room to adjust the landscape painting. It had driven her crazy the whole time. Satisfied that order had been restored, she walked back toward the stranger and for the first time she got a look at the man.

Martha would later describe the tourist as, "A very unusual and colorful young fellow, mid-thirties in age as best as I could detect, and tall and handsome no doubt, but rather unkempt. He wore an awful brown colored ball cap atop a hideous yellow blond wig and his wrinkled corduroys hung loose, as if he had slept in them for days. But aside from his looks what I found most disturbing was that he was quite lacking in interpersonal skills. Off-putting would best describe his demeanor. He was very guarded, hiding what I have no clue."

Now to be fair, Martha felt that all her guests at the Hibiscus Inn were unique in some fashion or another. After all she reasoned, they had the discriminating taste to have chosen her pristine nine suites Inn over the other two, rather ordinary, B&Bs in the village. However, she was extra fascinated with, "This curious young man who showed up on my doorstep like an apparition around midnight, on a Friday, and without, heaven forbid, a reservation."

I'm not sure what got more of a rise out of Martha, the fact that he was odd and disheveled and appeared out of nowhere, or that she had a vacancy in the popular month of September, and on a weekend no less.

Martha, a supreme busybody, didn't mince words as she launched into a rapid-fire interrogation of the man, she pressed him for explanations. What was his name? Where was he from? Why had he arrived so late? Why had he assumed that her Inn would be open at midnight? She deduced that he had arrived on foot and found that to be quite unusual she informed him. Why had he not called for a taxi? Again she asked, "What is your name young man?"

The traveler rubbed the side of his right temple and winced in noticeable pain, as if he'd just been stabbed in the eye by an ice pick. Seconds later, when it appeared that his discomfort had subsided, he walked right past Martha and into the cozy living room. He acted as if he hadn't heard a word that the ghost of an innkeeper had just asked.

She followed right behind him and gasped when she spotted dried mud caked all over his shoes. She became anxious, afraid that it would soil her precious Persian carpets. She demanded that he remove his shoes at once, but again he paid no attention to her.

His aloofness bothered her and she became frustrated. She felt like telling him to take a hike but she dismissed that thought at once, because it was more important to her that she rent him the room and have a full house. She wasn't concerned about the additional revenue, no, she was excited that her impressive twenty-year streak would remain intact, of having no weekend vacancies in September.

But she had had enough of his silent game and she told him so. She needed to know right now what his intentions were and how long he planned to stay at her five-star Inn (her own rating system).

The man became upset and spoke at last. "Please stop your annoying chatter. I have a splitting headache and your babbling isn't helping any. If you must know, I'm tired, I've traveled a long way, and I just want to rent one of your rooms. I haven't slept for a couple of days and need to crash. So, would you please just tell me what you charge for a week's stay and rent me a room? And if I like your Inn and your little village, and if all the people here aren't as nosy as you, maybe I'll extend my visit."

"How dare you young man! Why it is quite proper, if one runs a reputable business, to know with whom they are transacting. The nerve to suggest that I am prying." Martha, born in the USA and educated in the UK, always exaggerated her affected British accent whenever she wanted to make her point.

"Look Miss I apologize. I know I'm a bit cranky. My head's pounding and I'd prefer to be left alone if you don't mind. Please, just show me to my room and I promise that I won't bother you anymore ."

He had just fled a small town's wrath and his positional vertigo and throbbing head were constant reminders. He shuddered to think that this little village might be as narrow-minded and as claustrophobic. "I just need to regroup. I hope they'll leave me alone," he thought.

Martha was intrigued that he had spoken of a possible extended stay yet he had so little luggage with him. He carried a small, handsome Tumi black leather suitcase and a well-worn saddle bag, also in black, that was strapped over his right shoulder. She thought that perhaps he had other baggage en route. "He said he was up for a couple of days straight so he may have had a bad flight and his bags were lost or misplaced by the airlines. Who knew?" she pondered.

Martha also wished to get the room occupied and get some sleep as operating the Inn required her to rise at five a.m. to prepare a substantial breakfast for her guests. The traveler's intrusion had severed her regimen, she would have been fast to sleep by now.

She spoke very businesslike. "We charge one hundred eighty dollars per night which includes all taxes and a full American breakfast. It makes it easier on our guests, and on us, that we charge in this fashion. So, I will need some form of identification and a credit card number in case there are any additional charges or damages. I am sure a man of your obvious education can understand these requirements."

Again to her he seemed not present, in a dreamy drift, from sleep deprivation she guessed, because he didn't acknowledge her requests. Instead he reached into his pocket and pulled out an immense wad of one hundred dollar bills. He peeled off fifteen of them and attempted to hand her the stack and said, "This should cover a week's stay don't you think?"

Martha didn't grab the bait. She was taken aback, stunned, on the sheer principal that it felt as if this were some sort of bribe, *hush money* as she would later tell everyone. After all, her guests paid the civilized way, by credit card. She hypothesized, "He must be up to some sort of criminal endeavor. His behavior is far too suspicious. Whomever deals in cash except those detestable terrorists?"

However, when Martha looked at the mass of currency in his hand and sized him up once more, she felt confident that he meant her no harm, so she dismissed her distrust. But she did scold him. "Do you know how dangerous it is these days young man to carry around loose money? I am very uncomfortable with such a large sum of cash. So I will, at the very least, need to see some form of proper identification, credit card, driver's license, or the like, in order to process your stay. I am certain you can understand my concerns, you arrived at such a peculiar hour and without a reservation."

He mocked her overdone British accent. "Madame Innkeeper, I do not have a credit card and nevermore intend to carry one. They are just another trap set by greedy bankers for the innocent and naive to be imprisoned within. Therefore, if I pay you in cash does it matter who I am? Please, take this legal tender", he shoved the bills into her left hand, and gently closed her right hand over them, "and by my calculation this is more than enough for a one week stay and a security deposit. Wouldn't you agree?"

He said over her attempted protest, "Please realize that I didn't ask for your identification or proof from the Board of Health that your Inn is sanitary. Sometimes we have to accept what our good instincts tell us and trust our fellow women and men. Now, for the third time, would you please show me to my room, and if you are still troubled with my presence we can settle the details when I am up and about much later today. I'm shaking and I must get some sleep."

Martha was affronted by even the slightest insinuation that her Inn was in questionable condition, but with the hour so late, she stuffed the money into her housecoat pocket, walked over to the key board above the check-in desk and reached for the vacant room's key.

Martha was anxious to gossip with her friends about this unusual tourist and his inauspicious arrival. It'd be certain to kindle the locals' suspicions, if for no other reason than his actions were out of the ordinary, not of proper conduct. The man was different, and the villagers didn't tolerate different very well. In fact, they pretty much distrusted anyone who didn't look like them, act like them, and believe like them. It was how they validated their own cemented ideologies. The eccentric stranger would be more apt to be treated as their enemy than their welcomed guest.

The innkeeper escorted her secretive guest to the top floor (there were two floors in all) and opened up room number six, the *Harbor Light Room.* She boasted, "There is a pleasant view of the harbor and the *Nobska Lighthouse* that you will awaken to and…"

She was about to give her usual spiel about all of the Inn's and village's amenities, when breakfast was served and how to sign up for it etc., when he stopped her in mid-sentence.

"I'll be happy to pay you an additional one hundred dollars if tomorrow you would relocate me, for the remainder of my stay, to a room on the first floor, one with or without a harbor view."

Martha was baffled by his request.

The stranger took Martha by the elbow with care and moved her towards the door. But before he could close it behind her she said over her shoulder, "By what name do you wish to be called young man?"

"I'm thankful for your compassion. I know this has been a major inconvenience for you," he said as he held the door open.

He wished to allay her fears. "Truth is concrete. It isn't subject to interpretation. Our perceptions often reflect the truth, but our misperceptions are always false. I promise I won't be of any trouble. I'm just here to change the world one village at a time."

2

Martha had risen at the crack of dawn, as was her custom, to shower and dress before she headed to the kitchen to prepare her acclaimed full course breakfast. The stranger's arrival had given her a full house, all nine rooms were let, but she figured that he wouldn't be taking breakfast since he had gone to bed so late and he had said that he lacked sleep for two days. Besides, as was her unwavering rule, breakfast was served between seven and nine, no exceptions. She was certain he'd sleep well past then. So she erased the name *Mr.X* from her dining list.

Martha was an accomplished pro and had learned her trade well these many years. She could write the book. She knew that if you didn't require your guests to sign up the night before to indicate if they wanted breakfast the next morning, you'd be asking for trouble. So much food, and therefore, money, would go to waste. She had found out the hard way that many of her guests didn't always care to eat a large breakfast every day and many wished to eat at a local restaurant, or leave early to go sightseeing. It didn't take long for Martha to tire of preparing fresh food that went straight into the trash bin. What's worse, she found that if you didn't have them commit their intentions the prior night human nature would take over. Lodgers would sleep late or dally about in their rooms, and then at their leisure, not hers, walk into her kitchen, at any hour, and announce that they'd like to have breakfast served on the terrace right that moment. They'd expect her and her staff to drop all their other important duties and cook breakfast for them at eleven o'clock or whenever. Inefficient! No, she vowed to put in a system where such wastefulness would never happen again. So if you didn't sign up the night before or if you showed up after nine, you were encouraged to help yourself to the basket of fresh baked muffins, a bowl of fruit, cereals of all sorts, a variety of fruit juices, and a cup or two of tea or coffee. But like Seinfeld's *Soup Nazi*, "No American breakfast for you." She and her staff had other crucial chores to attend to.

Her staff, Sonia and Lizavetta, two gorgeous, blond, twenty-five-year-old Russian women, worked for Martha from mid-May until November. Sonia had been doing so for the past four seasons while this was Lizavetta's inaugural year. With their hair tied in perfect ponytails, the young ladies would do all the prep work. They'd cut the fruits, onions, peppers, potatoes, tomatoes, meats and cheeses. Then they'd tend to the table placements and flower arrangements both inside and out. Martha hand-picked the flowers each morning from her authentic English gardens that had been designed in memory of her late husband, Harold. It was an exact replica of the gardens where Harold and Martha had first met in the sixties, in the Cotswold District of England.

Martha and her staff loved to host and to show off her wonderful property. She often told guests when asked how she managed to stay so enthused for over twenty years that, "The average owners work at it less than three years. They become disillusioned right away. They are in it for the wrong reasons. They fantasize that it will all be jolly conversations, wine and linen. They never take into account that it is a very competitive business; that margins are tight; it is a twenty-four-hour responsibility; and, yes, toilets do have to be cleaned each day. They lament that every week they have to deal with another set of strangers in their home. It can be very disconcerting, I know. But where I differ from these dilettantes is that I feel grateful to be able to meet people from all around the world, ..and get this, they come to me! How wonderful is that?"

It's true. Anyone who had ever been a guest at the Hibiscus Inn could tell you that Martha had a knack for making you feel welcome and important. She and her staff had a genuine interest in people and strove to assure that their vacations were memorable.

The Hibiscus Inn was a substantial size measuring well over five thousand square feet. There were three high ceilinged guest rooms on the first floor, and the other six suites on the second floor all had nine foot ceiling heights as well. Lots of space to keep spotless. All the rooms were furnished with impeccable taste and each offered quality amenities similar to a fine city boutique hotel. Martha lived in her own spacious two bedroom owner's quarters which was on the first floor, adjacent to the kitchen. Liza and Sonia shared the medium sized one bedroom which was located in the clean and spacious basement. It was bright and cheery thanks to three large above ground windows. They also shared a bathroom with its shower and double sink.

On this particular early Fall weekend room number one, the *Honeysuckle*, was occupied by a gay couple from Wisconsin who were in their mid-forties. They were registered under the name of Trevor Miller. They told Martha that they'd just been wed in Boston and that this would be their honeymoon. Despite Martha's views being a bit on the conservative side, when it came to marriage, this was good heavens Massachusetts, in the United States of America, where all were created equal in God's eyes. If same sex marriages were approved by the state, that would be good enough for her. Love is love. She wished them all the best.

Rooms two and three (*Petunia* and *Iris*) were occupied by a very quiet group from Berlin Germany, the Stroebels, (Father, mother, son-in-law and daughter). This was the eighteenth time this season that Martha's Inn had attracted clients from Europe, another indication that the Hibiscus had a far reaching, worldwide reputation for excellence.

Upstairs we know that the stranger was rooming in number six, the *Harbor Light*, at least for one night, as he had made an unusual request to be moved to the first floor.

Room number seven, *Birds of Paradise*, the Inn's signature room, which was often used as the honeymoon suite, with its' sweeping views of the harbor, the village square and the ocean beach beyond, was let for the entire month of September to a couple who had been returning to the Hibiscus Inn year after year for the last sixteen years. What loyalty. They were the Mantz, she a school teacher and he a scientist. They were a very charming couple in their mid sixties, whose visits Martha looked forward to each year. They had been good friends with Martha's husband and were a great help to her when Harold had passed away during one of their stays. But what Martha liked most about Baltus and Lily Mantz was that they were doers, never letting a day pass without exploring the Cape and its surrounds. They were the ideal guests, demanding little and offering a lot with their cheerful attitudes.

The occupants in the other rooms, four, five, eight, and nine were as follows: *The Dogwood*, was let by a Ms. Perry, a single, good looking, nerdy woman, in her fifties, who was visiting from Georgia. *The Forsythia*, was rented for one week to a young married couple from Surrey England, Charles and Mary Spring. *The Maple* was let to a sweet, hunched, little old white haired gentleman from Boston, Robert Foley.

He kept to himself. The *Dahlia* was rented to three beautiful Vermont women, the Adams sisters, Gardyne, Bristol and Lee. They were very pleasant and full of vim and vinegar. They enjoyed a good conversation and a glass or three of *Pinot Noir*. Martha much appreciated their company.

At around ten a.m., once they had completed the breakfast cleanup, the staff would begin tidying up the guest rooms. This particular Saturday, like most days, Sonia began on the first floor. She instructed Liza to start upstairs on any room except for number six, but Liza had misunderstood Sonia's directive. She put her master key into the keyhole of room number six and opened the door.

To her horror the new guest stood stark naked in the middle of the room. She panicked and said sorry as she blushed at the sight of his erection which pointed due east toward the bathroom. Mortified, she slammed the door shut and dashed off. Her ponytail beat her on the back in self-flagellation as she ran down the stairs to seek Sonia's advice.

Inside his room, after the initial surprise, the stranger yelled after her that he would be dressed soon and that she should come back again in five minutes. If she had heard him it wouldn't have mattered though, because Liza spoke and understood very little English.

The stranger in fact didn't mind the intrusion as he'd been up for a few minutes already. Despite the fact that he was still very tired, after he had thrown open the curtains and witnessed the wonderful sunny harbor view before him he determined that he'd go out for a while to explore the village. But first he would have breakfast. He paid no attention to the time and wasn't aware that the breakfast service was already over.

He was very happy to be back on the Cape, so he'd leave all thoughts of his recent troubles behind. Lupita was right when she had encouraged him to slip away. He'd try to enjoy himself here while he awaited good news from her back home.

He walked into the bathroom and took his deodorant stick out of his Dopp kit and stroked a few rolls. He took a deep whiff of his under arms and seemed satisfied that this *instant shower* had succeeded to mask his three-day body odor.

He went out into the bedroom and put on underwear, a pair of blue jeans and the same white Polo shirt that he had worn the day before. He threw his fine light brown, crumpled linen sport jacket over the shirt and walked back into the bathroom.

He thought he looked rather handsome as he viewed his reflection in the mirror. Although the three-day growth on his face was quite noticeable, he felt that it made him look rather appropriate for this seaside setting, so he didn't bother to shave. He ran a dab of gel through his gnarled mane (he let it do what it felt like, sort of an Einstein-do) which in fact today was his natural color, medium brown. He had stashed the pathetic blond rug into his bag last night.

It was then that he remembered he had asked the innkeeper to change him to a room on the first floor, and that in turn reminded him that he had left all his money in his corduroy pants. So he went over to the bed where they lie, reached into the left front pocket and removed the wad of hundred dollar bills. Next he went over to the tiger maple desk, grabbed the Hibiscus Inn labeled ball point pen and on the face of a white Hibiscus Inn envelope he wrote in capital letters IAN. He had a little chuckle. He peeled off a one-hundred-dollar bill and placed it in the envelope. He flinched as he licked the medicinal tasting glue on the envelope's flap and sealed it. He put the wad of bills into his left front pocket and proceeded to stuff all the clothing, that he had taken out of his bag the night before, back into his small suitcase. He had to kneel on the bloated bag in order to force the clothing to flatten enough so that he could zip it shut. With his right hand he took his unopened saddle bag and flung the strap over his shoulder, picked up the suitcase with the same hand, looked around the room one more time and sang to himself the Beatles, "Good Day Sunshine". He exited the suite.

When he stepped outside the door he spotted Liza down the hall-way fumbling with her key chain, in her failed attempt to get into another guest's room before he had seen her. He yelled to her as he spread his arms out wide, luggage and all, "Look mom, I'm all dressed." She had no idea what he meant.

Once on the first floor he perused the pleasant interior with greater attention than he had the night before. He loved what he saw, and the tantalizing smell of baked goods that wafted in the air seemed to erase whatever state of anxiety had brought him here.

As he passed through the great room he leaned his bags next to the Baldwin upright piano that stood erect at one end. He tickled the keys and sang aloud, "Things have changed."

Ian's stomach growled and he spotted the full basket of fresh muffins and rolls that sat in the middle of the serving table. He reached for a poppy seed bagel but stopped himself when he remembered that he had paid for a full breakfast. He looked around for where breakfast might be served and determined that the kitchen was straight ahead where the door was marked with a large wrought iron letter *K*. He paid no attention to the *Private* sign that was also affixed to the door.

Ian listened at the door but heard no sound on the other side. He knocked three times and walked right in. What a wonderful cook's kitchen, but no innkeeper.

He went into the walk-in pantry and he could see through to a small porch on the other side that there were two very large freezers that stood side by side and a powerful looking Honda generator. He raised his voice, "Hello innkeeper, anyone home?" No one answered.

Next he walked back into the kitchen and opened the screen door that lead to the backyard gardens. It was there, standing on the steps, that he spotted Martha far below. She was on her knees hand-picking veggies from an abundant row. She had two beautiful straw baskets next to her that were almost full.

He walked down the twelve steps, took a left around the gargoyle fountain and didn't want to startle her so he boomed, "Excuse me. Your weary traveler is alive and well and ready to eat a horse."

Martha remained on her knees and said, "Well dear weary traveler all the horsemeat has been eaten. We serve breakfast between seven and nine and it must be well past ten by now. So you are out of luck. However, as is the case throughout the day, there are plenty of fresh baked goods in baskets on the serving table in the dining room, fresh fruits, cereals, coffee and tea brewed as well. If you wish to drink juice please have a look in the fridge. Your choice. I have tomato, orange and mango today."

"So it is," he said, as he looked at his watch for the first time.

"I am surprised that you are up already. How are you? Did you get a good night's sleep I hope?" she asked in rapid succession.

He didn't answer her as he remembered the envelope. He handed it over to her and said, "Here's the one hundred dollars that I promised, for the room change to the first floor."

She answered, "Well you are fortunate. I spoke at breakfast with the two kind gentlemen who are occupying the *Honeysuckle Room* and they agreed to exchange with you."

She took the envelope from him and couldn't help but notice the name IAN printed on it.

"So Ian is your name is it?" she asked.

He grinned. exposing his bright white teeth..

"When will I be able to move?" he asked.

Martha answered him somewhat disinterested, "Sonia and Liza will see to it that the room is ready by noon."

"Tell them that both my bags are downstairs next to the piano and that they're not to open them or touch anything except the handles," he demanded.

"I can assure you sir, Ian, that I have the finest staff and they are upright in all that they do. Your precious bags will be in room number one, *The Honeysuckle*, undisturbed!"

He felt bad that he had raised his voice and said, "Thank you. It's just that I have some very important papers that are in a particular order and if they got mixed up it would cause a real hassle for me."

They were uncomfortable for a few seconds then Ian broke the silence. "I'm in the mood for a hot breakfast so I think I'll take a nice walk through your little village and find a good eating spot. Any suggestions?"

"They serve an excellent breakfast, well for a coffee shop that is, until noon at the Eatery up on Main Street," she answered.

"If it would not be too much of a bother would you mind delivering an envelope to my brother, Dr. Nickerson?" It was the sympathy card for the Baker family that she wished for her brother to sign and deliver in person.

"He will be there at the Eatery, with his *Round Table Group*, until noon. It is rather important that he gets it soon," she said. Ian was amenable.

She told him that the envelope was on the kitchen table and that she would go fetch it for him.

It took quite an effort for Martha to rise to her feet. Still hunched over, she brushed off the dirt from her apron and her knees and waited for her arthritic back to straighten. Martha was a big woman but not an overweight one. If she were a dog perhaps she'd be a hearty mix of Saint Bernard and bloodhound, attractive, curious and durable. She was a woman of impeccable style and grace, and even there, toiling in her *English Garden*, she wore a fashionable floral dress and a black shawl that matched her black garden gloves. She topped her appearance off with her handsome beige colored Tilley hat that was perfectly positioned on her thick gray hair, in order to protect her baby-like skin from the sun's harmful rays. She knew how to dress and how to make the most of what God gave her. She looked a number of years younger than seventy-six. If you viewed the entire package she was still a very fine, confidant woman, a real catch for any widower, if she would ever have him. However, for Martha, no one could compare to Harold, he was her rock.

Ian accompanied her back to the Inn and she was thankful that he acted as a gentleman, carrying both baskets for her. Once inside he asked, "Do I have to keep referring to you as Madame Innkeeper? Now that you think you know my name, may I call you by yours?"

Martha wondered what on earth he meant and said, "Martha is what I know my name to be Ian, or whatever your real name is and you would be welcome to address me as such."

She handed him the envelope and gave him the simple directions to the restaurant.

Martha watched the young fellow walk down Harbor Street and disappear when he took a left turn onto Main Street, in the direction of the Eatery.

She thought, "This is why I adore the hospitality business so. I get to meet such characters. I am certain that he made up the name Ian just to keep me off the scent. If you have been in the people business as long as I have you have seen this cover-up a hundred times.(but usually with adulterers..um).

"He does seem to be much more pleasant and at ease today though. If only he would shave that horrid stubble on his face I bet he would look just like that movie star..." She couldn't remember the actor's name.

"Perhaps I should not have been so fast to alert the others to his odd behavior?"

3

Ian couldn't remember the last time that he felt so good. He inhaled the refreshing salt air and gawked at the understated elegance of the Village Green and the sea captains' homes and shops that aligned its perimeter.

For a brief moment he stood under the shade of a large elm and stared at the marvelous ivy covered Episcopal Church that stood its proud watch. Funny, the past often reminded him of his pain, but this was different. He liked what he saw and felt in this historic community. He determined, at that very moment, that he would extend his stay until he got word from back home that all was clear.

He didn't care if anyone was in earshot when he shouted his faux decree, "Destiny will have to wait."

Ian reached into his pocket and pulled out the vial of pain pills that his doctor had prescribed after the assault. Even though his head felt somewhat better the past few days, the blackouts were intermittent of late, it was more out of habit, prevention, and the desire to feel a good rush of energy, that he coaxed a small blue colored tablet loose from the bottle and into his left palm. He forced himself to swallow it without the aid of a liquid.

He spotted the Eatery sign up ahead, on the same side as he, but instead of going straight there he decided to walk across the Village Green and have a look at the quaint shops that formed an inviting chorus line on the opposite side. En route he picked up a broken oak branch and threw it as far as he could for the two dogs to fetch (the excited Golden Labs that had come up to sniff at his heels). Their owner smiled a warm thank you and he nodded to her. He felt weightless the remainder of the stroll.

He walked into one of the cottage style shops, a musty home goods store, and browsed around for a few minutes. The owner was busy at her desk and didn't bother to acknowledge his presence. This made him feel even more relaxed because, unlike most people, he reveled in the role of stranger.

As much as he would have liked to go into the tiny hardware shop next door, a family owned operation for over one hundred years, not some ripoff franchise, his empty stomach reminded him that he should trot over to the Eatery to get breakfast before they stopped serving. Perhaps on the way back to the Hibiscus Inn he would pay a visit to Dimmock's Hardware and Necessities Shop.

The entrance to the Eatery was at the rear of the one story gray clapboard building. He passed by its steamy windows and could see that there were diners inside and that a couple of them, men, had turned to stare at him. When he had reached the wooden entry door he walked in and lingered to get his bearings.

Ian stood at the far end of the elongated restaurant which was much more narrow than it was wide. Opposite him was a thirty-five-foot-long wooden counter with its' aged red leather stools, about sixteen in all. It was rather nondescript but inviting. The space behind the counter was very tight with just enough room for two wait staff to pass by one another, if each were turned sideways. The newly painted white walls were covered in colorful signage, with all the breakfast choices written in the two left hand columns and the luncheon selections written to the right. There was a large cash register affixed to the countertop down at the other end from where Ian stood. The restaurant was spotless.

There was one male patron at the counter, at the end stool there near the entry. The scene seemed *Hopper-esque* to him. He forgot that it was after eleven a.m. and in between services, so no wonder it was more than three quarters empty.

Along the windowed wall to his left, that he had just walked past, there were five veneered tables each with accommodations for four patrons, all unoccupied. Down at the very end, opposite the cash register, was a large round veneered table that was meant for a party of eight but was cramped with, he counted them, nine occupants, all male.

He hadn't noticed that an elderly waitress had limped in obvious discomfort on her bunion covered toes down to a spot opposite him, on the other side of the counter. She wore a black hair net on top of her dyed short length silver locks. With a large menu tucked under her flabby arm and a pot of coffee in her opposite hand, she spoke with a thick Massachusetts accent, "Sit anywah ya like hun." But before he made a move she set the menu down on the counter and turned over a coffee mug and poured a fresh cup, in a blatant attempt to manipulate him into sitting right there. She wanted to save herself the potential marathon walk all the way around the counter to a table on the other side. As if in a hypnotic state he took her cue and sat down on the stool in front of her.

However, seconds later, when he saw an attractive waitress dash out from behind the kitchen doors and plant herself near the cash register, without saying a word to the older waitress, Ian stood up and walked down to that end. He took a seat on the first stool in from the cash register. His back faced the always boisterous *Round Table Group*.

The older waitress was annoyed by his rude action and yelled to her counterpart, "Heads up Caroline, heah comes a real gentleman ya way." She whisked the mug off of the countertop and dumped the poured coffee into the sink underneath.

Caroline, who had worked with Dorothy for two years, knew from her tone that this guy must be a real winner. She nodded back to her senior colleague.

"Hi. What'll it be?" Caroline asked him.

She was drop dead perfect. A natural beauty, she was twenty-five and wore her long blond hair in a casual ponytail and her olive skin set off her baby blue eyes. She was gorgeous.

"Whatever you suggest. I can see that you have fine taste," he flirted.

"How about the check then," she shot back.

When she gathered that he hadn't gotten her quip she asked, "First off, would you like a cup of coffee or tea?"

"*Earl Grey* would be fine, no lemon please."

She yelled down to Dorothy, "Any *Earl Grey*?"

Dorothy shook her head in disbelief that the jerk had ordered a name brand tea. She had trouble bending down but managed to open a door underneath the rear counter and fumbled through the basket of loose tea bags. She shouted to Caroline, "Lipton, Lipton and Lipton. No wait, there are two bags (she butchered the pronunciation) of Chamomile."

Caroline said, "You heard her. What's your pleasure?"

He smiled at her, not to make her uneasy but to let her know that he liked her. He didn't answer her question but instead said, "I can see I've made you feel a bit uncomfortable. I apologize. It's just that it's uncanny how much your looks and mannerisms remind me of someone."

He could see that Caroline didn't know who that someone was, so he clarified, "My ex."

"Don't hold that against me please," Caroline said.

She raised her hand in front of herself with her palm facing him and said, "Hold on to that thought I'll be right back," as she responded to a shout that had just bellowed out from the cook in the kitchen, "Orders up!"

Caroline served the nine men, came back to the counter and removed her order pad from her apron. She ribbed him, "Made up your mind? We do close at three you know."

He had a vacant look so she reminded him once again of his tea choices.

Ian snapped to and answered, "I'm very particular. No Earl Grey um. Do you have bottled water?"

She spun around, took a step and grabbed a Poland Springs bottle from the cooler and set it down in front of him.

"Thank you Caroline. May I bother you for a glass as well?"

"You are a particular one aren't you? It's nice to have a gentleman at the counter for a change." She smiled at him.

She reached for an eight-ounce glass on the shelf underneath the counter and asked, "So what'll it be?"

She pointed behind her to the menus on the white wall. "Breakfast choices on the left are available 'til noon. The rest you can have any time after eleven."

"I'd like to have breakfast please. Do you have a few specials that you can recommend that aren't the usual eggs and toast?" he asked.

"I guess you can't read *Massachusetts*," she laughed as she pointed to what was written on the wall under the heading *Hank's Specials*. "My favorites this time of year are Hank's pumpkin nut pancakes and maple syrup. You'll come back for more I promise you."

"Sounds good to me. Set me up with them please and I'd like whatever berries you might have. One more thing, could you ask that *loudmouth* asshole behind me to take it down a decibel or two?"

She chuckled and said, "He's mellow at the moment, wait 'til he gets into a conspiracy theory or two then you'll need ear plugs."

"Conspiracies are games little-minded people play. They want you to know that they alone are privy to inside information that the rest of us mere *numb nuts* are blind to. It's their desperate need to feel important. And have you noticed that they're always bitter, blaming someone else when things don't go their way. The football game was *fixed*, the election was *rigged*, immigrants are evil. *Whinny victims*. Avoid them. They're just *vacuum vampires* who suck the reality out of the room. What's the guy's name?" Ian asked.

"He's Bob Maxwell, he owns the Village Realty. Bob and Doc Nickerson own half of the village, the best half of course."

"The mouthful always grabs another helping," he muttered.

Caroline turned away and put his order on the tray at the kitchen window and tapped on the bell to alert the cook, "Cummin' in Hank."

The patron at the other end of the counter had left so Ian and the *Round Table Group* were the lone customers.

Ian reached for Friday's newspaper that was next to the cash register, the Falmouth Enterprise, and scanned through the paper. As was to be expected for such a small population, the articles were about simple, small town matters; tourist attractions, fishing charts, high school sports, school lunch menus for next week, cooking tips etc. He came upon the two-page section that was devoted to events in this nearby village so he took the time to read them. It all seemed somewhat familiar to him and it was easy to grasp the pulse of this cozy village that he had happened upon. Well, it wasn't happenstance that brought him here, as he did know that he would arrive on the Cape, just not to this tiny community located in the shadows of beautiful Falmouth.

When he had finished the paper and its' *townie* gossip he noticed a stack of large pink colored flyers propped up against the side of the register. They had a large picture of a child on the front. She looked so innocent. The headline read, "Baker girl's body found in Palmers Pond."

He read the article and paid close attention to the details of the little girl's tragedy. She had lived in Marblehead and had been on vacation visiting her grandparents for a long weekend. His eyes teared up and his heart felt heavy. The sad news had considerable effect upon him. He felt the child's loss and the family's grief.

He started to unravel a bit. He massaged his temples as his head started to pound. Soon he became irritated by the noisy group seated nearby, they seemed to be mocking him. Annoyed by the fear bullshit he could hear Maxwell spewing, Ian swiveled around on his stool and shot a menacing glare that managed to stop his monologue for a brief moment. Maxwell would later tell his colleagues when he looked into the stranger's eyes there was evil written in them. It caused him to shudder.

Bob Maxwell's reaction to the stranger wasn't out of the ordinary for him. He saw terror around every corner. He trusted no one, except for his immediate friends and colleagues. He was a married man, fifty years old, tall and thin, had a slight paunch around his belt and his black hair had grayed at the temples, which gave him a more distinguished look than perhaps he deserved. He felt it his duty, as a role model in the community, to always maintain a squeaky-clean image, so no one ever saw him wearing anything but a pressed sport coat and tie in public. He was a sound businessman, citizen, unwavering patriot, and member of the Town Council. His political affiliations (although he didn't trust any of them) were more Conservative Republican with the occasional dash of fascism sprinkled in.

Maxwell was a reactionary if ever there was one. He was convinced that the *progressive liberal subversives* running the media were leading the country into its rapid decline. In his nostalgic mind the clock needed to be turned back to the times when people were respectful and knew their proper place (his bigoted code-speak). And in order to accomplish such a daunting task he was confident, like the true *tunnel-visioned narcissist* that he was, that he alone could straighten things out, if only people would get their heads out of their asses and listen to him. Be clear, that if you didn't see things his way you were considered an unpatriotic, *socialist lefty* (Maxwell always painted with a wide *red* brush.) Hell, he even once accused the town's esteemed librarian, Mabel Bourne, a sweet eighty-seven-year-old lady, *Daughter of the Revolution* chairperson, of poisoning the minds of the local youth when she had displayed books of filthy liberal propaganda at the front entry of the public library for all to see. He was referring to Obama's *Audacity of Hope*, which had just come out at the time and which was displayed in the *Recent Best Sellers* rack where it belonged.

Now to be fair, Maxwell did have a likable side to him. He was a nice enough guy and if he called you friend he would be loyal to his death. But as the ultimate *know-it-all*, for as long as the villagers could remember he'd been obsessed with warning them of one ill intended conspiracy after another, both national and international. He blamed Bush and the infamous *Families*, whom he believed ruled the world along with their government cronies, for the attacks on the World Trade Towers. He knew they too had schemed to cause both Wall Street and the real estate markets to crash, so that they and their friends could get better deals for themselves.(By the way, many of the villagers laughed at the irony that Bob was the largest beneficiary of the downturn. He had swooped up as many foreclosed properties that he could get his hands on.)Furthermore, he distrusted the *Fed* and the soon to be extinct U.S. dollar, so he urged everyone to buy and stash gold.

Maxwell was anti any social programs as well. He'd be damned if deadbeats and illegals weren't out to abuse our healthcare system, take our jobs, and drain our resources. And he warned that letting any Syrian refuges, or any Muslims for that matter, into this country would have dire consequences, with all the terrorists that hid in their midst. He despised the Germans and other immigrant welcoming countries, and without question he loved the *Wall* idea between Mexico and the U.S. You see, Maxwell felt entitled. He never subscribed to the notion that all people were created equal, just American white people were afforded those constitutional rights.

If you really wanted to wind him up just ask him how he felt about our first black American President. Maxwell *knew* that Barack Obama was placed in power by the aforementioned *Families* as their *politically correct* puppet. He called Obama's transparent nomination the ultimate homage to affirmative action. He hated the man, not because he was black of course. Maxwell, who considered himself fair and honest, and definitely without a racist bone in his body, was adamant that President Obama was a closet Muslim, a non-American citizen born outside the U.S. and therefore ineligible to hold office. Obama's sole purpose he warned, was to take away our guns and open our borders so that his terrorist buddies could take over America.

Fear and hatred had gripped him at a young age and even though most of what he warned hadn't yet materialized, like many wide-eyed conspiracy theories, some proved true and others were very believable and held kernels of truths. They validated his belief that the world was in the anti-Christ's hands.

His wife Gail became very concerned. "Honey, the world's such a different place than you see it. I'm worried because you've become so obsessed with these deep dark plots. You're so angry and distrust any-one who doesn't hold firm to your beliefs. It's not healthy Bob. You're the one who harbors the negativity inside. It's bound to take a toll on you darling."

For a brief moment Maxwell wondered if Gail was one of *them*...

Ian's stares were interrupted when he heard Caroline set down the utensils on the counter. He swiveled around, caught a glimpse of her bright smile, and his mood changed back again.

She said, "I can see you're a real feisty one. What nerve to scowl at one of our esteemed town leaders." She figured that this must be the guy whom Martha had phoned her about earlier that morning.

Then she changed her tone a smidgeon and warned him, "They're a powerful bunch when they're all together, and a bunch of *wussies* when they're on their own. I wouldn't advise you to pick a fight, not if you plan to have a quiet stay at the Hibiscus for more than one night."

She didn't hear him ask as she walked back into the kitchen, "How did you know I'm staying at the Hibiscus Inn?"

This was the same small town mentality that he had just fled. Everyone knew everything. How fast it could all close in around you. He had worked with people for so many years and understood what motivated them and he also knew himself all too well. He wouldn't be able to keep silent, even though it was imperative that he do just that. He wasn't naive. The inevitable confrontations were around the bend. Although he decided, at least for a while, that he'd try to concentrate on Caroline and the amenities of this beautiful village, not on those know-it-alls behind him. He'd explore the town for as long as he could, before he tackled the tainted, human sideshow that inevitably spoiled all things of beauty.

When Caroline served him the sumptuous pumpkin pancakes she put down a maple syrup container on the table as well. He folded the Baker girl flyer and attempted to put it into his inside jacket pocket but it met with resistance, as the envelope that Martha had asked him to deliver already occupied that particular slot. He put the flyer in the opposite inside pocket and removed Martha's envelope and asked, "Caroline that's not real Vermont Maple syrup is it?"

"No," she answered. "Doc Nickerson has the real stuff, I'll go get it."

"No, please, don't bother I'll do it. I have to give him this letter from his sister," he said, as held the envelope up in front of him.

"Which one is he?"

Caroline took the pencil from behind her ear and tore off a check stub from her pad. She drew a circle and made several x marks around its perimeter. "They call themselves the *Round Table Group*. They've been meeting here six days a week for the last fifteen years I'm told. Let me give you the layout."

She pointed to the twelve o'clock position on the circle and moved clockwise to the adjacent positions around the dial. "They always sit in the same seats. Doc sits here at twelve o'clock; on his left is your friend Bob Maxwell; next the very tall, balding man, is Stuart Holmes, the president of the Village Bank and Trust; next to him, the very short and stocky guy, is Gilbert Andrade, he's a real estate attorney, and chairman of the Planning Board; next to him, that powerful looking dude is Police Chief Carl Nickerson, Doc's cousin; on his left is the editor of the *Enterprise*, Silvio Medeiros; the vacant seat is, was, always occupied by Dale Baker, owner of Baker Construction, but he's devastated by the loss of his granddaughter who drowned yesterday. She was such a beautiful little girl. I don't think he'll ever be the same."

Ian asked, "Why was she all alone by the pond? Where were her parents?"

"I see that you've read about the terrible tragedy. The family has sequestered themselves as you might expect. The details will come out in a few days I'm sure," Caroline said.

Since Ian didn't react further, she resumed her clockwork. "At nine o'clock sits the buttoned up, bowed tied Bill Dimmock, Doc's brother-in-law and owner of Dimmock's Hardware and Necessities. His wife, Doc's sister Eileen, owns the Village Bake Shop across the street. That's where all the restaurants in the area get their baked goods from. Next to Bill, the guy with the long brown hair, is John Turnbull a fine architect. To round out the *Round Table*, on Doc's right sits the always stoic

Michael Small, owner of The Village Funeral Home. There you have it."

"Thank you for pointing out the particulars of the *All White Honky Group*. The privileged few. Not a person of color amongst them.."

Ian swiveled one hundred eighty degrees, got off the stool and stepped the three paces to their table. Caroline watched with heightened curiosity.

The conversation at the table had remained frisky, but when Ian sat down at the table in Dale Baker's vacated seat and began to speak, they all went quiet. They wondered what he had to say and were amazed by his rude behavior, that he hadn't introduced himself or even asked them to pardon his interruption.

"I am sure you will welcome this brief interlude. You couldn't possibly want to hear another sentence of fictitious bullshit spewed by this fear-goat," he said as he pointed to Bob Maxwell, but all the while he looked straight ahead at the doctor.

Many at the table muttered as they waited to hear what this odd stranger had to say next. They didn't know what to make of him.

"Oh, Doctor Nickerson your snoop of a sister asked me to deliver this important envelope to you." He held the envelope above his head, as if to indicate that it was out of reach.

"I'll trade it for that pitcher of real Vermont Maple Syrup that I see you are finished with," he said to the doctor.

They were all dumfounded by his sarcastic tone. The doctor, with his short cut grey hair, who always dressed as neat as a pin and looked as if he had just come out of the shower, maintained his self-control and responded," To whom do I have the pleasure of making this exchange?"

Ian shot back, "My rude disruption causes you pleasure? Well that's rather weird and not my intent. Have you tried therapy Doc?"

Doc Nickerson and cronies ganged up on him, "Jerk. Asshole. How dare! Who the hell do you think you are?" they lashed out.

Ian said, "I am a guest at your sister's inn. You can call me the *nameless lodger* if you need to label me. Now please just pass me the maple syrup before my pancakes get cold."

With that, Ian stood up, bent way over the table to accept the pitcher that the doctor had passed down to him and placed the envelope on top of the table and gave it an aggressive shove in the Doc's direction. It fell off of the edge and landed in the doctor's lap.

With an automatic polite response Doc said, "Thank You."

"Please Doc don't thank me. Instead you should thank all of your pathetic patients whom you've hooked on one pill or another and your pharmaceutical cronies for the fat commissions."

Doc and all his companions were outraged and they said so. Chief Nickerson told him he'd better go back to his seat and not be a bother again, or else.

He didn't pay much attention to their threats as he grabbed the pitcher and turned to walk back to his stool. Once seated at the counter he swiveled back towards them and apologized, "Sorry. I meant no harm. Please forgive me. Feel free to continue your pompous *circle jerk* without any further interruptions from me. Have a great day." He turned back around to enjoy his breakfast.

As to be expected he caused a genuine commotion at the dignitaries' table and a cacophony of protests rang out. However, the kind Doctor raised his hands and begged his colleagues, "Gentlemen, Martha warned me about this guy. Let's use our better judgment and not lower ourselves to this troubled man's level. It's obvious that he's off his meds," he reasoned.

Meanwhile, Caroline leaned over the counter and whispered to him, "You're a crazy one. That was terrific! I've never seen Doc and his apostles so rattled. What's your game?"

He said, "They're all the same no matter where you go. People just want to hear themselves talk. Brag, brag, me, me, me. They feel they have to tell you whom and what they know, where they've been, how successful they are. I'm sure you've gotten one of those awful self-centered end of the year letters. No wonder social media is the rage. All they want is to use you as their audience, for their own vanity. They're good at masking their insecurities from you and from themselves. They could care less about any other human beings in this world, except for their inner circle. Separation no connection. They don't care how genuine or how loyal you are. They get so caught up in their own sense of self-importance, that's what sickens me. They always want to show you that they're the smartest person in the room. And when you put several like minds together, well they're near impossible to tolerate. They become dangerous to others and to themselves. Look at that pathetic narcissist President and all the hate he spews; they're all so full of themselves. They have so many sycophants who worship them that they start believing that they must in fact be anointed. The *many chosen few*. They're such a joke. I'll take an honest, real person like you any day of the week."

Caroline blushed. She glanced over to the *Round Table* and whispered to him, "If looks could kill as they say, you'd be a dead man. Why don't I move you down to the other end of the counter, before this gets any uglier."

He agreed and picked up his bottled water and the syrup pitcher. Caroline grabbed his plate and utensils and set him up at a counter stool which was at the other end, opposite the entrance, where he had first sat down.

Caroline left him and went back to service the *Round Table Group*.

He glimpsed at her in an animated conversation with them, and wondered if she would defend him, or take the easier path and side with the regulars. In his heart he wished to believe that she wasn't one of them.

After he had eaten breakfast he removed the pink flyer from his jacket pocket and reread it. The little girl's plight touched him, tears flowed down his cheeks. He paid particular attention to the descriptions of her parents and brother who were left behind. "The survivors are the unfortunates who'll pay the price of death. It's how they react that matters now. How well I know". He crumpled up the pink flyer and placed it on the plate.

A few moments later Caroline brought him his check. She noticed his tears, so she reached into her pocket, pulled out a clean tissue and wiped his face. He acted as if he hadn't noticed.

She put the tab on the counter, it totaled under ten dollars, but he handed her a one hundred dollar bill and said, "Keep the change. You've put up with me and them, so you've more than earned it. I'm sorry if I've caused you any grief. I don't know what's gotten into me."

She thanked him for the excessive tip, and said, "Don't worry about me I can take care of myself."

She changed subjects. "What's your name, and what are you up to today?"

"My name is Garrett, he felt like a Garrett just then. What am I up to? Well, I think I'll walk off this delicious breakfast and check out the town, see the sights," he said.

Caroline shocked him when she said, "I work the breakfast shift and will be off in a minute or so. If you can wait you can walk me home. On the way I'll point out all the interesting details of our quiet, but handsome village." She picked up his plate and mug and put them in the gray plastic bin on the shelf underneath the counter.

He was excited with her offer to be his guide and told her he'd wait an hour if need be.

She left to cash out and to get her sweater.

Caroline did find him unique, not as a love interest, but as a man of the world, a breath of fresh air. A complete opposite from the predictable, upright citizenry of this hamlet (older people most of them) where she was born and raised and had seldom ventured from. She could see that his use of *shock value* was his primary weapon and although it made her somewhat uncomfortable that she had taken his side, she wished to know more about what made this unusual man tick. Besides, Doc Nickerson and the others had encouraged her to find out what this peculiar guy was up to, so a little walk couldn't hurt.

Too bad for her that her invitation would appear to our dreaming man to signal that she was attracted to him.

He still wasn't thinking straight after all that had happened to him. His wife had also come to him out of the blue and he felt that perhaps it was a good omen that brought Caroline to him.

He would misread her intentions and begin to obsess on her.

4

Garrett's eyes crossed and chills shivered through his entire body. The OxyContin had kicked in. His headache had subsided and now he couldn't sit still. He almost jumped off the stool and started to pace. He was excited with anticipation of his walk with Caroline.

Maxwell noticed Garrett's jitters and warned his comrades that they should all be wary of this nut. The doctor chided him, "Maybe he's an Iranian plant, or worse, runs an *ISIS* cell that wants to recruit our naive teenagers and waitresses and turn them into heroic suicide bombers. Falmouth is such a hot bed of intelligence it very well might be a target for al-Baghdadi's boys."

"WHOI (Woods Hole Oceanographic Institute) could very well be of interest to terrorists," Maxwell said.

"We shouldn't let Caroline, or anyone else for that matter, out of our sight when they're alone with him," Maxwell added.

"Caroline's a smart girl and can handle herself. She won't stray from the public eye," the Chief said.

Caroline was the first to speak once they were outside the coffee shop. "I wouldn't say you've endeared yourself to the ruling fathers. If Bob Maxwell had his way he'd have Chief Nickerson lock you up on suspicion of intent to incite a riot," she laughed, as did he.

Garrett was antsy as the pill provided an extra wallop to his brain and increased his energy twofold. Unable to control his actions he began to ramble. "Gosh you're so pretty, do you know that? Of course you know it, how couldn't you? I mean, I'm sure everyone tells you that all the time. But do they tell you that your real beauty is in your personality and your kind ways? The minute I saw you I was struck dumb by your presence," he confessed.

As they turned right onto Main Street and walked facing the bright noonday sun she was agitated. "Look Garrett, let's get this straight right away ok? I'm engaged and will be getting married soon. I offered to give you a mini tour because you interest me and I thought you might enjoy a local's point of view."

He seemed hurt by her harsh tone so she corrected, "I thought it would be fun to get to know you. You're shaped from so different a mold than the men in this town are cast from. I can tell that you've traveled and seen a lot and perhaps I can be of help to you. You know, introduce you to some people, if you promise to behave. Show you around, that sort of thing."

"Oh please don't think that I meant any harm. It's difficult for me, as you have seen, to keep my thoughts to myself when I feel moved by something, someone. I must admit that I did think, or should I say hope, that maybe you did like me in some small way. I know it sounds crazy but it's not often that a gorgeous and heady woman asks a stranger to take a stroll with her without having some level of interest in him. I know, I know. I need to filter my words, that's what I always told my wife that she needed to do, but I find it near impossible to do so myself, if that makes any sense. Sorry to rant but I am a bit nervous in your presence," he admitted. He was conscious of his speedy chatter and became vexed with himself.

"Don't get all freaked. I just wanted to be out front with you that's all. Chill, I won't bite," she said.

Caroline wondered if this tour was such a smart idea after all. She decided to change their discomfort and pointed across Main Street. "That's our well stacked Village Book Shop. Do you read? I'm sure you do, you look like a reader or writer."

He nodded but didn't speak. He hoped to control his nerves. He did appreciate that she didn't ask him any personal questions because he felt helpless before her and knew that he was liable to spill the beans if she were but to ask. He must be guarded, but why? He knew from all of his years in practice that someday he'd have to let it all out. Release his dark ashes like a once dormant volcano that had turned active.

"But not now. Stay silent. The time is not right," he scolded himself.

"Remain anonymous, don't get too familiar. You're way too vulnerable and she's too dangerous for you."

Garrett stared at her, he couldn't help it that his eyes traced every inch of her beautiful being. Even in jeans and a simple pale pink sweater she looked magnificent.

Caroline wasn't looking at him and continued, "The owner's a beautiful single woman in her forties and I think you'd enjoy each other's company. Her name is Annie Temple. She's very witty and smart as can be. After work I often spend some time at the book store with her. We exchange book ideas, gossip. She has several comfortable lounge chairs and offers free coffee or tea. Matter of fact I'm pretty sure she has your favorite, Earl Grey. She is so talented too. She decorated the store herself and it's as cozy as the Hibiscus Inn in my opinion."

He spoke somewhat perturbed, "Why are so many businesses here called the *Village* this or the *Village* that. Where's the creativity, the imagination? Don't the *Round Table Goons* allow any new ideas around here?"

She heard his shock attempt but refused to be suckered in, she didn't answer him. Instead, with her slender, long index finger she directed his attention to the home store and flower shop, the arcade, the record store etc., and gave him the quick backgrounds as to who owned them.

As they walked further up Main Street she pointed to a figure a block away and said, "See that woman who just got out of the blue station wagon? She's Amelia Nickerson. A very unique person." Many in town were not as kind as Caroline as they referred to Amelia as the *Village Idiot*.

When they got closer to Amelia he could see that her Audi wagon was filled to the brim with boxes and stuff, a quintessential *junk lady*. The car looked as if it hadn't been washed since nineteen ninety-eight when it had first came off the showroom floor. Amelia was rather tall and attractive, with long white hair that often didn't look well on an older woman but she somehow pulled it off. She wore a pretty long floral red and white dress that matched the red leather belt and a white sweater worn over them. But on her feet were rolled down, frayed white bobby sox and filthy, once white, sneakers. With great effort she leaned into a large ribbed metal waste basket and rummaged through the debris as she honed in on the three empty beer cans on the bottom. He could see her panties.

He asked Caroline, "Another Nickerson? She's not related to the Doctor or Martha is she?"

"He wishes she weren't I'm sure, but...well I don't know that for certain. I shouldn't have said that. He's in denial, in public anyway. You know he's a very nice man underneath that professional exterior. Angie Bowker, a teller at the Village Bank and Trust (we do have a lot of businesses named *Village*, you're right) told me that he had set up a dual bank account with Amelia some time ago and that he manages it for her. I've never seen them together, nor has anyone else that I know, but. So yes, Amelia is his older sister," she said.

"I'm twenty-five, and as long as I've known her she has been on her own and looks and acts just as you see her now. What I do know is that the Nickersons had five children and the father was a Boston lawyer and a bit of a runaround. Their mother had become very fragile after the birth of their last child (Doc) and was bedridden for a few years thereafter, right up to her premature death in fact. Poor Amelia, since she was the second eldest, and at age fifteen I think, was forced to quit school and run the household. She cared for Gregory, Eileen, Doc and her sick mother. Sad. I hear that she did an excellent job and was devoted to Doc in particular, who was the baby. Martha was the eldest and was away in England where she went to university and stayed on and met and married Harold Lawrence. What a kind man he was. Martha and Doc have always been very close, she's been sort of a mother figure to him, but they're not close with Amelia.. I said there were five children but make that six, because her father had another kid. The story goes that he got Amelia pregnant, the son of a bitch. Imagine your own father. Anyway, at around age eighteen he threw Amelia out on her own when she was about to give birth, of course he denied that it was his and made it seem that Amelia was some sort of slut. He gave her enough money to take care of herself and her new-born child and he bought her a little house on Palmers Pond. That's where she's lived for over fifty years. Doc was around three years old at the time I think and doesn't recall much.

"Amelia never was the same once her mother died and she went downhill when her father threw her out on her own. And although she acts as if she were absent a few marbles (camouflage for survival I think) she managed to raise her son Darren and send him off to college with the money she had saved from what her father had given her and the bottles and whatnots that she had collected. Darren meant the world to her but.. Her's is a dreadful story for sure when I tell you that as far as anyone knows she hasn't heard from him since he left for Hartwick College over thirty years ago. He was embarrassed by her is what everyone in the village figured and always was as a kid. Since he was little he told his friends that she was his loony aunt."

They remained silent as they walked past Amelia who had just gotten back into her station wagon. She nodded hello to Caroline and to the stranger with her. Garrett just stared at her.

"Where are Amelia's other brother and father?" he asked.

"Gregory died in a plane crash years ago, somewhere in Spain. Mr. Nickerson moved to Argentina in the seventies I think and nobody heard another word from him. I'm sure he's dead by now," she answered.

They walked a few more blocks and Caroline stopped and said to him, "Well here we are. This is my corner. I live down there," she pointed to a row of two story sea captains' homes on Sea Street, none in particular. She didn't want him to know which one was hers.

There was a very awkward pause, neither knew what next to say or do.

Caroline began to walk away but then she turned back and yelled, "Hey Garrett. The wonderful *Church Bazaar's* tomorrow. You must come. It's loads of fun; card games, music, rides for the kids. The whole area comes out in force and each year it's for a different and wonderful cause. This year it's in memory of Carrie Baker, the little girl whom you read about in the paper."

When he heard that it was for the girl's benefit he said, "I think I will. What a worthy cause. What time does it begin? When will you be there?"

"It starts at noon but until six or so it's mainly for the kids. You'd best arrive after six that's when the food, beer, wine and adult games begin. And please Garrett behave yourself and spend lots of money for the *cause*," she said.

Then she said, "You seem to be touched by Carrie. That's so sweet. You're just a soft, sensitive man underneath that fake annoyed exterior. See you tomorrow."

Ian, Garrett, whomever he had them call him, felt elated. She had invited him to the *Bazaar*. She saw through his irritated exterior that he was a good soul. There was a ray of hope he reckoned.

He always needed the approval of a good-looking woman, and the disillusioned prospect that he could somehow lure Caroline into liking him caused him to feel guilty about the commotion he had incited at the coffee shop earlier. He determined that he would be on his best behavior tomorrow at the *Bazaar* and apologize to all whom he might have offended. After all, they were Caroline's friends and if he was to get anywhere with her it'd be best not to have them as enemies.

He turned back in the direction from where he had come, put his right hand over his brow to shade his eyes and surveyed the village to see where he might walk next.

As he was about to cross the street he saw Amelia's station wagon turn off of Main Street and disappear down a narrow road which was located between the pharmacy and the record store. He walked two blocks straight to that road and read the Palmers Pond Lane sign that hung above his head on the iron post. He looked down the lane and got a peek of the pond some five hundred yards away. The paved lane he noticed turned into a seashell covered track about half way to the pond.

"So this is where little Carrie died and where Amelia lives," he thought.

He leaned against the pharmacy's wall and took in the view down the lane. It beckoned him. He jogged in its direction and hoped to get a glimpse of Amelia. The lane looked perfect to him with its' *Mohawk haircut-like* grass center that stuck up in a perfect row between the two tracks of white seashells for an auto's tires. It was bordered by lilac trees on either side, that had long ago in June lost their purple flowers, but looked great nonetheless with their shinny green leaves.

He hummed a tune aloud that rather pleased him, although he didn't know if he had just made it up or had heard it once before. It didn't matter. It was twelve thirty on a glorious afternoon.

The lane ended and he reached the tranquil pond. He scanned the expansive mowed lawns that led to the water's edge and his eyes were drawn to the two grey wooden benches that were set in strategic viewing positions. They faced the pond and the lone wooden raft with its colorful buoys that bobbed in the middle of the water. The pond was glassy still. For a brief second he felt as if he were stuck inside a live painting.

He could see across the small sized body of water to the five large clapboard homes on the other side. They all had large porches that faced the pond and he squinted to see that all had steep wooden steps that connected to their own wooden docks. Small canoes, paddle boats and kayaks were moored to each.

Because the Cape is much further south than the upper New England states just a few trees had begun to show off their magnificent orange and red fall colors, a prelude to the brilliant landscape that wouldn't engulf the entire area for another month or so. To his right he noticed a couple of homes spaced a good distance apart and to his left, a few yards away, there was a single weathered shingled house which sat high up on stilts. Underneath it the blue Audi wagon was parked.

He stared at Amelia's home and didn't see that she had pulled back the curtain and that her two suspicious eyes peered down at him as well.

Garrett turned his attention to the pond and felt a little uncomfortable, confused as he wondered why no one else was here on a Saturday and on such a perfect *Indian Summer* afternoon.

He walked closer toward the pond, all the while looking about for any evidence of the little girl's recent drowning. He could sense her presence. When he reached the pond he was surprised to see that there was an abrupt and dangerous fall off into the deep water. This was more like a lake he thought.

Garrett was miffed that he hadn't brought the *Obit* along so that he could reread the scant details and perhaps determine her precise entry point. He played detective and at first concluded that she must have seen the raft ahead and thought that she could swim to it. He remembered that she was found a mere few feet off shore. She mustn't have known that the pond's entry was so steep right from the start. It was man made and was the deepest pond on the entire Upper Cape he had learned in the article.

She must have been disoriented when she went down. "Why didn't she know how to swim and where the hell were her parents? How could they've let her out of their sight?"

He sat down on the damp grass next to a few noticeable tire tracks. He crossed his legs and inhaled a deep breath of the crisp air. As the sun warmed his face he closed his eyes and fell into a meditative state. He hoped to get her vibration.

But in a few moments Garrett's tranquility was interrupted when he sensed the presence of another person. He turned his head around and was startled to see Amelia standing a dozen feet away. She held a shotgun that was aimed straight at him.

"Ya trespassin'," she snarled.

Before he could figure out what to say to her she said, "This heah is private propatee. Yah don't think the damn town would mow the lawns so good do yah?"

"I am sorry. I thought this was a public park," he attempted to placate her.

"Well it's not. This is myin' the last I knew and has been for moah yeahs than you've been alive."

She saw that he meant no harm so she used her shotgun as a pointer and indicated, a few yards away, where the Town's land began. "Past that wooden stake is wayah the public propatee begins."

"Thanks."

Then he proposed a burning question since she no longer had taken his presence as a threat. "Do you know about the little girl who drowned here? I bet you don't miss a trick around here. I mean, where the kid went into the pond and why she was alone, that sort of stuff?"

She didn't answer but asked him, "Was you the guy I saw snoopin' out heah yestaday? What's yah name?"

Garrett didn't speak.

"I saw you walkin' in the village with that beautaful waitress and pointin' at me. Then you show up on my propatee. Why?"

"Caroline showed me the village and pointed out some of its wonderful people and sites. You happened to be on our walk. I asked her about the little girl's death and she told me where the pond was so I decided, out of curiosity, to see it for myself."

"My momma told me it's nevah propah ta staah at anyone. Specially an outsidah shouldn't staah like you did at me in town."

"Oh, I'm sorry. I wasn't aware that I was staring at you. Although many times I've been told that I intimidate people with what they say is my *intense* stare. They've said that I looked through them when in fact I was looking for them."

Amelia looked bewildered by his statement. "Ah you some kinda cop nosin' about? The Chief and his fools have ahweady investigated. Nothin' else ta be done."

"No..no. I'm just an interested tourist fascinated by the fact that misfortune visits small Cape Cod villages too. I can't imagine how a six year old could wander hundreds of yards from her mother down this lane and walk or jump into the pond. Or how her parents didn't have a clue that she had disappeared?"

"She didn't walk she was on huh bicycle," Amelia wished she hadn't said that.

"The obituary didn't mention that she was on a bike. Are you sure?" he groped for more.

"She rode it on my damn lawn I should say I know. That's enough about huh. God called for huh so young cause she wasn't payin' attention I guess," Amelia said.

He knew there was more, much more to her story, but also he knew, from his years of experience, that it was best not to push too hard right now. There would be an opportunity some other time.

Still energized he talked about how perfect he found this village to be and how he might consider a much longer stay than he'd at first planned.

He thought about what Caroline had told him about Amelia's sad upbringing and he felt close to her. Then he remembered that Caroline had said the *Bazaar* was tomorrow, perhaps..

He formed a plan. "I heard that there is a wonderful event in the village tomorrow, at the church. I'd love to go but I'm too shy, a stranger and all, and because just an hour ago or so I caused an uproar with those stuffy know-it-alls, at the Eatery. You know who I mean? *The Round Table Group*. I'm sure that they'd try to get even with me if I went alone."

There was silence for a few seconds, then he asked, "Will you be there?"

"Waayah?" she replied

"The *Church Bazaar*," he answered.

Amelia said, "Neva been befawh, why go now? I'm not like them. I'm as much an outsidah as you in this town."

"Well two strangers make a couple and to hell with anyone else. Would you give me the honor of being my date tomorrow? I'd be very grateful," he said.

For a good ten minutes they went back and forth debating why it would or would not be such a great idea for her to join him. But he hadn't lost his persuasive skills because she did start to wear down. He knew she would love to go to the event since she had been ostracized from it these many years.

Her main concerns were down to just three. What would she wear? She didn't have the proper shoes and scarf. Second, that she was old enough to be his mother, so why did he want to go with her? And her third concern was that the Doctor and the Innkeeper would disapprove. She told him that she had a past history with them that she didn't wish to discuss and for his part he didn't let on that he knew they were her brother and sister. She told him it might be too uncomfortable for both she and them.

Garrett assured her that he could handle uncomfortable situations and he convinced her that there would be hundreds of other people at the *Bazaar*, tons of stuff to do and plenty of grounds to walk around on, so it would be a piece of cake to avoid any unpleasant moments. Besides, he reminded her that she had as much right as anyone to enjoy the festivities, maybe even more so as matter of fact.

He closed the deal and against her strong protest he handed her three one hundred dollar bills and insisted that she buy herself a new pair of shoes and a scarf. He made no mention of her other concern about why he wanted to go with her. He didn't want to burst the bubble of happiness that had enveloped her, so he failed to tell her the real reasons he had asked her out. He hoped to make Caroline jealous, as if he could, and he hoped to find out all that Amelia knew about the the Baker girl's accident. But he also did very much want her to have some fun. He felt that Amelia deserved to have the slight fantasy that he wished to date her, that she was still attractive to men. He always rooted for the underdog no matter how long a shot. They agreed to meet in front of the church the next evening at six.

He watched Amelia walk back to her cottage and climb the steps. It took a bit of an effort for her to push the front door open wide enough so that she could slither in sideways, because there were so many stacks of boxes and debris piled high in her entryway.

"What a *packrat*," he laughed to himself.

He stayed by the pond for a few moments, then jumped to his feet, excited with the prospect for fun tomorrow. He walked back up Palmers Pond Lane and stopped a couple of times to look back at the pond to gauge just how the little girl might have mistaken the danger.

Once back on Main Street he stopped to get his bearings. He noticed that the large roman numeral bank clock indicated two ten. The excitement at the pond had further drained his energy and with the effect of the pill waning he needed to head back to the Hibiscus Inn, fast.

5

Despite his lethargy, when Garrett came upon the Village Book Shop he couldn't resist stopping in to take a look around. Book stores always brought him comfort and there was a particular subject matter that he hoped he'd find, that might shed some light on the girl's tragedy.

Garrett held the door open for a man who was leaving the shop. The man's clothes reeked from the smell of old cigarette smoke, so Garrett kept the door open long after the man had passed, to be sure that all the nauseating odor exited with him. Once he stepped inside he noticed that there were two other customers at the counter and that a pretty black-haired woman, who wore an attractive deep purple blouse, was ringing up their purchases.

Garrett strolled the aisles of the small shop with a distinct purpose to his browsing. He was hoping to find information on Palmers Pond. He was in luck, because in another moment he came upon the travel section. He disregarded the majority of colorful books which were about Cape Cod's history and its beaches, and his interest perked when he spotted a small pocket sized hard cover book entitled, *Upper Cape Lakes and Ponds.*

He reviewed the table of contents and thumbed his way through to the chapter on Falmouth. But before he was able to read it the woman in purple approached him from behind and asked, "May I help you?"

"Thank you, but I think I've found what I'm after," he held up the book for her to see.

"Are you a fisherman? We have several other books over there that might be more informative."

"Any about Palmers Pond?" he asked.

"No, I don't think so. Does this one mention it? What's your interest in Palmers Pond if I may ask?" the woman said.

"Not much, other than the fact that small children seem to drown in it."

She could tell that he was the character whom Martha had phoned her about earlier.

"Yes poor darling. Very sad. Carrie was such a precious girl. So I take it then that you're not an angler?" the woman asked.

"No. Well, I guess you could say I'm just fishing around for information. I can't fathom how her parents could let her off on her own. You let a small child ride her bicycle unsupervised and no good will come of it."

There was a pregnant pause as she digested his statement that Carrie had ridden her bicycle.

She changed the subject. "How rude of me not to introduce myself. My name is Anne Temple, I'm the owner. Please call me Annie." She found him rather attractive and he found her appealing as well.

"Garrett here. Well Annie it's my pleasure to meet another beautiful woman in your village."

She smiled. Annie Temple was the real thing, heady, outgoing, and fine looking.

Garret asked, "As the owner of such a magnificent book shop am I right to assume that you are also an expert on the village's history? "

"There are many others whose histories far outdate my family and who take pride in assembling the village's heritage, historians in the true sense of the word. Matter of fact, we have a marvelous Historical Society that is opened on Tuesdays and Wednesdays this time of year. It's opposite the Village Bagel Shop on Front Street. If you have the time you might want to pay it a visit. There are a number of old photographs of Palmers Pond and a few notes about it as well that you might find interesting," Annie answered.

"History bores me. It's already happened, can't do shit about it. I'd much rather make history than read about it," he said.

She was somewhat taken aback. Martha was right, he was unpredictable. So, to relieve the awkwardness, Annie excused herself and approached another customer who had just walked in.

Garrett took off his jacket, sat down in a very comfortable upholstered arm chair and turned the pages of the book to chapter six, entitled, *Falmouth area Lakes and Ponds*.

He was disappointed. Palmers Pond was mentioned just a few times with drab information about when it had been dredged, it's unusual depth and when the raft was donated by Doctor and Mrs. Calvert Nickerson. Useless.

Garrett decided he must leave. But when he stood up and put on his linen jacket he felt light headed. He had to grab hold of a nearby book shelf to steady himself. He became sick to his stomach and belched, which brought the taste of maple syrup up his throat. Stabbing heartburn followed and he had to wait another minute before it subsided. He wished he had a *Tums*.

He needed to get back to the Hibiscus Inn, but before he left the store, even though the book seemed rather worthless to him, he walked over to the cash register and slapped it on the counter. He awaited Annie's return so that he could buy it for Amelia, as a thank you gift for accompanying him to the *Bazaar*. She might find it more useful since she lived next to it.

Once back behind the counter Annie took his cash and opened the register. He asked her if she wouldn't mind gift wrapping it.

Annie made one more attempt at friendliness when she handed him his receipt, change, and the wrapped present. "There's a wonderful *Church Bazaar* tomorrow. It's quite the end of season happening for our small town. If you're available it'd be a pleasure to accompany you and I could introduce you to some of our fine people. It should be a fun time."

"Damn! I already have a date." he said.

Why had he asked Amelia? He found Annie to be a pleasant person, and more attractive bait.

"I hope to see you there though and have some laughs," Garrett said.

As he said goodbye Annie thought, "Who sank her tentacles into him already? Anytime a catch stumbles into town we single women descend upon him in seconds. There are just too many horny women in this village to go around," she laughed to herself.

Garrett squinted when he stepped outside into the light. The large yellow sun seemed too close in the cloudless sky. It produced an instant sweat over his entire body. His skin felt clammy. He was overtired and weak and was aware that he was crashing. His head pounded, the pain was back. He felt achy and quite disoriented. He didn't recognize much.

He wanted to get back to the Hibiscus Inn and get more sleep. Why had he been so stupid to have chanced his health?

He became so preoccupied with his anxiety that he hadn't realized that he'd stopped in front of the Village Realty. He loitered for a spell and with a vacant look on his face he stared at the faded pictures of properties for sale that were affixed to the window. Meanwhile, inside the office, the owner, Bob Maxwell, was shocked to see the stranger looking in on him. How dare he show his face after hurling his terrible insults. Bob pulled out his desk drawer and removed his handgun, just in case the madman went *postal* on him.

But seconds later, Garrett, unaware of Maxwell's presence, turned away from the picture window and proceeded down Main Street. Maxwell threw on his blazer and ran outside to look after him to make sure that he didn't pull anything nasty.

Garrett hadn't noticed him, nor anyone else for that matter, and headed in the direction in which he thought the Hibiscus Inn was located, but he had little conviction that he was right.

However, it wasn't much later that Garrett managed to stagger into the Hibiscus Inn and take a seat in an arm chair opposite the piano. He read the note that he had picked up at the front desk, that Martha had written to him. She informed him that his new room was number one, the *Honeysuckle*, and that it was open and the key was on the end table inside the room.

It took quite an effort for him to rise from the chair and as soon as he was able to steady himself he headed straight for his new room. Once inside, he locked the door and then dashed to the bathroom because he felt an extreme wave of nausea rise up. He just made it time to lean over the toilet bowl and upchuck the pumpkin pancakes. Weak and listless, he slid to his knees and his head remained over the bowl for the next several minutes.

When the nausea had somewhat subsided, Garrett positioned his hands on either side of the toilet bowl and managed to leverage his entire body weight by pushing against the commode with what little strength he could summon. This propped his limp body up and onto his feet. He stood there and dry heaved a couple of times, then went over to the sink, brushed his teeth, cleaned his face and exited the bathroom. He avoided his undisturbed luggage that was placed in the middle of the room and stumbled his way en route to the queen-sized poster bed that was perched on the opposite side. He managed to yank back the bedcovers and dove face first onto the bed. He would remain in that same position, with shoes, socks, and clothes on, well into Sunday.

Earlier, at the Eatery, Bob Maxwell was angry with the stranger because of the embarrassment that he had caused. "This man has to be stopped."

So before the *Round Table Group* had adjourned and against the others' protests, he had excused himself and rushed out of the coffee shop to tail Caroline and the *madman* as they strolled up Main Street.

There wasn't too much to observe until he noticed that Caroline had pointed to Amelia and he could see that the *nut* was interested in her. "Why would she catch his fancy?" he wondered.

After Caroline had said good bye to Garrett and disappeared from view, Bob felt emboldened and slithered up closer to his prey. He stood no more than a block away from him. He knew that this man meant trouble to the community and if the others didn't see it that way to hell with them. He was the self-appointed protector of the naive and wouldn't be derelict in his duty to see to it that this wicked man be brought to justice. Normal proud American citizens didn't act so disrespectful and rude the way this guy did. He was certain that this *loose cannon* of an ingrate planned to use his insults and detestable behavior to distract the villagers so that while all their attention was drawn to confronting him, his evil-minded cronies, plotting no doubt right now as we speak, could sweep into the village undetected and enact their harm.

His thoughts seemed to always be focused on the dark side of human capability. He trusted no one and felt that all, except for the *Round Table* crew, needed to be under constant surveillance. Therefore, when this mysterious stranger wandered into his village and caused a raucous, Bob Maxwell had no doubt that he was part of some terrorist plot or a socialist deviant group set on the overthrow of the *American Way*. Or at the very least he was just another unbalanced mental loser, like the West Virginia mass murderer. Whatever. Maxwell knew that he would have to uncover the secretive events planned by this *evil doer*, before the bell tolled.

Maxwell's curiosity was heightened when he watched the psycho cross Main Street and walk down Palmers Pond Lane. He was after Amelia he figured.

"What does he want with her?" he thought. "She lives by the pond and off the beaten path, so maybe he's cased her home as a hideout for his gang. Maybe he stashed his weapons on her property. He could see that she's not the sharpest tool in the box."

He had watched the stranger walk down to the pond and sit on Amelia's lawn, as described earlier. Bob lurked behind a maple tree for a few more moments, long enough to see Amelia point her shot gun at the jerk and then put it down and talk with him.

Maxwell had seen enough, so he left the area and returned to his real estate office.

It was another hour later when the stranger stood outside his office, gawking at the property pictures in the window.

After he had stepped outside and watched the guy wobble off toward the Hibiscus, Maxwell was beside himself and felt the need to tell someone else of his mistrust. So he jaywalked across Main Street to have a chat with, and forewarn, Annie Temple. Even though Bob was a contented married man he would leave his wife in a heartbeat if the talented Annie Temple ever gave him so much as a wink.

Annie told him that the handsome man had stopped in a little while ago. "He was a bit peculiar I admit but that must have been from lack of sleep. Martha mentioned that he'd been up for a few days."

Bob then told her of the upset and insults at the coffee shop, and of his theory that Garrett wasn't to be trusted.

Annie laughed, pinched him on his cheek and said, "Bob Maxwell you *Chicken Little* you. When have you ever trusted an outsider in your entire life?"

"Come on Annie, I didn't make this shit up. This guy's bad. He has a cloud of dread looming over him. I tell you it doesn't bode well for any of us. We need to keep a close eye on him believe me. You don't want another *San Bernardino* massacre here do you?"

He continued, "You said he was a bit peculiar, how so? What did he say? Any weird stuff?"

"Well he seemed to be fascinated with Palmers Pond and little Carrie's death," she said.

"So that's why he followed Amelia," the doubter thought.

"He was just interested in books about Palmers Pond. I didn't know of any except that I told him that there were a number of old photographs of the Pond at the Historical Society and notes that he might wish to look at. He said, "History bores me. It has already happened, can't do much about it. I'd much rather make history than read about it.""

"Ah ha! Make history! My God he's tipped his hand. But you said that he also mentioned Carrie's death. What'd he say?" Maxwell probed.

She remembered Garrett's words. "He said something about him not being a fisherman but that he was fishing around for information. He said he wondered how her parents could have let a small child ride her bicycle out of their sight for even a moment; that no good ever comes of it.

"I didn't know anything about a bicycle,"she said.

Bob almost leapt out of his skin. "Bicycle? What bicycle? I never heard that she rode a bicycle to the pond."

She ignored Bob's remarks and said, "Oh! I told him about tomorrow's *Bazaar* and offered to escort him to it, but he said he already had a date. I wonder with whom?" she mused.

Bob was about to speculate on the Garrett's date reference but Annie had to wave off any further conversation and pardon herself, as she needed to leave the shop and meet up with Martha to prep for the *Bazaar*. She and Martha were the supervisors.

When she said goodbye he cautioned, "We need to alert the others tonight before he gets hostile.

"Who the hell is this guy?"

6

Annie and Martha had been supervising the *Bazaar's* entertainment preparations for the past fifteen years and they had the process down to a science. They remained at the church until seven or so, then the two good friends, satisfied that all was in order, drove off at dusk to Dr. Nickerson's home for the traditional *Big Event* dinner. The kind Doctor and his wife had been the gracious hosts at their Penzance Point mansion for the past ten years. Annie and Martha would be back on the church's grounds first thing Sunday morning to oversee the food prep, and any final, and inevitable, unattended issues.

Night had fallen as they drove up to the Nickerson's mansion in Annie's Prius. Once out of the car, they wound their way along a well lighted white seashell path that led them to the seven-foot-high, egg-plant colored front door. They rang the doorbell and were greeted by a waiter. As was always the case, because of their responsibilities at the *Bazaar*, Martha and Annie were expected to be the last guests to arrive. The hostess, Helen Marr Nickerson, the Doctor's wife of thirty years, made certain that the staff planned to serve the meal no earlier than eight o'clock. Helen wanted her friend Annie and her altruistic sister-in-law to have time to acclimate once they arrived, to chat with the others, and to indulge in a cocktail or two.

Inside the mansion it was quite clear that the party had begun without them. There were twenty-one attendees, including the hosts, and they were all rather animated, their conversations loud and enthusiastic. The Doctor bounced about from guest to guest and told a funny joke or two, patted them on the back and thanked them all for their support.

The caterers from *All Food Fresh* had once again outdone everyone's expectations, as they presented lobster appetizers and eel sushi in a variety of dishes. The wine served was, as tradition for this party, a variety of Cape Cod and Martha's Vineyard premium stock.

Martha and Annie split up when they arrived. Martha joined in on the conversation with Bob and Gail Maxwell and with Bill and Eileen Dimmock, her younger sister. They were listening to Bill describe the details of his new Boston Whaler. But Maxwell seemed preoccupied, he wondered where Annie had drifted off to.

Annie had snatched a glass of *Sauvignon Blanc* from the tray that a passing waiter was carrying and sat down to listen to Pastor Adams discuss his high expectations for tomorrow's seventy second *Church Bazaar*. Caroline and her fiancé, Sean Garland, Stuart Holmes the banker and his wife Lynn were also listening.

The Andrades, Gilbert and Erika, and Chief Carl Nickerson and his wife Millie sat in the parlor on a handsome wood carved, blue velvet Victorian sofa and were having a boisterous laugh, about what it's not clear.

John Turnbull, the architect, was single his evening, because his wife stayed home with the flu. He was in deep conversation with Annie Temple's son Nick, the young twenty-eight-year-old golf pro/savant, who practiced his craft at a local country club.

Mike and Ashley Small were alone out on the ivy-covered veranda. They held hands and admired the tiny diamonds in the sky on this star-lit night. They were newlyweds (second time for both) and they savored their good fortunes for having found real love for the first time in their lives.

Absent from the festivities were core members of the *Round Table Group*, Dale and Katie Baker. If it weren't for the misfortune of their granddaughter's death, the affable Bakers would have been the center of attention per usual. If a vote were taken last week they would've won for being the happiest people in the entire village. But now that their granddaughter, little Carrie, had perished, that unfair twist of fate made them, no doubt, the saddest people in town.

At the stroke of eight o'clock Helen rang the dinner bell and announced, "Hear ye, Hear Ye! Our dinner in honor of this year's *special recipient*, Carrie Baker, will be served in the *Cabot Room*. All be so kind as to join us now and please leave your unfinished cocktails with the wait-staff."

The committee had to move at lightspeed to install Carrie as the Bazaar's esteemed honoree. She bumped the scheduled recipient, a famed former assemblyman who had died several years ago. He'd be next year's posthumous guest of honor, unless another tragedy struck before then.

After consuming the sumptuous salmon entrees along with their accompaniments and while they awaited desert and an aperitif to be served, Helen again rang the damned dinner bell, the loudness of which attracted everyone's attention, and annoyed quite a few.

The guests stared in her direction as she waxed lyrical about the night's star, Carrie Baker. It was a wonderful and moving speech they all agreed. When she had finished, she turned and gave a nod to Gail Maxwell who stood next to a shrouded easel, to Helen's left. As was choreographed, with a sense of drama Gail took great care and removed the canvas cover and unveiled the exquisite four foot by four foot oil painted portrait of little Carrie, done by renowned local artist Mark Everett Valentino. He'd worked through the night to complete it.

After their initial gasps of pleasure, silence ensued as the guests gazed with reverence at the portrait's understated and perfect likeness. Helen informed them that it would be the main prize at the *Bazaar's* auction.

To break the ice, as was scripted by Helen, Gilbert Andrade stood up from his chair and raised his wine glass to propose toasts to Carrie, to her parents and brother, and yet a third toast to her grandparents. A few other people chose to speak in remembrance of Carrie. They took turns sharing heartwarming stories about the little girls short time on this planet.

When everyone was finished speaking, Helen encouraged her guests to resume the night's festivities. They all sat back down and tried to concentrate on the scrumptious bread pudding that had just been placed in front of them. But since most of them still felt a bit saddened for Carrie and her family, Bob Maxwell, knowing that he had a captured audience, leapt at the opportunity to stir up the pot so to speak. He appointed himself to be the town crier and to connect the dots of the girl's mysterious death, (his words), to the visit of a confrontational stranger.

"I find it more than a coincidence that a vile stranger appears out of the blue and that there just so happens to be a suspicious drowning of a precious little girl," he said.

Helen was quite bothered by his remarks that her death was mysterious and said to her sister-in-law, "Martha please tell us more about this peculiar guest, this stranger whom Bob referred to, who was deposited on your doorsteps late last night."

Martha, ever the dramatist, rolled her eyes skyward and appeared to be pained in her attempt to draw from the chambers of her memory the details of the young man's arrival last night, as if it had happened fifty years ago.

"Well yes... Let me see," she contemplated.

Martha related her observations with great embellishment of course. "This young man arrived without reservation, with but two small pieces of luggage, at the stroke of midnight or thereabouts, and acted quite distracted and disoriented. His appearance at first had given me pause, because he was rather unkempt. He donned an obvious blond wig, which he did not wear today, and mind you he has a full head of hair so why the need to disguise it I will never know? Also I noticed that his shoes were caked with mud and I feared that he might traipse all over my antique rugs and soil them to no end. When I asked him to remove them he flat out ignored me. Furthermore, what was most bothersome was the fact that he would not give me his name, nor any form of identification, no credit card or the like. Can you imagine my distrust? And he tried to force a large sum of one hundred dollar bills into my hand whilst he demanded to be led to his room, because he said he had been sleep deprived for a number of days.

"How startled I was to see a disheveled man at my door step at midnight, who acted very odd and aloof, who presented no form of identification, and paid me a thousand dollars in cash. It felt as if it were *hush money*! I was sure he must be up to some sort of criminal endeavor. It was not right. I considered phoning Carl but I did not want to cause a ruckus for my other guests, so I decided otherwise. When I escorted the young man to the *Harbor Light Room* on the second floor, he attempted another bribe, if you can imagine. He told me that he would pay additional money the next day if I would relocate him to a room on the first floor. Well before I could answer him that all the rooms were let and that he should know how fortunate he was that I even had this room available this time of year, and on a weekend no less, he damned near slammed the door straight in my face whilst he said good night."

Murmurs from the crowd.

Martha remembered one more detail and said, "Oh! I forgot to mention that his last words to me were, "I am just here to change the world one village at a time."

Maxwell jumped in. "See? Very odd behavior wouldn't you agree? Carrie dies less than twenty-four hours before he shows up at the Hibiscus. He hasn't a reservation and refuses to show any form of i.d., or give Martha his name, and his shoes are covered in mud, from the pond no doubt. Remember that Mohammed Atta and his dastardly group paid cash and showed no ids to board the plane in Boston. It smells fishy to me. And this morning he showed up at the Eatery and unprovoked he proceeded to insult every one of us at the *Round Table*. At one point the guy gave me such an evil stare that I shuddered."

Caroline seemed irritated and scolded, "Oh come on. His name is Garrett and he's harmless. He uses his shock value sense of humor to get your goat. The way he mentioned his ex-wife to me it made me think that he's just gone through a nasty divorce and is still troubled by it."

"Harmless perhaps, he did seem more at ease this morning I have to admit. But he remains very secretive. This morning he wrote his name down as Ian, not Garrett," Martha said.

Doc Nickerson asked, "Caroline you said it was his sense of humor. Really? I find no humor in what my sister and Bob have related, nor in how he insulted me today. No one found it humorous at our table I can assure you. You took a walk with him. You didn't find him to be peculiar?"

Caroline had to admit he was very unusual. "He did tell me that his name was Garrett, but Martha had called me earlier and said his name was Ian. I didn't bother clarifying it with him. Who knows or cares?" She failed to mention that he seemed infatuated with Carrie's drowning.

Bob egged Annie on. He asked her to share her encounter with Ian, or Garrett, that afternoon at her book shop.

Annie told the interested listeners that he had a laser focus on finding out information about Palmers Pond. She related how it took her aback when she had encouraged him to visit the Historical Society and he told her that history bored him and that he'd, "..much rather make history than read about."

Helen gasped at this statement, as did several others.

Maxwell added to Annie's story. "You told me that he said his interest in the pond was, "Not much, other than the fact that young children seem to drown in it."

"Yes he said that. He also wondered why her parents had let her ride her bicycle down to Palmers Pond," Annie concurred.

Chief Nickerson sat up wide eyed, he looked engaged for the first time in the account of the odd man. "Bicycle? We made no mention about the bicycle. We withheld that key piece of evidence on purpose. There's only one explanation for how in the hell he could know that!"

No one thought to ask the Chief why Carrie's bike was never divulged, they were all too caught up in the strange fact that maybe Bob Maxwell was onto a real problem this time.

Bob added, "After he and Caroline had ended their walk I saw him stalk Amelia. He followed her down to the pond. I watched him lie down on the grass and just stare into the pond. Chief isn't it true that criminals always return to the scene of their crime?"

The *Newtown catastrophe* as their reference, Maxwell said, "We don't need any sick copycat murderer of children on the loose in our village do we?"

"Not to make a big deal of it, but he did seem preoccupied with Carrie's drowning. At one point while we talked about her he teared up," Caroline said.

There was noticeable silence at the table as each one of them attempted to assimilate all that they had just heard.

Nick said, "I'm uncomfortable with your perceptions of this Garrett guy and feel that we all should proceed with a little caution. You must see that to jump to conclusions is rather irresponsible. This man has been here less than twenty-four hours and you think (he looked directly at Maxwell) that you know the truth about him? Misperceptions are not the truth," he emphasized. "He sounds different no doubt, and I'll give you with all the accounts that I've heard tonight that he may be an enigma, like Kasper Hauser, but since when is that a crime Chief?"

No one knew this Hauser person whom Nick had referred to, nor did they care to ask. Caroline agreed with his overall assessment. Then she chastised the group. "Let's not encourage Bob to get us all hyped up over a harmless man's peccadilloes. Yes he's a quirky guy, but come on now."

But her reprimand seemed forced. They felt that she too had her doubts.

"Peccadilloes lead to massacres if you ask me," Maxwell had to add.

Bill Dimmock asked the Chief to pay the jerk a visit and put him on notice. Many of his fellow diners agreed with his suggestion.

However, Chief Nickerson, always the cautious one, told the group that Nick was correct, that the stranger had, as of yet, done no wrong. So it could be perceived that the police would be harassing the man. But he assured them, "We have our ways of finding out what he's up to."

Doc offered a better option. "Why not have Nick or Annie pay the man a visit and see what they can uncover. Has there ever been anyone who didn't want to spill their soul to the Temples?"

Gail Maxwell wished to end the conversation, she said, "Well aren't we a rowdy mob? I agree with Nick. The man has been here a day and he has us all in the palm of his hands. Let's forget about him.We have the *Bazaar* to focus on tomorrow, and I bet all of us would love to hear from Martha and Annie all the details of what's in store for us at this year's event."

While Martha prepared to take center stage, and in essence tell them what she had told them before the *Bazaar* last year and many years hence, the Chief, Maxwell, Doc, Sean Garland, Stuart Holmes and Bill Dimmock retired to the wraparound porch for a cigar break. With a nip in the air the gentlemen, of course with Maxwell's fear-based leadership, picked up where they had left off in the conversation about the Garrett. They determined that they had to find out more about this infidel before it was too late.

The Chief had a good idea. "I'll ask Chief O'Connor if he'd conduct a fake fire drill at the Hibiscus. Once the stranger's out of his room we can have my men rifle through his luggage."

In the meantime, Doc reiterated that Annie or Nick should talk with Garrett soon. "They'll uncover a whole lot more about the man than we will."

Nick joined them on the porch and agreed to have a chat with Garrett, but only from the standpoint of protecting the visitor from all their farfetched, paranoid theories.

7

The seventy second *Church Bazaar* was in full swing by the time a very attractive Amelia and a clean shaven and dapper Garrett met each other in front of the tent entry. He gave a slight bow to her and she a semi curtsy.

"I am very navus." she said. "I can ahwedee feel the stahs."

"Don't pay any attention to them Amelia. The most powerful person in the room is the one who remains silent. It drives the others crazy. They'll obsess wanting to know what you think about them, so don't worry about what they think of you. Besides, the festivities are for everyone and no one has more of a right to party than you. Heck, the event should be dedicated to you for all that you've sacrificed. So let them stare. Stare at the *Queen of the Bazaar*!"

She wondered what on earth he meant. Sacrifice?

Once inside the massive white canvassed tent (it was a series of rental tents in fact) they found themselves in front of the raffle table. He turned to Amelia and asked, "Are you feeling lucky my dear?"

"Yes," she answered.

He spoke to one of the four ladies who sat on the other side of the table. "I'd like to purchase one hundred dollars' worth of raffle tickets please."

"How generous of you young man. We're so pleased that you both could join us," the kind white haired woman, who was dressed in a handsome fall colored burnt orange sweater, said. "Best of luck to you, and to you too Amelia. By the way, be sure to check out all of our incredible silent auction items over there as well," she pointed to a line of large tables along the church's outside wall on which were displayed the special prizes. "All the proceeds go to the Baker family. Enjoy," she encouraged.

Garrett fumbled with the cumbersome roll of red numbered tickets that the woman had given him. He and Amelia laughed at his poor coordination as he attempted to keep them from unraveling. He looked like he was trying to put a new spool on a weedwacker and was losing.

"Hurry Amelia open up your hand bag please." Garrett managed to stuff the entire unwound, spinal column looking roll into her purse and she snapped it shut before any could escape. Neither of them noticed that one ticket did manage to stick out its red tongue and would hang that way for the remainder of the night.

"Where should we start Amelia?" he asked.

They were a bit overwhelmed at first as they surveyed the more than sixty two tables in front of them, both unable to choose a direction to begin. Man was it noisy and packed.

"Amelia, where would you like to start?" Garrett asked once again.

"Don't much cayah just as long as it's not ova theyah," she pointed in the direction of a group of dignitaries who stood in a tight circle on the empty sawdust covered dance floor. They were deep in conversation and he could see that Amelia's estranged sister and brother were amongst them.

There was a white clothed table near the entry just a few steps from the raffle table and Garrett said, "Then let's begin right here."

"Hello ladies. It is such a wonderful night to be with you for such a worthwhile occasion. In honor of the young Baker girl. Tragic, tragic. Don't you agree?" he said.

When Garrett noticed the confused looks on their faces he clarified, "I mean don't you agree that it is a wonderful gesture to pay honor to that dear girl and her grieving family?"

They all perked up and in unison told him that yes it was.

The women giggled as Garrett put a one-hundred-dollar bill in the middle of the table and helped himself to just two of the fudge nut brownies that were for sale. He handed Amelia the larger of the two and a napkin as well and nodded to the ladies as he said goodbye. They thanked him for his generosity. He waved off their gratefulness as if to say please it's the least that I could do.

When he had taken his first bite of the scrumptious delicacy he shouted back over his shoulder to the ladies, "Magnificent. Worth every penny."

Amelia clung to his arm and had a huge smile on her face and they both seemed to grow more comfortable with one another as they bounced from booth to booth. Although, she was still cautious because she couldn't decipher why he wanted to be with her. But what the hell.

Garrett played every damn game in an attempt to win her a prize and he encouraged her to try her hand at a few as well. At various booths, of which there were several on the perimeter of three sides of the tents, he bought her all that he could: dolls, fried dough to eat, gift certificates to various local restaurants, tee shirts, candied apples, trinkets, you name it. There was no way that they could tote all the stuff around with them, so they had to leave them with the respected attendants and told the teenagers manning the booths that they'd be back to pick them up at the end of the night.

Amelia was all aglow from the attention he was giving her. An hour or so had passed by but to her it felt like seconds. And her happiness was noticeable to many in the crowd. Some were excited for her, while others were suspect of why Garrett had escorted her. There were even those miserable few who were uncomfortable that she had been allowed to attend, prejudiced because of her slow mental capacity.

At some point the peculiar couple stumbled upon the silent auction tables with their very special prizes. Garrett dragged Amelia down the lengthy row and stopped at each of the first thirteen auction items and put a healthy, over-sized bid on each one of them. A high bid that would almost be certain to win a number of the prizes, or if not, it would at least drive up the offers of other bidders, ensuring that the Baker family would take in even more money. Amelia hadn't noticed that he had written her name as the bidder on everyone.

Amelia was no longer concerned about what his motivation might be. She was ecstatic, happy to be caught up in the gaiety of the moment. When was the last time she had laughed and giggled she wondered?

It was after he had placed the last generous over bid on a free hairstyling a month for one year, at the Marky Lucky Cuts Salon in downtown Falmouth, that they found themselves in front of the haunting portrait of Carrie Baker the deserved honoree. The grand prize.

Garrett was drawn to the painting. He combed over the brush strokes as if it had been painted by a fine Dutch Master. He was so engrossed that he hadn't noticed that Amelia had wandered off. He wrote down Amelia's bid of two thousand dollars even though the suggested retail value was listed at eight hundred and fifty dollars.

As time passed he turned to ask Amelia what she saw in the portrait. He wished to know if it was accurate and captured the essence of the little girl. But to his surprise Amelia wasn't there. He looked around and spotted her, shoulders slumped, leaned up against a tent pole several yards away.

He walked up behind her and put his right hand upon her shoulder. The contact made her jump and when she noticed it was him she asked, "You like huh bettah than me, don't yah?"

"Who?" he asked.

"That Bakah kid."

"Baker? Carrie?"

Relieved that her reference wasn't about Caroline, he gathered his thoughts.

"I've been mesmerized by her story ever since I heard how she died. That portrait sort of brought me into it. The more I looked into her eyes the more it didn't make sense to me that she would ride her bike into the pond. She was six years old and must have been able to differentiate between where the land ends and the pond begins. It wasn't dark at the time, so I just can't figure it out. It seems weird to me. The poor, poor child."

Then he thought about her question and asked one of his own. "Why would you ask me that?"

"Nevah mind."

At that very moment Caroline and her fiancé Sean Garland walked by arm and arm. They seemed to be unaware of the world around them. That is until Caroline happened to glance over at Amelia and Garrett. She was startled because on impulse Garrett swung Amelia into his arms and planted a long, passionate kiss upon her lips. Amelia blushed in ecstasy, she hadn't noticed that her escort had his eyes opened and was focused the whole time on the true object of his desires, Caroline. Garrett was beside himself with delight when he saw that Caroline had walked off with jealousy written all over her face (his misguided interpretation).

"I don't know what came over me Amelia. Please forgive me if I have offended you. I am just so over the top happy tonight that I can't control myself," he half lied.

She was still in a swoon and raised her hand and waved off his apology, as if to say don't bother about it, or do it again please. It hadn't taken much to put her head over heels for a man who was younger than her son.

But a minute later, without announcing his intentions, Garrett left Amelia standing all alone and self conscious, as he headed straight towards the group that she had pointed to when they had first entered the tent. The one that had included the Doctor and Martha. However, the Doctor was no longer there.

Martha saw Garrett approaching and gave a slight poke in the ribs to Stuart Holmes. The conversation stopped as the group of six braced themselves for whatever havoc this strange man might wreak upon them now. But Garrett was of a different mindset. He was bent on being on his best behavior and not causing a stir of any kind. He was having such a wonderful time and his good intention was to thank them for such a fine event and to apologize to all for his prior indiscretions.

He stood in front of the muted group and as he prepared to address them he gathered his thoughts and coaxed himself to stay in control and, at the very least, to be kind. But as he was about to speak his cheeks began to twitch and his heart raced when he noticed that Caroline had also joined the group.

Garrett's face reddened as he proceeded, in all sincerity, to ask them to accept his apology for his poor behavior.

Stuart Holmes reflected the group's sentiment when he said, "Apology accepted young fellow. Garrett is it?"

However, to their chagrin, he felt the need to offer more. He asked their forgiveness for yesterday's outburst at the Eatery. He blamed it on his unrest and lack of sleep; on his headache and jittery reaction to the pain pills he takes; (he didn't tell them that he was on one now as well); on his shyness that seemed to manifest itself in an aggressive behavior whenever he was tired and cranky; and on his poor sense of self confidence because he felt that the group had made fun of him when he had first entered the restaurant.

They were uncomfortable and didn't know what to say or do next.

Garrett continued, "To be honest with you" (he knew he was rambling too much but couldn't keep the words inside his mouth) "with all that stuff in my head the ultimate blow that unnerved me was when I saw this vision, this free spirit of a woman, on the other side of the counter. It always makes me very nervous to be in the presence of pure unadulterated beauty," he announced, while he looked straight at Caroline. She was stunned and the others were aghast at what they perceived to be his inappropriate flirtation.

Garrett noticed the scowls on their faces and knew that he must have said something offensive. That was not his intent, damn it! He panicked and stammered and stumbled as he tried to right the ship, but instead seemed to make matters worse. He went on and on with what appeared to be a stream of unconnected thoughts and stories of woman who reminded him of other women he had known; about sleep depravity and its harmful health risks and about how beauty inside a person always reflects itself on the outside as well, on and on.

The Dimmock's felt that the man must be high on some kind of illegal drug. They were disgusted with his behavior and walked away, but Caroline decided to take a stand.

"For the life of me I can't figure you out. You offer us your sincere apology, then proceed to humiliate me and my friends with your crude remarks. Remarks made to a woman who is engaged to be married. It's good for you that my fiancé had just gone for drinks or I am afraid you would feel the ill effects of his brute strength. So why don't you run back to Amelia before he returns and leave us normal people alone."

He was confused and asked all of them to forgive him once again. "I never meant to harm Caroline or any of you, please believe me." But the group wanted no more of Garrett and en masse turned their backs and muttered as they walked off.

He was beside himself with confusion. "This isn't how it was supposed to be. I wanted to make peace but I created more enemies, Caroline too."

Garrett needed someone to comfort him and soon gathered his wits when he remembered that he had left Amelia all by herself, poor soul. Guilt and anxiety consumed him as he looked around in search of his date.

He approached the table where the women had sold him the brownies and rushed over to it. "Excuse me ladies. Have you seen Amelia?" he asked them.

One woman answered, "I'm pretty sure she stepped outside for some fresh air. She did look a bit pale if you ask me. Her hands were quite full of prizes, the lucky girl. She left out that flap," she pointed to an exit.

He ran out the tent opening that the woman had indicated. It was dark and it took a few seconds for his eyes to adjust their focus. He saw no sign of her. "She must be back inside," he concluded. Although he figured that if she had a handful of presents with her, it was doubtful that she went anywhere else but home.

He turned his attention to another tent entry where Pastor Adams, the host of the gala, stood alone outside smoking his cherry tobacco filled pipe. He was a very tall, handsome man of fifty-five years, dressed in his black and white holy man's uniform. Garrett was pleased to see that there was a black man in this town.

He approached the clergyman and without so much as a hello, or an excuse me, he asked, "Pastor have you seen Amelia?

"Well hello to you too sir," he chided.

When Garrett didn't laugh and looked rather concerned, the Pastor told him, "No I have not. Aren't you the young man who escorted her here? Shouldn't I be the one to ask you that question, not vice versa?"

Garrett became irritated. "Yes. Yes of course you know that I came with her. I saw you point at us awhile ago inside the tent."

The always chipper clergyman said, "I am sure she will turn up soon. Why don't you go back inside and wait for her? I'll bet she's searching for the lost member of her flock as we speak."

Garrett had no time for his humor. "Well I guess you'd know how it feels to lose some of your flock. If they don't run from the phony biblical stories you preach at them, I'm sure the pedophilia will drive them out of the pews."

Pastor Adams scolded him, "That's a Catholic problem! Not every man of the cloth is a molester for God's sake. Not every child needs to fear that their mentors are their predators. Have we become that small minded young man?"

Garrett tried his best not to alienate another person. "Fear is an illusion. I know. I've worked with the paranoid much of my adult life. So too are the fantasy stories told by organized religion illusions, illusions steeped in fear, in order to keep the flock fenced in. Aha! So I guess that we've come full cycle in our short, but pleasant discussion. Well I must return to my flock, albeit a tiny one. We agnostics need to stick together."

8

Garrett felt guilty that he'd used Amelia as a decoy. He scanned the crowd but there was no sign of her. He picked up his pace and paid little attention to whomever he bumped into.

At some point he was distracted by a woman's voice who called to him, "Mr. Cashmere, Garrett."

When he turned he saw that it was Annie Temple, not Amelia, waiving her hands over her head in an attempt to get his attention. He was amused that she had called him by the clothes that he wore. He decided to walk over to her and ask if she'd seen Amelia.

When he reached Annie she sat back down at the poker table and gestured for him to take the last seat. "Please. We're in need of a tenth player for a spirited game of *No Limit Holdem Poker*," she said.

"Won't you give us the pleasure of your company, and cough up twenty-five bucks for a good cause?" He sat down as directed.

"For those of you who haven't met this handsome gentleman, he's a guest at the Hibiscus Inn, Garrett Cashmere. Of course that's not his last name, but maybe if we play our cards just right we can get him to lay his on the table and tell us what his real name is," she said with a smile.

The players at the table said hello and Doc Nickerson, who was seated at the other side of the table, asked him where Amelia was. But Garrett never answered, he just stared at the plastic placard in front of him.

The young man seated to his left, Nick Temple, introduced himself to Garrett and said, "This is a charity poker game and you'll be the sponsor for," he leaned over in front of Garrett to read the card, "*The Veterans. of Foreign Wars*. All of your winnings will go to that charity and all of your antes will go to Carrie Baker's family."

Garrett asked Nick, "Would you mind changing seats with me? I detest war."

They both stood up to oblige Garrett's strange request and traded seats, while some of the other players at the table seemed pissed. They hadn't heard of Garrett's apology gone wrong just a short while ago or if they had they might have confronted him for being so disrespectful to our vets. Instead they remained quiet, not wanting to spoil the fun.

Garrett looked at the new placard and asked Nick, "What's the *Jimmy Fund*?"

Nick told him that it was a charity located in Boston and was focused on cancer cures for children.

"That sounds right to me. Anything for kids," Garrett said.

Annie, as it turned out, was the volunteer card dealer. Seated clockwise to her left at the semicircular table was Bob Maxwell, he always tried to get as close to her as possible; his good friend Dr. Nickerson; Police Chief Nickerson; local newspaperman, Tip Garland, soon to be Caroline's brother-in-law; Janice Downs the very mellow, and rubbery bodied yoga instructor; Sybil Keating, a short and plump waitress who worked at the Skull and Bones Steak House and was Janice's love partner; Bob Townsend a weather-beaten pool contractor by trade; Baltus Mantz, Martha's guest at the Hibiscus Inn; Nick Temple and Garrett.

Annie doled out a thousand dollars' worth of chips to the new player and asked that he ante up twenty five dollars, in real money, as the *buy in*.

"Shuffle up and deal Annie," Bob Townsend barked.

She picked up the deck of cards and reshuffled them like a professional.

Bob Maxwell flirted, "Just slip me a couple of Aces Annie."

Garrett had his poker face on. He stared in silence at the authentic green clothed table and thought that Amelia must have gone home and that he would play for just a little while before he followed after her. He was feeling more calm at the moment.

The game progressed and the group enjoyed themselves, even Garrett. Annie and Nick made the effort to get him comfortable and engaged in conversations and he proved receptive. He seemed to be thankful. He could see the similarities in their looks and the liveliness in their spirits. Nick was at the very least six foot three inches tall, had a short thick head of black hair and his long muscular body seemed to be the model of a pro golfer. There was no doubt that Nick was Annie's handsome son.

To everyone's surprise, except his, it took Garrett a mere forty minutes to win all of their chips. He wiped out the table! They were stunned. He had accumulated all ten thousand dollars' worth and had them piled in a neat stack in front of him. He had a large grin on his face and appeared to be feeling quite full of himself.

But they all were disappointed when he announced that he must leave in order to catch up with Amelia.

Others reached into their pockets to ante up another twenty five dollars for more chips when Garrett said, "Thank you all for allowing a humble stranger to win all of your chips. Please, let me give each and every one of you a gift."

With that said, he reached into his pocket, pulled out his wad of hundred dollar bills and handed Annie three. He announced, "This is to pay for all of the players' next antes and the extra money I wish to be donated to Carrie's parents." He was feeling generous, per usual, and peeled off another three hundred dollars and placed them on the table too. "For the Baker family," he said.

He gave a slight bow, patted Nick on the shoulder, asked for Annie's hand and kissed the back of it. Garrett turned and waved good bye to his competitors.

But before he could disappear Bob Townsend pleaded with him, as he had done so once earlier, to explain how he had been able to wipe them all out in such short a time.

"You never once looked at your two hole cards. How's that possible? Please tell us."

Garrett reconsidered leaving at that moment, and because he was in such a cheerful mood he agreed to honor Bob's request. He told them that he'd do a brief synopsis. They all cheered him on.

"First of all, forget that I didn't look at the first two cards dealt face down. *Texas Holdem* is much more a psychological game than a game of luck. It's about reading your opponent's tendencies so that you can confidently guess what their two face down cards might be, while at the same time you make them believe that your two hole cards are altogether different than they actually are. It's controlling perception and turning it into misperception. Remember they are but two cards and even if you're dealt two Aces, unless you play the hand just right, you're often in for failure. Because five more cards will be dealt to the benefit of the entire group and these cards can change the strength or weakness of your two hidden cards pretty fast. Any two hole cards can grow into a powerful hand using the additional five community cards that are dealt on the table. Matter of fact, I think that many famous poker tournaments have been won with hands that started with a ten and two in the hole, more so than with Ace-Ace.

"So what was my advantage? It's that you all were oblivious to observation. You focused on your own cards and yours alone. Contrary, I looked at the flop and the last two community cards and determined, in accordance with my seat position, what I wanted you to believe I had. I toyed with you and didn't look at my two hidden cards because, in all sincerity, I knew that you were all new at the game and it would be much more of a challenge for me. After I'd observed the first five hands we played I could see that you were all *easy meat*. If I had looked at my two private cards I'm afraid to say, in all modesty, that the game would have been over much earlier."

They all laughed along with him at his inflated bravado.

"Could you give us an example or two of what you read our weaknesses to be?" Nick asked.

Garrett thought for a moment, he didn't want to be too honest and offend anyone, again.

"Let me go around the table and point out one *tell* that each of you are guilty of."

"What's a *tell*?" asked Sybil.

"It's a subconscious quirk players broadcast when they're under duress or when they're excited. It tips off the observant players in the group as to what kind of cards they're holding. You get the point?" he said.

He could see that Sybil hadn't understood his explanation, so Garrett clarified, "I'll go around the table and do a quick exercise. You'll get the picture I'm sure."

He thought of Amelia and looked at his watch to see the time. His heart rate raced.

"Let me start with you Nick. You're not a bad player and I believe, just in the short conversations that we've had tonight, that you incorporate many of the observation skills you've developed in giving golf lessons, into your poker game. You are gifted I can tell. But your main flaw is that you play in far too many hands with marginal cards. It's the amateur's number one mistake to think that average cards will catch *lightening in a bottle* when the flop and fourth street come. Play fewer hands and bluff once in a while.

"Mr. Mantz, twice you had a good hand and you sat erect in your seat, then slumped back down as if to make us believe that you had very little. I knew not to mess with you on those two occasions."

Garrett turned his attention to Bob Townsend. "Bob, what's your profession?"

"Pool and spa contractor. I've been in concrete all my life," Townsend answered him.

Garrett and the others laughed at the hilarious mental picture his unintentional remark conjured up.

Garrett said, "Well then, that explains it. Now I know why your play is so erratic, because you're always plastered. You're all over the map Bob. Don't worry about when your next drink will be served, pay closer attention to your opponents' quirks and *tells* instead. Alcohol kills the powers of observation. Sorry, was I too harsh?"

Townsend was bent over with laughter and waved for Garrett to continue fleecing the others.

Garrett felt that he was on a roll, happy to entertain in a good, not combative way, for a change.

He continued. "Sybil when you first looked at your cards and said, "Yes"! I think that even these poor players knew that you had high picture cards. Perhaps you could not get so excited and say something like, "Oh drat!" Everybody, Sybil included, had a good chuckle.

"Janice you curl the hair by your right temple when you think you have good cards and run your fingers straight back through your hair when you have zip. You have several other *tells* but I don't want to get too critical," he smiled.

"Let's see umm, Tip is it? You're like every young, aggressive cowboy card player. Because your *tell* is that you fill up every pot with chips. You think that you can run us over no matter what cards you hold. You bluff way too much. You could win ten hands in a row but if you always fill up the pot with all of your chips, you're almost certain to go broke. *All in* doesn't mean all the time.

"Chief Nickerson you twirl your wedding band when you plan to place a sizable bet. That tells me to get out of your way and wait for another hand when you have weaker cards.

"Doctor you were the hardest of all to get a fix on."

Doc smiled, puffed out his chest and slapped Bob Maxwell on the shoulder.

"Hardest because, and I mean this in the kindest way, you have so many *tells* it just took more time for me to register them all."

Again they all roared, except for Maxwell. He sat up with a pinched look on his face. He was defensive. He braced because he knew that he was the next to be evaluated by his enemy.

Garrett addressed him. "And now for my good friend and confidant *Mr. Conspiracy*, I mean Mr. Real Estate Broker. You strike a mean pose and glare right through your opponents whenever you have zero, nada. You're the consummate bluffer. Kind of the way you are in real life too."

The players at first didn't know whether to howl again or what. But when Garrett winked at Maxwell and shot them all a big grin and waved goodbye, they all let go a hearty laugh at Maxwell's expense.

Annie saw that Maxwell was pissed and reached over and gave his arm a soft squeeze, "Dish it out but can't take it Bobsie?"

Maxwell pretended to lighten up and joined the others, albeit with a fake grunt.

Garrett turned to leave but the Chief caught his attention. "Say Garrett, did we play our cards well enough so that you could tell us your last name and where you're from?"

Garrett didn't answer him.

"Why so secretive? Your past couldn't be that troubling could it?" the Chief pressed.

"The present is much more interesting, you can do something about it. It's who you are, not were. Besides Chief, don't we all look back over the years and remember when we were kids say, and think that that was someone else altogether, another person's life?" Garrett said.

"Sounds to me like your dodging the Chief's question," said Maxwell.

The others at the table seemed very uncomfortable.

"I must be going. I've got to go to Amelia," Garrett said.

He turned to Annie and said with a wry smile, "Cashmere, Garrett Cashmere's my name if you must know."

Most of the players laughed once again.

Nick meanwhile, had gone over to Doc and whispered in his ear. The Doctor struggled with Nick's request. Nick had suggested that since Pastor Adams had hurt his back and wouldn't be able to join in the Doctor's playing group for the *Carrie Baker Golf Scramble* on Thursday that Doc should ask Garrett to complete the foursome. Nick told him that Garrett had mentioned how much he loved golf and that he once held a single digit handicap.

Nick implored, "I'm sure he would be on his best behavior. Besides, he says he likes to walk the course so no one would feel uncomfortable in a cart with him. He might be a *ringer* and you know your team could use the help. I'll lend him a set of clubs. What do you say Doc? The charity is for such a good cause and it's the last event for Carrie Baker. Every dollar raised is important and he's proven to be a very generous guy."

Doc was reluctant at first but caved-in and said, "Why not?"

Garrett would round out the team, joining Doc, Tip Garland and Katie Keenan, the Novartis rep, for Thursday's charity *Scramble* at the Donald Ross designed Woods Hole Country Club.

"Tell him to be there for lunch at eleven. The *Scramble* is a shotgun format and we need to be on our designated tees for the noon start," Doc said.

Nick slapped him on the shoulder and ran off after Garrett.

Maxwell, who had heard the Doctor's last remarks to Nick, leaned over to him and said, "I'm not fooled like the rest of you by this sudden change in his behavior. I'm worried for Amelia and everyone else in this town. I know he's up to no good. But if he's in your group we'll at least know where the monster is on Thursday."

Doc said, "Come on. See. He can be a real charmer if he wants too. Garrett's got some admirable qualities. Maybe Nick's right. Let's give him the benefit of the doubt and see where it goes. He's not always a complete ass."

"Just a half ass," said Maxwell, still wounded.

Nick caught up with Garrett as he was about to exit the tent. He told him of the invite but Garrett wasn't that interested. He told Nick he'd think about it. But Nick kept at him with the same persistence that he had just used on Doc.

"I need to give them an answer now. It's the last and most successful event for Carrie Baker. The biggest money raiser of all. And besides, the group really needs another good golfer."

Without a moment of hesitation, Garrett agreed to play in the *Scramble*. "Why didn't you say it was for the young girl and her family? Of course I'd be delighted to play," he said.

9

Garrett dashed back outside the tents and was greeted by a cold wind, it was the end of September. He headed straight for Amelia's where his guilt told him he should have gone an hour ago. But he had to admit he did have a wonderful time playing poker.

When he reached Palmers Pond Lane he walked down the jet-black road, and with sparkling moonbeams filtered through the trees as his lone source of light, it was an eerie atmosphere that he was engulfed within. He paused for a moment and questioned whether he should proceed. "Is it too late, and is it fair to Amelia?" He came to the rationalization that since he had come this far he might as well continue. Amelia deserved an explanation for his poor behavior.

In another minute, as he neared the end of the path, he caught a glimpse of a silhouette of a person sitting on a bench, body slumped forward. He was certain it was Amelia, who else could it be? He heard her sobs as he drew closer to her.

"Is she crying because I left her to fend for herself at the *Bazaar*, or is she concerned because of what happened to Carrie? Maybe when she saw Carrie's portrait it brought her back to that awful day? Or maybe she's afraid of what will happen to her once the truth is discovered? As if I know the truth."

He didn't want to startle her, so he cleared his throat loud enough to let her know he was there. She jumped up off the bench and turned in a panic to face the trespasser.

"Amelia, it's me, Garrett. Don't be afraid."

He could see her relax her shoulders and loosen her guard. He walked up to her. He talked fast in apologetic terms and asked her to forgive him for abandoning her at the *Bazaar*. After all the hurt levied upon her for all these years by the others he wanted her to know that he wasn't one of them. That wasn't his intent. Yes his actions were selfish but in no way were they meant to put her down. He pledged, "I promise Amelia I'll never be so egotistical, ever again."

But she surprised him when she told him that she wouldn't hear of his regrets. She said that it was she who had chosen to leave the party and not because of his disappearance. In a very soft and concerned voice she told him that the *Bazaar* had became too much for her to handle, with the crowd of people, people whom she knew wondered what right she had to be there. They were right. She never fit in before and what made her think that it had changed overnight. She told him that when he had kissed her, as much as she enjoyed it, she knew that it wasn't right. She told him she knew he meant it for someone else.

"But I want yah to know that it meant so much ta me. It's the fust kiss I evah tasted."

His heart felt so heavy for all that he imagined Amelia had endured in her life.

After a spell of silence Amelia asked, "How can the Chuch Bazah be so festive an occasion when it's theyah to honah such a sad event as the Bakah gul's death?"

This was the opportunity he had been waiting for. "I know, it doesn't make much sense. But most people choose to forget the traumatic stuff by burying it with alcohol and music. Or just block it out of their minds altogether, as if it never happened. Denial.

"You know, a lot about Carrie's death doesn't add up to me. I get the feeling that you can make some sense of it though. Am I right? Amelia would you like to tell me about what happened that day here at the pond? I don't think you've told me or anyone else the whole story? I promise to keep it between us."

To his surprise his question opened up the flood gates. She straight away told him what had happened that tragic afternoon right near where they now sat.

Amelia related how the little brat had driven her bicycle onto her precious lawn and that when she yelled down to her from her bedroom window to stop, how Carrie giggled and continued to crisscross her bike back and forth over the moist grass. It created deep unsightly ruts. She laughed at Amelia and shouted that she didn't have to listen to her because everyone said she was a *nutty lunatic*. Carrie told her that everyone called her *squirrel turd*.

When Amelia came down the stairs to confront her, Carrie dragged her bike over the lawn again and proceeded to inflict more damage.

Amelia told Garrett, "I can still heah in my mind the kid's mockin' laughtah."

She told him the more that she scolded the girl, the more Carrie scorned her.

She stopped to draw her breath and told him that despite her pleas the little witch didn't care that she had damaged Amelia's land. Amelia wondered why had she been so naughty? She told Garrett that she wouldn't have tossed her damn bike in the water and Carrie wouldn't a gone in after it, if she had only listened and apologized.

"She'd still be alive taday and they'd a had ta figyah out whom else ta honah at the *Bazah* tanight," Amelia said.

Garret was so moved. He thought, "Poor Amelia, with all that she's gone through. It's not fair. She acted as best she knew how. She reprimanded a child who disobeyed an adult's orders. When the girl had defied her Amelia aped the poor role model she had known, her abusive father. She must have lashed out with blind force at the little brat, as she referred to Carrie. Hum. She just said that she threw the bike in and that Carrie went in after it, so she wasn't physical with the child. She didn't push her in. She's not of sound mind and reason, but she wouldn't harm anyone, on purpose anyway," he thought.

Garrett swore to himself that he would not let anymore harm come to Amelia. He was sure she hadn't told anyone else and he would go to his grave with her secret. She didn't mean for the girl to drown. Her mind couldn't have calculated that Carrie would have jumped in after the bicycle. But would the others see it that way? "They're so self righteous and superior acting that they'd punish her to the maximum extent of the law I'm sure," he told himself. He vowed to stay silent and be her protector.

Amelia told him that the reason she had opened up about the accident was that she had overheard Bob Maxwell tell people in town that he thought the stranger had something to do with Carrie's death. Amelia wanted Garrett to know and to be on guard.

But he just brushed it off as another crazy rant by the village fearmonger. "I can handle that conspiracy peddler any day of the week," Garrett boasted.

Garrett decided that if it ever came to it he'd deflect their suspicions off of her and upon himself for a time. After all, so many of them distrusted him and Maxwell, blind with revenge, already suspected him as he had just learned. "It should be a snap to get them off of her scent and onto mine if need be. It'd even be easier than bluffing them at poker," he thought.

"Ironic", he thought, "to save Amelia's life had value, but to be vengeful for Carrie's death wouldn't raise her from the dead and therefore, was worthless."

He saw another poignant paradox in all of this. He'd been under suspicion back home and had been beaten for his questionable innocence. He knew how cruel angry people could be. Their malice could be uncontrollable. And now, one hundred percent innocent in the drowning death of a precious little girl, he'd be putting himself into a similar destructive cyclone in order to protect another.

As nine o'clock arrived Garrett handed Amelia the Palmers Pond book that he had carried with him in his jacket pocket and gave her a soft kiss upon her forehead, this time as a protector would. They said good night and he waited for her to ascend the stairs and slide her way into her clutter-filled home.

As he walked back up the path and onto the road, tears ran down his face. Tears for Amelia, for Carrie and for what he knew was in store for him.

10

Rock music pulsated from inside the church tents and Garrett stopped on the sidewalk to have a listen, before he continued his walk back to the Hibiscus Inn. He felt quite low after his visit with Amelia and the music provided a needed distraction. He was pretty certain that it was a live band playing and he decided to take a seat on a wooden bench on the Village Green and listen for a while. He told himself that it wasn't that cold.

Garrett could hear the patron's voices mixed in with the music, they seemed to be singing in unison with the band. It sounded like a lot of fun. He closed his eyes and pictured the crowds of people dancing on the sawdust covered floor and soon, without any manipulation on his part, a vision of Caroline came into his mind. Everyone else on the dance floor moved at slow motion speed and he could see Amelia and his ex-wife amongst them. They reached out to him as they began to fade into the background along with the others, while Caroline's figure brightened and took center stage. She threw her head back and he felt her long flowing golden hair swipe across his face. He could smell her essence as she and her colorful skirt twirled around him.

The image of her seemed so real that it drew him up off of the bench, as if his heart were made of metal and she its powerful magnet.

"I should apologize to her," he said in half sincerity.

He knew he was fooling himself, he just wanted to hear her voice and feel her glow once again. It made no sense for him to remain a spectator out there in the cold. He convinced himself that he ought to go inside the tent for a few minutes and experience the excitement for himself. He still had energy to burn, so why not enjoy the music and get warm again? It wasn't that late.

When he re-entered he was pleased to see that a majority of the three hundred or so patrons were on or near the saw dust dance floor. The young band on stage cranked out *Beast of Burden* and people danced, clapped and sang in various pitches along with the female lead singer.

He looked for a familiar face or two but before he could spot anyone, Annie Temple came up from behind him, linked her arm in his and proceeded to drag him toward the dance floor. He put up a little resistance at first but succumbed to Annie's determination to have a dance with him, as the happy smile on her face melted his defenses. He was in the moment.

It was reminiscent of a rush hour traffic jam in downtown Boston, bodies bumper to bumper on the sizable dance floor. Garrett and Annie managed to find a sliver of it to stand on and just shuffled in place, both with big grins on their faces. She yelled something to him but it was impossible to hear, because her words were hijacked by the wave of loud music and the singing herd around them. He just shrugged his shoulders and gave her a flirtatious smile.

The band played three more *Stones* songs nonstop and Annie and Garrett gyrated away. At some point they were able to work their way out onto the middle of the dance floor, and now, in the eye of the storm, they couldn't dance as they had bonded together in one big rhythmic blob with the throngs around them. They just swayed back and forth to the beat. It was a blast. He sweated a lot and figured that this was the first exercise he had had in months. Wow was he ever out of shape! But that wouldn't stop him.

Garrett was glad when the band decided to take their break. Annie thanked him and he put his arm around her for a brief second. Almost breathless he told her, "You're quite the dancer. I had all I could do to keep up with you." They walked off the dance floor and looked for refreshments.

Annie said, "You held your own quite well Garrett. Although I can see that you haven't done this for awhile." He chose to nod so as to conserve his breath.

Just then a distinguished looking gentleman, somewhere in his mid fifties Garrett presumed, appeared on stage and shouted into the microphone in an attempt to get everyone's attention, but without much success. When he repeated his plea a few more times, the word began to spread throughout the spirited crowd that a major announcement was about to be made. The sounds of, "Hush" and "Be quiet please," were able to overtake the swarm's exuberance. It was another full minute before the audience went dead silent and the man on the stage loosened his tie and began to speak in a normal manner into the microphone, "Is everybody happy?"

Their cheers and hoots answered his question.

Garrett asked Annie, "Who's he?"

She told him, "Caroline's father, Ned Cassidy. He's a great guy."

Ned, a tall man of six two didn't adjust the mic and instead he leaned forward with his lips up against the device. "Tonight I have a very special announcement to make and I know that you will all agree this was well worth me having the balls to interrupt the festivities. Pardon my French Pastor Adams."

Cheers and mock boos rang out from the crowd, all in good humor. Ned laughed into the microphone and it caused an excruciating screeching noise. Startled, he jumped back as if he had just been electrocuted.

He was more cautious as he approached the microphone a second time, he didn't want it to notice him and bite back again.

Ned said, "Sorry. I'll be brief. I promise. My wife Kitty and I are proud to announce that our beloved, engaged daughter Caroline and her wonderful fiancé, and soon to be our son-in-law, Sean Garland, have decided to forgo their June nuptials next year and instead they will be wed right here at St. Barnabas Church next Saturday!"

He held up his hands to quiet the frenzy but it took a full minute before they calmed down. When they had at last followed his request to wait he added, "Sean ships out next Sunday on a second tour of duty to the Middle East and the two lovers wish to tie their bonds in honor of his commitment to serve our great nation. So let's congratulate two wonderful kids!" he shouted into the microphone, which screeched once again, while he raised a glass, of what, the crowd couldn't tell.

Garret began to wander off, he was in total disbelief. Shock would be a more apt description of his state of mind. The clamor of congratulations and cheers caused his head to spin, his pounding headache had roared back. He felt as if he was on a bad trip. It was all too surreal. His mind raced. "Why the hell did I come back? This is madness. Caroline can't be serious. She wants to marry another village clone? I thought she was different from them?"

Before another *woe is me* thought could find space inside his head he was spun around again by Annie and tugged back in the direction of the dance floor. She paid no attention to his sincere protests as she maneuvered him through the sea of well wishers in an effort to reach her dear friend Caroline to congratulate her.

As they reached the edge of the dance floor he no longer opposed her, resigned to the fact that he would at least see Caroline again.

Caroline chatted with the doctor's wife; then she was hugged by a young teen; then by several other familiar faces who gave her their best, the cook, Hank, was one of them. Annie ran up to her and gave her a big hug and kiss and told her how thrilled she was for her young friend and her fiancé. Annie then walked over to Sean who stood with his back to her a few feet away. He was ecstatic as he shook hands and received congratulations from his friends and admirers.

In an awkward twist of chance, Garrett was left standing eye to eye with Caroline for a brief few seconds. He had no idea that he was about to make a jerk out of himself once again. His lips moved and the words leapt out, "As your most passionate devotee and head of the *Caroline Cassidy Fan Club*, I will do all in my power these next several days to show you that I'm your best choice for the future, not that empty-headed warrior whom you've been tricked into marrying."

Caroline had no clue what could be in his brain. She was stunned by his audacity. But before she could gather herself to lambast him, her *husband to be* came back to her side and gave her a kiss on the cheek. She decided to just let this fool's comments evaporate.

However, others whom had gathered around her and had heard most of what Garrett had said, gasped with disapproval at his most inappropriate remarks.

Meanwhile Sean, who had not heard Garrett's comments, whispered in Caroline ear, "Who's the lightweight next to you?"

Before Caroline told him, Annie was back and introduced Sean to Garrett. With a noticeable lack of enthusiasm on Garrett's part they shook hands. Garrett didn't congratulate Sean.

Sean looked Garrett over for a second and with a huge smile on his happy, *soon to be married to the most beautiful girl on the planet's face*, he jested, "You've been here less than forty-eight hours mister and you're already a celebrity. You'll have to determine if that's a good thing or not. What a commotion you've caused man. Although I wouldn't let it go to your head Garrett. Even if my love Caroline seems fascinated with you., the others aren't so taken..."

Caroline elbowed him in the side so hard that he knew enough to stop in mid-sentence. She didn't want her fiancé to give Garrett any false encouragement. She also decided not to mention the uncomfortable confrontation of a moment ago, she didn't want to spoil the moment.

But Garrett, with a little fight still left in him, said to Sean, "How is it that you, an average mortal at best, was able to convince the goddess Caroline to accept your proposal?"

The lieutenant was not used to being teased. No one dared. But he decided to leave well enough alone, as this was the greatest night of his life to date and with just seven days left until his departure he felt grateful and wanted to spend every last hour with Caroline.

Seconds later the young couple was engulfed by a tsunami of well-wishers that swept them away with their gentle undertow.

That left Garrett in the company of the Doc's wife Helen, Martha and several of their friends who had gathered and waited for Caroline and Sean to be out of earshot. Martha wanted to set the record straight and echoed the genuine discomfort of the group after they'd all had heard his most improper flirtations.

She scolded him, "It is most uncivil of you to have made a pass at a young woman, whose very wedding announcement had been made just a moment earlier! How dare you! I cannot imagine what is inside that head of yours. How could you be so insensitive and so brash? And as for your noticeable disrespect for her fiancé Sean Garland, well let me tell you Garrett...Perhaps you are not aware that lieutenant Garland is an upright local boy, football and lacrosse star, top student at West Point, and a true hero, not just to the people of our fine community, but to the citizens of this great nation as well. This unselfish man has chosen to leave his wealthy and privileged life behind and with the utmost bravery, in one week's time, is about to embark upon his second tour of duty, off to protect us from those heathens in that dreadful Middle East, Iraq, Afghanistan, Syria, or wherever those prehistoric *beheaders* roam. He is prepared to sacrifice his own safety in order that you can feel secure here at home. He is a true American hero and you should be honored to be in his presence."

The group had grown by a few more people and they all seemed to say in unison "I agree. Hear, hear! Well said Martha."

Garrett was already irritated by their engagement announcement, so it didn't take much for him to become inflamed by Martha's reproach. He mocked her. "Dear Mrs. Nickerson, and I mean this with the utmost respect to you, your neighbors and the lieutenant as well (too bad he isn't present to hear this himself). If I'm not mistaken the good lieutenant has joined the armed forces on his own volition. No one dragged him to the recruiter's office, am I correct? This is a volunteer army after all. And please excuse me if I overlooked anything, but he does seem to be in tip top shape, with all his limbs and eye sockets intact. As far as I know he never had an occasion to defend himself, let alone anyone else for that matter. So I take offense with you and everyone else in this blindly patriotic, violent ridden country of ours, when you hand out the title hero to someone just because he or she is in uniform, or has had a tour of duty over there. He is a soldier, he is trained to kill and does as he wishes."

He was deaf to their protests.

"It's not that I don't feel for him and his colleagues, as it's a certainty that they will be put in harm's way. I hope for their safety and wish them a quick return home. But come on now people. They signed up to be in a profession that, from the very start, describes the possibility that they might be put in danger at sometime in their employment. It's their responsibility too. I would rather say that they are good men and women who fight and destroy someone else' property in a far-off land, so that we can feel our life-style will be kept intact and that our mega corporations can continue to earn their big bucks.

"And don't get me started on the real reasons we're always meddling over there. The lives of our soldiers and the taxpayers' money is spent to protect corporate interests. Of course they should be protected if they wish to risk doing business in terrorist riddled countries. But the taxpayers shouldn't fit the bill, the corporations should. If they want military protection, they should pay for it all themselves. So too should our so called friends and allies around the world. If Japan wants us to be their army, then it's only fair that they pay the whole tab.

"Look if I had my way there would be no war. Whatever has come of it besides domination and widening the gap between the haves and have-nots? Don't you think that we face far more danger today because of our presence over there, than we did prior to Sept.11, 2001?"

He was lathered up and wanted to complete his rant.

He emphasized, "To me a **hero** is someone, who through self-sacrifice and with no personal gain, protects the lives of others. Someone who puts his or her own life in jeopardy in order to save those in peril. Firemen and policemen at the World Trade Towers for example.

"Sure there are a few acts of heroism in Iraq, Afghanistan, wherever, but they're the exceptions. Most of the military over there just does the job they are paid to do. And they do their business very well. We are the strongest and the best. But they're not immune to the effects of all the stress they have to deal with. Some snap and go out of their way to inflect pain on the locals and our enemies, just for kicks. War is hell!

"There's a frightening idol worship in this great country of ours for those in military uniform. It's not healthy to paint each and everyone in military dress as a hero. It degrades the status of those who were, and are actual *lion hearts*. It makes it too commonplace. Everyday there is some announcer who spouts off such bullshit, "His father is Semper Fi", U.S Marine, our hero, does it get any better than that?" "Or at a little league game, "We salute our heroes in uniform who protect our free way of life, our freedom protectors. Yeah, while they blow up some other country's freedom.

"We're conditioned by the military complex to believe that there is evil around every corner and that they're the heroes who fight it every day. Right, thousands of miles from our shores. Come on people. Look around. Every week homegrown terrorist' attacks are happening at schools, nightclubs and theaters right here in the USA. This is where we need the uniform protection. We need the military to protect our own shores, not to send our young ones over to the desert to protect the oil corporations' profits. Too many people have died and I mean ours and theirs. We can't just count our own dead. In Afghanistan and Iraq thousands of our military have died. And I've heard estimates that a hundred thirty thousand civilians, civilians have been killed. Syria is much worse. Enough!

"I can hear your protests because I know you buy into the propaganda. You're so selfish that if anyone messes with your beliefs, well then heck, he's either unpatriotic, or a socialist who wants to see the end of this great nation. Bull! Open your eyes and hearts to others in this world. Don't demonize them because they don't look like you and don't believe in your god. Admit that you're driven by fear and greed. You're afraid that someone else might take a piece of your pie. Your mouths are full yet you want second helpings while the others are left to fight for your crumbs. Sure there are some crazy bastards out there who hate us and our privileged way of life, but they're very few. The majority of humans roaming the planet want what you want. Cut them some slack for heaven's sake. If I were you I'd be far more concerned with the growing angst in this country over income disparity rather than the insanity on the other side of the globe. You can't just stock pile your automatic weapons and wait for the boogie man to come to take away your freedoms. It isn't healthy behavior. We're all in this together. Stop your superior, separation crap. We've got to help the good cops, the majority, weed out the bad cops. Stop the bad cops from killing defenseless black people. Open your eyes, stop hating on people of color. You can't turn the clocks back. You want it to be like it was. That's how civilizations crumble, going backwards. Show the least fortunate in this world how they can participate in the pursuit of a better life and they will strive to assimilate into your society. Build walls to keep the least fortunate out and they will storm your gates. Accept the new reality and embrace the new demographics not fight them. Unite!"

If he hadn't been already, it was now official, Garrett was their arch enemy.

As he walked away he laughed to himself, "That took a lot of balls. Does that make me some sort of *hero?*".

11

Garrett paced in his room. It couldn't have gone worse!

"Why do I always feel I have to set the record straight? Filter dammit! Can I just once let people wallow in their phony beliefs without having the compulsion to open my big mouth? Why do I have to challenge these impostors? I'm supposed to lay low and avoid attention, but I've done the complete opposite. I'm such an idiot. I knew I'd blow it sooner or later. They'll be all over me like flies on shit," Garrett thought.

"It's like someone's taken over my mind. I've got to change and get back to who I am, was. What am I thinking? Ever since the attack I feel I've been half here, half in a parallel world. Like life has changed back to black and white and I'm waiting for Buster Keaton to trip across the room."

He opened the curtains and gawked at the harbor lights as they were being dimmed by a fast rolling blanket of fog.

"As if I have a snowballs chance in hell with Caroline. I don't even know the woman. It doesn't have anything to do with Caroline. It's because she reminds me of Marlie. I'm so pathetic. Caroline seems to be a fine person and is already in love. Let her be."

He grabbed his hair with both hands and pulled outward as hard as he could.

He turned and looked around the room and walked over to his luggage. Garrett reached for his saddle bag and removed a manila envelope, took out a few important papers and looked them over. They were his bank statements and he was pleased to see, that despite his recent spending spree, he had about a two-hundred-thirty-eight thousand-dollar balance in his account.

Anxious, Garrett went into the bathroom and turned on the dimmer switch to its brightest. He stood up against the sink and leaned as close to the mirror as possible, so that he could better examine his soul. Then he said aloud to the mirror, not to his image, "You've seen so many faces, so much history. What do you think of me? How do I compare? Is there any hope?"

For a few moments he stood and stared at himself. He seemed to be waiting for his reflection, or the mirror, to tell him what to do next.

Once Garrett snapped out of the mirror's spell, he left the bathroom, undressed and crawled into bed. After an excruciating hour of tossing and turning, he fell fast to sleep.

He was awoken at dawn when a wedge of light squeezed its way into the room and shone straight into his eyes. He popped out of bed, cleaned up in the bathroom and without hesitation, packed his luggage. He went over to the maple desk and wrote the innkeeper a short note and left it on the bedside table. He downed a little blue pill and didn't wait for it to kick in.

Garrett exited the room. He snuck out the front door and left the premises unnoticed. He walked the two and a half miles to the bus station on Depot Avenue in nearby Falmouth, in order to catch the seven thirty bus to Boston. He had planned to take this short trip sometime next week, but after last night's fiasco, he thought it best that he get out of town so that the air could clear.

It wasn't until ten o'clock when Liza was cleaning his room, that she saw the note he had addressed to Martha. She put it in her apron pouch and intended to give it to Martha after she had finished with all of her chores.

Sometime around eleven Liza went into Martha's private residence and handed her the note. When Liza left, Martha unfolded it and read, "Dear Innkeeper and staff. I will be out of town and intend to return on Wednesday night. Please, no snooping around in my absence. Thank you! G."

"Well of all the nerve! You would think that after last night's poor display he would have learned to curb his rude behavior. Robert Maxwell's suspicions that he is a menace may not be without merit. At the very least, the man is a troublemaker," Martha said aloud.

She tossed the note into the fire and watched with pleasure as it curled up at its' edges when the flames began to acknowledge its arrival. She stared in deep thought while it turned into ashes.

Later, when she had put her routine call into her brother, Doc mentioned he'd heard about Garrett's poor behavior at the *Church Bazaar*.

Martha said, "The man knows no boundaries. But you will be happy to hear that we will get a reprieve from his awful deportment, at least for a couple of days anyway, because he left a note that said he had gone away and would not return until Wednesday night."

"Did he say where he was off to?" Doc asked.

"No. Just that he would be gone and for us not to snoop around in his room. Can you imagine?"

"Yes Martha I can. What could he be up to now? Why is it such a mystery with that man?" Doc wondered.

He continued, "Please be careful around him when he returns and be sure to report any unusual conduct to the Chief. See if you can find out where he went and what he's up to. He has exhibited a very odd and dangerous behavior. More people think Bob might be right this time, that he may have had a hand in Carrie's death. I know it sounds far-fetched, but he's so unpredictable, and what disturbs me even more so is that I believe he's even unpredictable to himself. He seems to be haunted, driven by demons. He's seldom rational.

"It's best that we all stay on our guard in his presence, until we can be sure of who he is and what his motivations are. He's an enigma, a real enigma."

12

That same day at the Eatery, the *Round Table Group's* conversation remained focused on Carrie's drowning and how the stranger could have known that she had ridden her bicycle. The thought of murder chilled them.

Doc Nickerson spoke. "Martha called me and mentioned that Garrett had left a note saying he'd be out of town until Wednesday night. He didn't say where to, or for what purpose dammit."

"Perfect," said Maxwell.

He said to Chief Nickerson, "You won't have to ask the Fire Chief to do a phony fire drill to get you inside his room for a look around. Let's go over and see what we can find."

"Just hold on a minute Bob. Neither you, nor anyone else at this table will go anywhere near his room. He hasn't been charged with a crime. Hell, we don't even know if there was a crime. I'd need a warrant to search his room and the D.A. would never grant me one based on a hunch. We need evidence, solid evidence," the Chief reprimanded.

Stuart Holmes, the banker, had a strategy. "Chief wouldn't it be quite proper to investigate the sudden disappearance of one of the Inn's guests? A guest who had just yesterday at the *Bazaar* displayed such poor judgment? A man, whom others would attest, had acted very bizarre. Aren't we afraid and concerned for his safety…and the safety of others as well? Maybe something untoward has happened to him? Perhaps he has taken his own life, or harmed someone else?"

"Great idea. That should work," offered several of the group.

"Well Chief?" asked Maxwell.

"I guess it could warrant, no pun intended, a quick peek. You know, and we must all be sworn to secrecy here, that if it didn't smell to me like someone had a hand in Carrie's death I'd tell you all to take a hike. But when I saw all those deep bicycle tire tracks on the lawns by the pond I could see that someone with a hell of a lot more strength than a little six-year-old had made them. I'm very suspicious because Garrett knew she rode her bike. We withheld that information from the public on purpose, until we could determine if it was material or not. Carrie's family, the police and the murderer are the only people who would know that she was on her bicycle. It was so damn muddy because it rained that afternoon that we weren't able to get any foot prints, but it wouldn't surprise me if he had cleaned them up with the side of his foot. That could explain the caked mud on his shoes that Martha said she saw when he arrived at her Inn Friday night- Saturday morning," the Chief said.

He then warned them all. "But look, this could all be a crazy coincidence. Let's not jump to conclusions until I see what's in his room, if anything."

He took out his cell phone and called the station. "Hi Susan. Can you put me through to Sergeant Scott please?"

When the receptionist told him that Scott had just stepped outside for a cigarette break, he told her, "Please tell him to meet me at the Hibiscus Inn in fifteen minutes, and Susan tell him I said he should quit the damn smokes."

The Chief got up from the table and told them all to wait, that he'd be back in a half hour or so. As he walked out the door, he turned to Doc, "Cuz, call Martha and soften her up a bit will ya? Tell her I'll be by in a few minutes for an informal look around."

When the Chief pulled his unmarked car into the rear lot of the Hibiscus Inn he saw that Sgt. Scott was leaned up against a magnificent oak tree. Scott didn't think that the Chief had just seen him flick his cigarette across the path.

The Chief exited his vehicle and scolded, "I see you have trouble following orders Scotty. Get over there and stomp out that butt before you start a three alarm fire," he laughed.

They walked through the rear gate and up the wooden stairs to the back door of the Inn and arrived at the kitchen entry. The Chief was in a hurry and banged on the screen door. They didn't have to wait very long when Liza came to see which vendor had arrived. She didn't recognize either of them, so she was wary and remained behind the locked screen door.

"We're here to see Martha please. Tell her that her cousin Carl has stopped by."

She was nervous and had no clue what he had just said, except for Martha's name. "Waits. I gets persons," she answered.

Liza came back accompanied by Martha, who greeted him and then cautioned, "Carl... You know that I do not approve of what you are up to. Calvert said it was routine police procedure but it sounds anything but routine to me. I cannot just go and open up a guest's room for any harebrained reason you know."

Carl was a big fan of Martha's and expected her to resist his request to case one of her lodger's room. She took pride in her first-class Inn and guarded her guest's privacy and their belongings. He respected that.

He cajoled her, "Martha my favorite cousin, if it were routine do you think I'd have come along? A patrolman would have sufficed. You see dear girl a few of our finest citizens have voiced concern for one of your guest's safety and a couple others are concerned for your safety and your other guests as well. So, would it be out of the ordinary if the door to his room just happened to be ajar when the sergeant and I walked past on our visit to see you?"

"If this was normal I would give you an emphatic no and you know that Carl. But with the stir he continues to cause around here and with the hurtful remarks that he had written to me today, I think for this one time and one time alone, I will turn my back. His room is through that door, the first one on the right. It is already ajar," she grinned.

When they entered the spacious *Honeysuckle Room* there wasn't much for them to see. Scotty went straight for the bathroom to check it out, while the Chief stayed in the main room. Carl looked at the Inn's stationery and magazines and he turned them upside down to see if there was anything hidden inside the pages, but nothing fell out. He pulled down the bedspread and sheets and looked under the bed as well. Nothing.

Likewise, Scotty came back into the main room empty handed. They were miffed.

They had just exited the room and before they closed the door they saw Sonia on the staircase. The Chief called to her, "Young lady, could you come here for a moment?"

She stopped at the bottom of the steps. She was a bit stunned to see the two strangers standing in front of Garrett's room. She was in no hurry as she walked over to them.

"Hello. I wonder if you would answer a few questions about Garrett?"

Sonia smelled *KGB* all over them, but if Martha had let them in she would cooperate. The thought occurred to her that maybe they were immigration agents, here to check up on her and Liza. If they were out to round up illegals she and Liza had nothing to worry about, they had their papers in order.

The Chief motioned for her to enter the *Honeysuckle* and he and the sergeant followed her back inside.

"Do you know where he has gone?" was his first question.

She shook her head no, "He somewheres not heres? He didn't tells me."

"Have you had a chat with him about where he came from?"

When she answered him no once again, Scotty gave it a try. "Have you seen any of his travel itinerary?"

"No sirs. But perhaps Liza seens them. She cleans room everyday." They figured that Liza must be the woman whom they had met when they had first arrived.

"I go to gets her, brings her here. She speaks little English. I shalls come interprets, no?"

The Chief sat in the arm chair while Scotty, anxious to light up another cancer stick, paced the room.

The women returned and Liza was very nervous and shy.

The next several minutes proved more fruitful. Sonia spoke in Russian to her friend and associate Liza, who had some answers to their questions. She mentioned that on Saturday when she had cleaned his room and emptied his waste bin, she had seen an airline ticket discarded in the basket. She reminded Sonia that she had brought it to her to read, because she herself could not. She wanted to be sure that it wasn't thrown in the trash by mistake. Sonia had told her that it was an email confirmation of the flight he had taken to Massachusetts and was of no use.

Sonia related, "Liza says she brings to me his airline ticket. Ah yes, yes. I remembers."

"What is it that you remember?" asked Scotty.

"I remembers she brings to me."

A little bit perturbed Scotty asked, "Do you remember what was written on it?"

"No."

At that moment Liza understood their banter and spoke to her friend. Sonia translated to the visitors. "Liza says I tells her Arizona, Phoenix Arizona. That's right. She remembers date too, September 19th. That's her mother's birthday she remembers thinkings at that time."

Sergeant Scott asked, "Did you or she read the name on it?"

Sonia, "No. You don't knows his name?"

The Chief intervened. "My friend wanted to know if Liza and you had perhaps read another guest's garbage by mistake."

Sonia said, "No, no it was ones she brings me I thinks."

Chief asked, "Where is the receipt? Do you still have it?"

"Why would I keeps used receipt that he throws away? No sirs, we empties rooms every day and Julio comes with truck and takes to dump," Sonia answered.

The Chief thanked them both and told them not to tell Garrett that they were there. On their way out of the Inn they stopped in the kitchen and asked Martha to reiterate to her staff that when Garrett returned they were not to say a word about them stopping by.

Outside the Hibiscus Scotty said, "I'll start a search of names of people who took a flight from Phoenix to Boston or Providence on the 19th."

"Don't waste your time. There are probably several flights a day and more connecting flights that go through Phoenix en route to the northeast. Do you know how many people from all over Arizona drive to Phoenix to catch their flights? It's a massive area that that airport serves. Millie and I have been there twice and it's the only airport for hundreds of miles. We need to uncover where he lives not where he flew in from. We'll find out soon."

When the Chief had rejoined the group and told them what they found, it was Maxwell who pointed out that September 20th was the Thursday that Carrie had drowned, one day before Garrett had taken a room at the Hibiscus Inn.

Maxwell said, "He told Martha he'd been up for a couple of days straight. Do the math. He arrived here on the nineteenth say, two days before he checked into the Hibiscus on the twenty first. Carrie drowned on the twentieth. He must have cased the village. Remember, Martha told us he arrived at midnight, disheveled and with his shoes encrusted in mud. Maybe he hid out down by the pond. There are lots of woodsy areas where he could have hidden with his cache of weapons. Maybe poor Carrie was unlucky enough to have come upon him and he feared his cover was blown. So he chose to silencer her and he made it appear to be an unfortunate drowning. Then he holed out for a day and a half, who knows where? Now he's off and disappeared for a couple of days, maybe to round up his terrorist cronies to go over their elaborate plan to attack the village, for what purpose I'm not sure? But we must find out before it's too late.

"He's a clever s.o.b., that evil bastard. Think about it, he's set up a brilliant diversion with his insults and shenanigans to make us think that he's just some unbalanced kook. He's drawn our complete attention to his behavior not to his actions. He has calculated it down to the most minute detail. But our gifted antagonist has made a few big mistakes I'm happy to say. First, he arrived late at Martha's unannounced and with the evidence of mud on his shoes. Thank God she was suspicious and so alert. Next, he blew it by letting his ego get the best of him when he had to show off just how easy it was to manipulate all of us and control our minds at *Holdem Poker* the other night. He was all puffed up with pride that he had conquered us. Remember? He has underestimated us and that will prove to be his *Waterloo*. The asshole's actions speak of his culpability in Carrie's murder. You know I bet Garrett's a phony name by the way. He's been back to the scene of the crime at least twice that we know of, perhaps more. And he asks anyone he talks with to tell him about the girl and how she died and he has given more money, than all of us put together, to her charity. Can you say guilt? Get this, he won five of the auctions the other night, Carrie's portrait the main prize and he outbid the next person by over a thousand dollars! Why would he, a complete stranger, who wants us to believe that he never laid eyes upon her, want her portrait and at such a hefty overprice? Because he didn't just lay eyes upon her, he laid his fangs upon her as well! And get this, he put all the auction bids in Amelia's name, as if to deflect the blame onto an innocent, challenged person. His disgraceful actions know no bounds. If all that weren't enough to convince you, he escorted Amelia to the *Bazaar* Sunday. Why is that suspicious? The more appropriate question is why isn't it?

"Maybe he wants to use her home as a refuge, to store his weapons, or use it as a safe haven for him and his band of thieves? Or perhaps she may have seen what he was up to, or his interactions with Carrie, after all she lives right on the pond next to the very spot where Carrie's body was found. He's clever this guy. He woos Amelia and asks her on a date to compromise her, she's not the sharpest tool in the shed, to keep her from telling us what happened that day. You could see that she was gaga over him. I think Chief that you need to question Amelia and you'll find your answers. He's the devil. He's your man Chief, mark my words!"

The Chief wasn't as convinced though. But he started to lean in that direction he had to admit.

Chief Nickerson said, "Very convincing Bob. But you left out the most important piece of the puzzle. Garrett knows that Carrie rode her bicycle. How?

Stuart Holmes added, "Say doc, isn't Garrett scheduled to play in Thursday's *Scramble* with your group?"

Doctor Nickerson answered him, "I wish that it weren't true, but yes."

Stuart said, "That's terrific. Because it'll be our diversion to have him watched by you and Tip, while one of your men Chief can do another *look see* in Garrett's room. He'll be back from wherever he just went and his luggage will be back too I presume. There has to be some piece of interest that you'll find Chief. At the very least you might discover where he returned from."

"Another terrific idea Stuart," shouted Maxwell.

The Chief once again sounded a word of caution. "Let's get solid evidence, not conjecture, and we can lock this bad actor up for the rest of his life. We need to exercise a little patience and of course vigilance, when and if he returns, and I'm not so convinced that he will. We all need to keep a discreet surveillance of the man and when the time comes for his crime to be carried out, we can pounce on him and his comrades and catch them red-handed in the act. Then we can squash them like the mere insects that they are."

13

Garrett returned to Falmouth by bus on Wednesday night from his Boston trip and took the lone taxi that was parked in front of the station. The cabbie looked Muslim to Garrett. They didn't exchange a word, other than where Garrett was to be dropped off.

He had visited his ailing mother in a fine Cambridge rest home on Monday, and since she was under the debilitating influence of Alzheimer's, he knew that that would be the last time he'd see her alive. He had arranged to met his mother's attorney in Boston on Wednesday afternoon to fill out all the proper legal documents and make arrangements for her end of life care. He also had several of his own legal documents drawn up and notarized. On Tuesday he traveled up to Marblehead on the North Shore, to pay his respects.

When he entered his room he noticed the large golf bag that stood in one corner. There was a note attached to the towel clip. He went over and read it. It was from Nick.

"Shit! I forgot tomorrow is Carrie's *Golf Scramble*." Well at least it wasn't scheduled until noon, so he could get some needed rest. He should have enough time to practice as well. It'd been a couple of years since he'd last played.

He lifted his attaché onto his lap and pulled out a thick file folder. He perused a couple of the legal documents that pertained to him alone. One was entitled *Last Will and Testament*, and with a smile on his face, he read every tedious sentence, just as he had done several times on the bus ride back to Falmouth. Then he read the other document, his *Living Trust*. If anything should happen to him, Garrett had seen to it that Amelia and Lupita would be the beneficiaries of most of what he owned.

He put all the paperwork back into their respected folders and the folders back into his attaché. He remembered to remove his driver's license from his leather wallet (he had taken it out of hiding because he needed to show identification in Boston) and brought it over to his suitcase and stuck it inside a black sock for safe keeping.

From the Boston lawyer's office he had emailed the Hibiscus Inn's contact information to Lupita back home. He now tore up the paper that he had written the information on and tossed the tiny, indiscernible bits into the waste bin.

Feeling that all things were in order, Garrett walked over to the bed, pulled back the covers, took off his pants and shirt and slipped under the sheets.

When he reached to switch off the table lamp he noticed that an envelope was leaned up against the base. It had Garrett written on it. He sat up, grabbed it and tore it open. A note had been typed by a person named Michael Castle CPA.

"Dear Sir,

Ms. Amelia Nickerson has informed us that at the Church Bazaar you made several bids on her behalf. We are grateful for your generosity. This is to notify you that you were the successful bidder on the following auctions:

*Carrie Baker Portrait	$2,000.00
*Marky Lucky Cuts Hair Styling	300.00
*Village Meat and Deli certificate	125.00
*Whale Watch Tour and Lunch for four	230.00
*Bikram Yoga 10 visits	400.00

TOTAL Due to the Carrie Baker Foundation upon receipt:
$3,055.00

Congratulations ! Unless you direct us otherwise, we will deliver all prizes to Ms. Amelia Nickerson's home on Palmers Pond Lane.

Garrett didn't flinch at the figure, he just wondered how he would get the money over to Castle, since he didn't have a check book or credit card with him. He did have loads of cash though, as he had just picked up more money on Tuesday in Boston. He had the funds wired in from his bank back home. He decided he'd get a cashier's check the next morning and have it made out to the *Foundation*.

At any rate, he needed to get some sleep, as he had a very busy day ahead of him.

When Garrett woke the next morning at seven he felt groggy, even though he'd slept for close to nine hours. He remained in bed and waited for his head to clear. But much later, when he re-opened his eyes, he was startled to see that it was a few minutes before ten. He jumped out of bed in a semi-panic.

He opened up his suitcase and took out a new shirt that he had purchased at a posh Newbury Street shop and a new pair of khaki pants as well. After he put them on, he realized that he might need a sweater or parka for today's golf. He opened the window to gauge the temperature outside and it seemed very warm, *Indian Summer-ish*. He disregarded the need to run out and buy a new windbreaker.

He was as nervous as a squirrel, he didn't have much time. He removed his other clothes from the suitcase and took out thirty-one, one hundred dollar bills from the bottom panel. Garrett counted them twice to be sure that he had the correct amount. He closed the suitcase after he had put back his clothing. He grabbed his attaché, opened it and placed the money inside. He threw the bag over his shoulder and hurried out of the room. When he exited he darn near ran over Liza who was en route to the kitchen.

Garrett rushed out of the Inn, ran down the street and headed straight for the Bank America branch office a few blocks away. Once at the small office he was able to procure a cashier's check made out to the *Carrie Baker Foundation*, in the amount of three thousand one hundred dollars. Garrett felt that the slight overpayment would act as a late fee for their troubles.

He returned to the Inn around eleven. When he walked in he saw Martha standing at the check-in desk, she was in the middle of a deep conversation with a person who had a familiar face. Whom it was he couldn't remember. He stood and waited until he could get her attention. She excused herself from the chat and asked him how she could help.

Garrett asked if she would be so kind to call a cab for him to arrive in fifteen minutes or so. He told her that he needed a ride to the Woods Hole Country Club. She told him that if he could wait twenty-five minutes or so that he could ride with her. He thanked her, but told her that he needed to get in some practice, so it was best that he arrive there sooner than later. He then reached into his bag and pulled out the cashier's check made out to the *Foundation*. He handed it to Martha and asked if she would see to it that the check got into the proper hands. She was excited and agreed to deliver it before she too went to the golf outing. She asked him how his trip was. But got no response. She called him a taxi right away.

It seemed that just a minute had passed when Sonia knocked on his door and announced that the taxi was out back. Before he left the room his sole thought was to grab his attaché and put it out on the fire escape outside his window, in case anyone came poking around his room.

Garret darted out of the Inn and headed for the rear lot. He hopped into the faded red cab and instructed the driver, whom he recognized to be the same Muslim guy who had driven him from the bus station the prior night, that he was in a hurry to reach the Woods Hole Country Club.

The driver asked, "Where are your clubs sir?"

Out of the cab jumped Garrett and he bounded up the stairs and back into the Inn. He went into his room to get the golf sticks and stopped for a spell to rethink his prior paranoia, that someone might snoop around in his absence. He worried that it could rain and that the attaché would get soaked, so in a quick and decisive manner he retrieved it from the fire escape and placed it in the bathroom tub and closed the curtain. Since Liza had already cleaned his room today no one would think to look there. Ever cautious, he rushed over to the closet, opened his suitcase and located the sock in which he had hidden his driver's license. He removed it and tucked the plastic card in his sneaker. He bounded out the Inn once again. He ran as fast as he could towards the cab with the golf bag slung over his shoulder. The bag beat him without mercy on the back of his legs with every stride he took.

The cabbie stood at the ready with the trunk wide open. He took the heavy bag from Garrett, grunted as he hoisted it up to his knee level, rested it on his knees for a brief second, took a deep breath and gave a mighty lift to his chest level, as if he were a weight lifter doing a *clean and jerk*. He threw the oversized bag into the trunk and the metal clubs clattered, they sounded like loose teeth in a animated cartoon.

The cabbie ran around to the front of the car and jumped behind the wheel and put it in drive. As he drove off of the property he told Garrett, "It is very poor for your health sir to rush so and be stressed. The good news is that we are but ten minutes from the golf club, and enough time for you to meditate to gain calm back to your soul. I have never golfed sir, but I am of the belief that you will play much better and enjoy the game more if you are calm in the mind."

"Is it a good omen that I have you once again as my driver?" Garrett asked.

"I do not know if it is sir, for I am the only cabbie in the village. What other choice is there? You will have to judge for yourself whether I am a blessing or a nuisance," he laughed.

Garrett was about to take his advice and deep breathe and meditate for the remainder of the ride, but the cabbie, full of coffee, who hadn't had a customer for the last two hours, was in need of conversation. He saw the possibility that this fare could be a convert and said, "While I waited for you sir.."

"Call me Garrett."

The cabbie said, "While I waited for you Mr. Garrett, I read an article about how the Western man and women are so obsessed with their features, they desire to keep a youthful appearance. They want to live longer on the earth. How the plastic surgery and Botox industries flourish and the pharmaceuticals, praise be Allah! They drug their citizens with little pills for anti-aging, for pain relief, to sleep through the night, to move one's bowels on a regular basis, on and on. You will all be two-hundred-year-old zombies someday, alive in body alone, is that what you want?" Again he laughed at his own joke.

Garrett answered him, "I ...," he looked at the cabbie's name on his Hackney license plate on the dash board in front of the passenger side, "Kassim, agree with you. The side effects that these drugs can cause are insane. The commercials they pound into our heads: doves gliding through blue cloudless skies; couples holding hands while in separate bath tubs under a waterfall; and gorgeous pictures of sunrises and sunsets. They're almost comical when the narrator's voice lowers and rambles off the litany of dire warnings, "Could cause blindness; may cause constipation; thoughts of suicide; there have been reported cases of liver problems; don't take if you're pregnant, want to be pregnant; know someone who's pregnant; or better yet, seek help if an erection lasts more than four hours. No shit!. And my absolute favorite is, if you're dead, they still warn," If **you** or a loved one has died..."

Kassim laughed and said, "The afterlife is *Paradise*. Joined together with Allah. Why should one be so foolish as to want to prolong this low consciousness existence I ask you?"

When Garrett didn't answer him, Kassim rolled on. "It is wrong to attempt to alter that which Allah has provided you with. Surgeries, drugs, body building are poor distractions. Go with what you have. You may live to ninety or to sixty, but do so with a pure and natural mind and body, not one masked by science. Whatever Allah has willed for you is all that matters for you to fulfill. No doctors, no insurance (what a rip off) no pharmaceuticals, just gratefulness and praise to Allah, Who you will join when He wishes you to. Do not deny His call. Then you will find true Paradise!"

Garrett, had paid close attention to this last diatribe against science and said, "I think you're on to something Kassim."

119

He wondered where this sage tutor hailed from in the Middle East, so he asked, "Where are you from Kassim?"

"Lowell Massachusetts, born and raised. But my parents are from Tunisia." Garret contained his snicker.

The cab had pulled up to the magnificent country club and heads turned, including Bob Maxwell's. They weren't accustomed to, nor did they approve of, seeing golfers arrive in such a shabby fashion.

The cabbie jumped out of his taxi, opened the trunk, and struggled to remove the golf bag.

Kassim said, as he huffed and puffed from the strain, "Mr. Garrett, that will be fifteen thirty please. I charged you one dollar for the heavy bag."

"Here, this is for your sound advice," he handed a startled Kassim a one-hundred-dollar bill.

Garrett added, "Kassim, now promise me that you won't go spending it on any Botox or funny pills."

Kassim thanked him a thousand times, bowed as he said, "Praise Allah."

He smiled from ear to ear, got back into his cab, and against club policy, before he sped off, he honked the horn in thanks for Garrett's generosity.

14

The other players in Doc Nickerson' foursome had already checked in by the time Garrett had arrived. He went up to the sign-in desk and paid his one hundred and thirty dollar entry fee in cash. He was told by the ticket person that the shotgun start would commence at twelve noon sharp and to please be on his golf cart in fifteen minutes. His group would start on hole number fourteen she informed him. Since he would be walking not riding, he knew that there would be no time for practice. He hadn't eaten yet, so he went into the dining room and grabbed a pre-made turkey sandwich, bottled water and some chips.

At twelve the fog horn was sounded and the golf tourney commenced on this most beautiful, circa 1899 Donald Ross designed masterpiece.

Garrett wasn't very social with his group. He walked the hilly course, to their pleasure, and the others rode in electric carts. But he did enjoy the game and the team did quite well.

All pleasantries aside, there were a couple unusual incidents that couldn't be ignored, however. The negative one was when Garrett accused Doc Nickerson of cheating. He claimed that Doc had placed his ball closer to the hole on the putting surface. It caused quite a stir, but the noise subsided when Tip pointed out that it was within the rules of the *scramble format* to place one's ball within an inch of the ball marker. Needless to say, Doctor Nickerson was not pleased with the false accusation.

The positive highlight occurred on the eighteenth tee when he was surprised to find that Caroline had set up a group photo shoot against a beautiful harbor backdrop. They said hello to one another and it was a nice exchange. She snapped the foursome's pictures and informed them that framed versions would be available at the end of the tournament, should anyone care to purchase one. Of course all proceeds would go the the Baker family. Seeing Caroline propelled him for the rest of the round.

Meanwhile, at the Hibiscus Inn, Sergeant Scott rummaged through Garrett's luggage. There wasn't much for him to go through, the closet clothes and the one piece with the wig in it, that they already knew about. He would never have considered looking in the bathroom tub where Garrett had hidden his attaché case with all his important and incriminating paperwork. Discouraged, Scotty was about to leave when he decided to go through Garret's suitcase one more time, to see if he had overlooked anything.

This time he chose to empty the suitcase's contents onto the bed and in such an order so that he could return them to their exact spot. He read labels on the clothes, searched through shirt pockets and pant cuffs, socks and underwear, but found nothing.

But before he put the clothes back into the suitcase, he thought it would be easier on his back if he put the empty suitcase on top of the bedspread and then placed the clothing in from there. He closed it shut, bent at both knees and lifted it up. That's when he got his first break. For such a small empty piece of luggage he was surprised at how heavy it weighed. Curious, Scotty held it out in front of himself with both hands and gave a few vigorous shakes. He felt and heard things rattle around inside and became very excited. Scotty carried the case around to the other side of the bed and opened it up. It appeared empty as before. But with the palms of his hands he pushed downward on the inside and noticed a little *give* to the bottom panel. He crawled his hands along the inside base and bingo! At the right back corner of the suitcase he found a tiny ribbon, camouflaged in the same black color as the bottom panel. He pinched it between his forefinger and thumb and pulled upwards. The bottom panel folded up and the false bottom compartment underneath was revealed. Thirty thousand dollars in cash! He counted it twice to be sure.

But Scotty knew that no matter how suspicious it seemed to carry around this amount of cash he could hear the Chief warn, "It isn't in and of itself an indication of guilt."

So, when he put the wrapped stacks of one hundred dollar bills back into their secret hiding place, he got a more promising lead. On the side wall of the hidden compartment there was a stitched label which read, "Brugman's Luggage and Potpourri, Sedona Az."

There were the initials AGM sewn in.

Scotty reached for his cell phone and called the Chief, who was out on the golf course, and left a voicemail message to inform him of the significant pieces of evidence he'd uncovered.

After the golf tournament was finished, Garrett walked the beautiful grounds alone for a few more minutes before he went inside. When he entered the large banquet room he had trouble distinguishing the members of his foursome, because every table was filled with the gaudy colors worn by hundreds of golfers. It was like looking through a kaleidoscope.

He spied the tall frame of Tip Garland across the room and walked over to the table where his companions sat. Chief Nickerson's foursome was also seated at the table and there were three empty chairs. Garret sat down on the middle one. A cocktail waitress came up to him and asked for his order. He told her that he like a "Glenlivet on the rocks."

At that very moment, the master of ceremonies held a mic in his right hand and asked the audience for their undivided attention. The man, a local radio personality, bombarded them with one golf joke after another. Garrett had to laugh, as the man's delivery and facial expressions were as good as the jokes he told.

After he had completed his five-minute act, he turned the mic over to the chairwoman, Martha Nickerson Lawrence of course, who proceeded to announce the winners of the *closest to the pin* and the *long drive* contests. She then announced the top three teams in the tournament, who were people Garrett had never seen before. The winners walked up to the prize table where they were greeted by Nick Temple, who handed them their one-hundred-dollar gift certificate to the over-priced pro shop. Caroline snapped their pictures with the young golf pro.

Martha then enlisted Annie Temple's help and they read off the winning numbers for the seven various golf related raffle prizes which were on display on an adjacent table. Garrett felt pissed that he'd arrived to late to have purchased any.

When Martha had finished, she congratulated everyone for a fine tournament and thought she had wrapped up that portion of the event.

But to her dismay, the radioman returned to the makeshift

podium and wrestled the microphone away from her. She was concerned that he had had a few too many already and that he would tell more of his filthy golf jokes.

However, she was relieved to hear otherwise, when he announced to the crowd that he had a very special treat in store for them.

He boomed in his deep theatrical voice, "Folks, before you dig into the sumptuous meal that the marvelous waitstaff is about to serve, since this *scramble* is the final event in memory of this year's beloved honoree, Carrie Baker, we are blessed to have her older brother Ryan step up to the microphone to say a few words on behalf of the Baker family and to conclude, what I know you will all agree, has been a most successful, although sad, fundraiser."

The golfers whooped it up. They cheered on the nervous ten-year-old as he approached the microphone. The radio celeb patted the boy on the back and whispered good luck in his ear.

Ryan looked back for a sign of encouragement from his parents, who hugged each other for support and they smiled back to him signaling their unconditional love. He unfolded the notepaper that he had written his speech on and stammered a bit as he began his simple and beautiful piece. "I loved my sister Carrie very very much," he swallowed hard. "So did Momma and Papa."

The silence was heavy as everyone pulled for the boy to make it through this most difficult assignment.

"Carrie was fun and always made me laugh and she was so smart, smarter than me, well almost."

The crowd roared with relief laughter. He gave a shy grin and lowered his head in happy embarrassment. He became a little more embolden.

"My family is so sad and my Momma in particular is having a hard time not cryin' every day. Sometimes we don't know what to do or say to each other. We just burst out cryin'.

"But we really want to thank all of you for your support and wishes, and for this great event for my sister. Carrie would have loved it, especially all the desserts over there." he pointed to a table full of parfaits and pies.

He swallowed hard once again and wiped the tears from his eyes with the sleeve of his dark blue blazer. "Thanks, it means a lot to my family to know how much you loved my sister. I miss her so much!" With that he flew into the arms of his parents and was swallowed up in their hugs and kisses.

The aroused crowd leapt to their feet and gave him a standing ovation, for what seemed to last at least two minutes. Garrett sobbed, as did many others. Maxwell and the Chief took special notice of his remorse.

It took quite a while before everyone was able to return to a more festive mood. But in due course people began to regain their composure and speak of subjects other than the boy's courageous speech.

The waitstaff scurried around as they served the first course to the diners and at the same time drinks were served at the two bars.

Their table of eight had been joined by Nick and Martha, who took the seats on either side of Garrett. Martha felt empathy for Garrett since she had seen his display of emotions and knew that he had connected with the Baker family's pain. However, the others weren't as taken in. They had conspired to look for clues and kept a close eye on Garrett's' each and every move.

When Garrett had gone to the bathroom to gather himself, he wiped off the tears from his face. On the way back to his table he stopped to visit with the Baker family and to offer them his heartfelt condolences. He returned to his table in a more upbeat mood.

He would remain in this good frame of mind and continued to drink as well. He downed just a little too much Scotch, as did most of his tablemates.

After the delicious meals had been completed and the plates removed, most of the golfers headed for the exits. However, Garrett, Doc, the Chief, Martha, Nick, Tip, and Katie decided that they would stay for one more round, which Garrett insisted he buy.

When Garrett left the table to place the order, Nick answered some of the derogatory questions and remarks that a few of the people had brought up.

Nick said, "Look, he's all about shock value. Pay his words very little attention but his deeds a lot. After all, he did escort Amelia the other night to the *Bazaar* and seemed to be genuinely concerned that she enjoyed herself. And he was very pleasant at the poker table remember; and his generosity seems to know no bounds. He does seem stressed and off balance, no question about it. But why not help him gain his equilibrium, rather than try to push him over the edge?"

Maxwell came over to their table, as the folks from his group had departed. He pulled up a chair.

Doc Nickerson said, "How many chances will we give this guy? How many times will we roll over and give him the benefit of the doubt, even when he disparages one or all of us? For no apparent reason the asshole accused me of cheating today on the course. He is not well, I'll grant you that Nick. But realize that sick people are more then capable of performing harmful acts. I have to agree with Bob, Garrett's up to no good. That's my conclusion. This is all a well planned diversion on his part. It's a *shell game*."

Nick felt the need to respond. "He's in a fight with himself more than he is with anyone else. If you must, then stay vigilant, but please, don't take this too far. Not to a level of fear and accusation. It will harm us all if that's our focus." The group was reticent to follow Nick's lead.

Garrett returned to the table with a waitress who carried their drinks and they all seemed to ease up a bit.

Martha entertained the group for a couple of minutes when she told of the comical time she had on the golf course when her group tried to find Cyrus Bates's golf ball, hole after hole. The old billionaire skinflint demanded that they look for his errant shots, even though the very beauty of a *scramble format* allowed you to go to the team's best ball and forget about the bad ones. They exploded with laughter when she stood up, hunched her shoulders over and waddled at the slowest speed, as she mimicked the old-timer looking around for his two dollar *Titelist*.

When she had finished her tale and everyone had settled down, the Chief (who had earlier listened to his voicemail and had spoken with Sergeant Scott to get further details) a bit tipsy himself said, "Garrett, you have been very generous with the attention and money that you've been so gracious to donate on behalf of Carrie Baker, our beloved honoree, whom you've never met I presume. Thank you from all of us. But may I ask you why you have such fondness for the girl and her parents? Yes her parents too. I'm sure it was you who delivered an anonymous envelope on their doorstep Monday morning, filled with several hundred dollar bills. Your calling card. And the Bakers just told me that after meeting you earlier today, that they're pretty sure they recognized you as the sun-glassed stranger who attended Carrie's funeral in Marblehead on Tuesday. Guilty are we? I'm also curious why you've placed the ownership of all of the fine prizes that you won at the *Bazaar* in Amelia's name. Why not enjoy some of them yourself? Why give them all to Amelia? Buying her off are you? Is she your beard of some sort Garrett?"

At first he stared back at the Chief, as if he hadn't heard a word. Meanwhile, the others squirmed in their seats.

The Chief pressed him further. "Come now man. Don't be so shy about it. I understand that you don't want attention for your kindness, but you have to admit it's very unusual. Don't you agree? You're a stranger whose just arrived here six or seven days ago, and you've become very attached to Carrie's plight. What gives? What catches your fancy man? Little girls perhaps?"

Garrett felt playful and wasn't the least bit threatened by the aggressive affront. He didn't answer the Chief's questions, because he'd forgotten them already, there were too many of them. Instead he addressed everyone at the table. "I would like to tell all of you a little story. Do you like stories? But it's not my story I hate to tell you. Or is it?" He burped. "Excuse me."

"You see, I met a man one day on a lengthy train ride through the beautiful countryside and he told me this most poignant tale that happened to his relative, whom I think you'll agree was the most extraordinary man who ever lived. Anyway, ever since he relayed the story to me it has often reinvented itself in my presence, in one way or another, year after year. But I digress. I know I'm drunk, but look, so are you. For once we are of the same mind I think. Pretty scary thought, no?" he laughed, as did a few of them.

"Oh yes, the fable. This particular man had incredible pain and grief dealt him throughout his life. He was born with a slight deformity in his right hip and despite all the heckling he took from other kids because of his noticeable limp, he was able to overcome the inconvenience and excelled in athletics through great effort and resolve. He was the third of seven children and was invisible to his parents. He had half an ear lobe on his left ear". In an attempt to demonstrate he fumbled, and grabbed his right ear first, then his left. "He lost the other half in a knife attack when he was eight, I believe the man told me.

"If that weren't enough, both his parents and his two younger sisters died in a horrible house fire when he was still a child of twelve. It was a miracle that he and the other four children escaped unharmed. But the sad result was that he and his siblings were soon split apart by the Courts. Each child was sent to live with a separate relative. He wouldn't see his brothers and sisters again until he was a young adult.

"Hard to believe but things got even worse for him, because his new guardians turned out to be an abusive aunt and uncle who both were *card-carrying* alcoholics. Love wasn't showered upon him. In fact, he was reminded every day of what a burden he was to them and how Christian it was of them to have provided for his care. Somehow, this unusual child survived their dysfunction and physical abuse for all of the six years that he lived with them in fear.

"But as incredible as it may seem, at no time in his life did he feel cheated or ever lose his optimism about what might lie ahead for him. He had gratitude for his lot in life nonetheless and wasn't in the least bit bitter for all that had befallen him. The great Winston Churchill once said, "A pessimist sees difficulty in every opportunity; an optimist sees opportunity in every difficulty."

"This person somehow had a bright view of life.

"At age twenty he married and in a short time his attractive wife gave birth to three beautiful girls in consecutive years. Life was tender and happy. He worked long hours as a landscaper and often was away from home. They lived a modest, comfortable life in the city.

"However, the dark cloud that seemed to always hover over him, would rain down upon him once again. Because during the birth of their fourth child, his wife miscarried and lost her life as well. He and his three daughters were devastated. How many losses could one man bear?"

Garrett had a vacant look on his face. He'd lost his train of thought. The others fidgeted in their seats. Nick broke the silence, "You said that the man's wife and unborn child died and "

"Yes, yes I know, thanks..Even though he was blown away, the man chose to focus on the positives, the three girls that were his wife's gifts to him and the reasons for him to live on.

"Wouldn't most men greet every day with distrust and hatred if all that had happened to them? Not him, he was ever grateful for his good health, for his past, and more so he was thankful to be the guardian of those three little loves of his life.

"He provided a fine household and the girls lacked very little. He saved his money and by the time the eldest girl turned ten, he was able to purchase a mountain chalet on a pond, so that they could retreat from the brutal Arizona summer heat. This was a wonderful source of joy for all of them."

The Chief shot Doc a nod when he heard the word Arizona.

"But in July of the second summer that they owned the cabin, disaster revisited them once again. It raised its viscous head. He was staggered by a blow of misfortunate so awful, that it almost crippled him. His youngest daughter, his precious little baby Gabbie, at age six and a half, was found drowned in the pond.

"The news of this tragedy spread and the local newspapers ran front page headlines. So when he returned to the city with his two girls and the body of his little dear Gabbie in her coffin, there were throngs of friends and strangers there to greet them. They offered their help and condolences and many gave financial contributions and welcome support.

"After the funeral he was asked inappropriate questions by a friend's judgmental wife. "How could you bear to go on any longer? What could possibly be life's lesson in all of this? Do you believe in God? How could you, with all the catastrophes that you have known in your life? Could you ever believe? It's so unfair."

"He gave a peaceful, honest answer. "There's no value, no benefit for me to keep this hideous pain in my heart for even a brief moment. I feel no remorse. Why should I cave in to it? I've let the dark clouds of this memory pass through my mind. I'm so fortunate to have my health and two wonderful girls to share my life with. Why would I choose to suffer more and continue to grieve for my losses? It's over, they have already happened. I encountered first-hand the grief when they occurred. I can't reverse them. If I played victim and carried the hurt around with me I would forever be their prisoner and be a worthless father to my two little darlings.""

"An older gentleman said, "You know, you sound a bit mad. How could you accept this horror? Wasn't this by far the worst that had befallen you, your youngest daughter's drowning?"

"It was awful yes, but there are no scorecards for such things. I loved her unconditionally and best of all she accepted my love and gave hers to me in return. How could one find fault with that? I know I will have her in my heart for eternity, so how is that a subject to mourn?"

"What then could possibly be more tragic than the loss of your daughter?" the same man asked.

"He didn't blink an eye and said in a kind voice, "When I first arrived here I was treated like scum by you people. Your looks said I was beneath you, an animal. And you still demonize anyone like me, who doesn't look like you. Your selfish thoughts are that I'm just another user, here to steal your jobs and grab your welfare checks.

"It was the unluck of the draw that I was born in Mexico and that you were born here. What if your circumstances were reversed and you were born, say, in Syria? Wouldn't you too try with every ounce of your being to better yourself and your family's life? You complain that immigrants don't spend their earnings here but instead send them back home. I pay my taxes, unlike so many billionaires. But isn't it commendable that if you have a wife, children, mothers, and fathers living in poverty back in your homeland, that you do the very same that the Irish, German, and Italian immigrants did in their quest for a small piece of prosperity?"

"Borders are fictitious. Share your wonderful opportunity, let good people have a chance. Let them in, let them contribute. We are in this together. That's what has always made America great."

"You may not understand this but my deceased Gabbie and my loving wife live inside me forever. But so too does the sadness I have in my heart for those greedy people who exclude other human beings."

Garrett stopped, he was quite dizzy. He announced that he must leave now and return to the Hibiscus Inn. He stood up from his chair and almost fell into Martha's lap. She had to push him to his feet.

Just then a wave of guilt floated over him, he felt bad for his past behavior toward the Doctor. So before he said goodbye to them all, he walked over to Doc and extended his hand. He apologized to him for everyone to hear. He then apologized to the others.

The question entered his head, "What is it about Doc Nickerson that causes such a negative reaction in me?"

The Chief was ready for a confrontation and wouldn't let up. "Garrett, your touching story was meant to distract us wasn't it? You are a real pro at that I must admit. But it still leaves me perplexed. You never did answer my simple question about why you've given all your auction winnings to Amelia?"

Garrett answered in a soft voice to the Chief, but all the while he looked straight into the Doc's eyes (he now had the answer to his question about why he always picked on the Doctor). "Can you answer me this travesty? How can one man have a billion dollars and the country of Haiti have millions of people who are penniless?

"You've taken over Amelia's privileges and have abused her and ostracized her from your precious society. Out of your own vanity you've discarded an innocent person's rights and ignored her existence so that yours could flourish. I have lavished her with gifts because she deserves love and I'm sad to say that she has no one who accepts her love."

He walked away.

The Chief didn't know what to say. The others were baffled by his remarks as well. Doc Nickerson seemed shaken.

It was almost six p.m. and the sun would be down soon. Nick chased after Garrett and offered to give him a ride, if Garrett could wait a little while. Garrett thanked him but said he looked forward to a brisk walk, since it was such a perfect late Fall afternoon. He wanted to enjoy the New England countryside along the way and he figured that the fresh air would sober him up.

It was almost dark, September 27th. Garrett's choice wouldn't turn out to be a wise one.

15

Garrett turned left onto Sippiwisset Road after leaving the Woods
Hole Country Club's property and he had trouble steadying himself. He
was quite unbalanced, so much so that he had to concentrate to stay
upright on the narrow country road. It was a less traveled route and he
became concerned that if he lost his footing, for even a second, he
might greet the front grille of speeding sports car as it rounded a blinded bend.

The road was canopied by magnificent two-hundred-year-old trees,
which prevented the sun's rays from warming him. He turned up his
collar and buttoned up his polo shirt to the neck. He was cold.

Garrett felt alone. There wasn't another person as far as his blood-
shot eyes could squint. The homes that were along this route had large
acre plus lots and were set back at least a hundred feet from the road,
which made him feel even more isolated. Most of them had their lights
on already, as darkness had already begun to pull its blackened shades
over the orange sun.

He scolded himself for not accepting a ride from Nick. "Bad move *ego man*." He walked on.

The solitude was soon broken by the roar of a car engine that came up from behind him. As the Mercedes rumbled near, Garrett stuck out his thumb in hopes to hitch a ride. But the driver slowed down just enough so that he could swerve away from the hitchhiker, then he gunned the engine and whizzed by, as if to tell Garrett to fuck off.

Garrett's legs began to ache. He had walked every inch of the hilly golf course and now, a half mile into this ill-advised journey, his hamstrings began to tighten up. They always did. So his pace lessened and he had to stop every few feet to massage his thighs and calfs. He succumbed to the inebriated thought that he couldn't go on much further.

A moment later, in the almost darkened silence, he spotted a large roadside boulder and decided to take a seat. The road at that segment was pretty straight, so he would be able to see an oncoming vehicle from this vantage point and should be able to get it to stop to give him a lift. He waited.

After quite some time, he jumped up in anticipation as a truck, with its headlamps looking like two flashlights in search of a missing person, headed towards him. It was upon him in a matter of seconds.

Garret took one step onto the ten-foot-wide road and waved his hands over his head. The small pickup slowed down, passed by Garrett several dozen feet, then came to an abrupt halt just off of the shoulder. The driver gave a soft honk on his horn, a positive signal for Garrett to come aboard.

He walked as fast as his aching legs allowed him and must have looked as if he had a load in his pants. Something inside his sneaker bothered him as well and he remember it was his driver's license that he had hidden there.

Garrett approached the rear of the pickup and the backdoor was flung open for him. He paid no attention to its two occupants, he was just happy to get inside and warm up. He thanked them twice for their generosity.

The driver looked in the rear view mirror and asked Garrett, "Back to the Hibiscus wiseass?"

Unsure, he didn't know how to react. Then the woman said, "You get crazier by the hour. What on earth are you doing out on this dangerous road and in those flimsy clothes?"

His heart pounded with excitement at his good fortune, he recognized Caroline's exquisite voice. Garrett remained speechless as he attempted to gather his thoughts.

Sean filled the silence as he floored the pedal of the Chevy, the sound of its squealing tires divulged his angry mood.

He spoke, "You must think we're fools to let you get away with all your surreptitious shit. You've pissed off one too many of us man. I should take you in an alley and play wall-ball with your head. If I were you I'd keep my eyes wide open and my big mouth shut."

Caroline pleaded with her fiancé to concentrate on the curvy road. She didn't come to Garrett's defense.

Garrett said, "I'm very sorry if I have offended you. But since I've already apologized to the Doctor and others, and since it was between them and me and not you, I'm sure Caroline would agree that, *Mr. Protector of the People*, it's none of your damn business."

Sean slammed on the brakes and Caroline screamed for him not to pay attention to this jerk. "He's baiting you Sean," she said.

Garrett braced for a fight, a fight that he knew he had zero chance of winning.

But to his surprise, Sean didn't say another word. It was quite obvious that he burnt inside with rage, but he quelled the eruption for Caroline's sake. He put the truck's shift back into gear and drove off.

When his truck had reached Caroline's street, Sean pulled up next to the curb in front of her home. He got out and walked around the truck and opened the passenger door for her. Garrett said good night to Caroline but she didn't acknowledge him. As they walked up the steps she cautioned Sean not to let Garrett get under his skin.

She told him, "Honey, take him straight to the Hibiscus. Promise? He's not worth the aggravation."

Sean told her not to worry, that he had things under control. He walked her up to the front door, gave her a passionate kiss and waited for her to go inside the house.

Meanwhile, Garrett didn't want another confrontation with this jock, and since he figured he was about ten minutes or so from the Inn, he rubbed his hamstrings to get them loose and decided to exit the truck and walk back. But just as he got out of the vehicle, Sean came up from behind him and grabbed him by the elbow. He forced Garrett to sit down on the front seat which Caroline had just vacated. Sean slammed the door and ran around the front of the truck and hopped into the driver's seat. He made a U-turn on Caroline's street and after he yielded at the corner stop sign, he turned left onto Main Street.

That's when he laid into Garrett. "Listen asshole, and listen good. I don't care for you or your yellow-bellied type. Think you're some sort of hotshot intellectual who can just come into our peaceful world and rattle up our naive citizens? Is that it? I'm on to you and so are the others. You're up to no good and whatever it is that you're hiding from us we'll find out. I can assure you, you'll feel the heat from the good people of this town. I've seen diversionary tactics played out by real pros, whom you couldn't hold a candle to. Your motives are so transparent. You've underestimated us.. Listen up fuck-head, everyone knows you have designs on my fiancé. What a dreamer, as if you could even be in the same room with her. She thinks you're pathetic. If you ever so much as utter another word in her presence, or an unkind remark to anyone about Caroline, the consequences will be dire. Understand?

"You don't fool us Garrett. We know you've had a hand in Carrie Baker's death. We're hours away from uncovering the proof. So you better not try any new stunts or you might not live to make the trial."

Garrett thought, "Bullies communicate with their muscles, but I have muscular thoughts." Although, for a flash, he considered what a rush it would be to smack this muscle bound *hero* upside the head. But he didn't feel well. He was sick to his stomach from the combination of the alcohol he drank and the rare meat he had eaten. So instead, he just nodded his defeated consent to Sean's threats.

Then to his surprise Sean slammed on the brakes once again. But this time he reached across Garrett and threw open the passenger door and gave him a violent punch in the left bicep. The force of which knocked Garrett out of the truck and onto the road.

Sean peeled out.

Garrett dusted himself off and looked around. He had no idea where he was. His left hand was bleeding and he wiped it on his pant leg. His head hurt from both the drinking and the former injury. He was so weak and he was stone cold drunk. His head began to spin and his stomach churned. He tried to focus but couldn't. With sheer animal instincts he stumbled over to a roadside bush, leaned over it and regurgitated several times.

He was drained. Even though the night was cold, the vomiting had taken so much effort out of him that he was sweating bullets. He no longer felt sick to his stomach, just drunk in the head. He felt relieved, but fatigued.

But it took just a few more seconds before it all reversed. The cold September night wiped off the beads of sweat from his brow. He shuddered from the nippiness. He thought of the time when his father had abandoned him at Old Silver Beach. He wrapped his arms around himself and sunk his chin into his chest in order to stay warm. He began to cough and could see his cloudy breath in the night air.

Still not clearheaded he didn't know what to do next, so he decided to rest for a moment. He walked around to the other side of the bush that he had just violated and found a small spot on the ground, between three other four-foot-high shrubs. He lowered himself to his knees and lied down on the cold, damp earth. He curled into a fetal position and was able to fall to sleep in seconds.

Hours later Garrett was woken by a mangy stray cat when it had licked his mouth. He swung his left arm at the dirty creature and happened to swat her on the tail. The emaciated cat arched her back and managed to eke out a feeble hiss. But when he attempted to get to his feet and shoo her away, she decided not to put up a fight with this cranky giant, and instead turned and trotted off.

He got up on his unsteady feet and surveyed the unfamiliar area once again. He was no longer drunk, but he was very cold and tired still. When he didn't recognize his surroundings, he went back down on the ground and again curled into a fetal position. He wondered what time it was? Throughout his life he had an uncanny ability to know, without the aid of a clock, what the time was; give or take a few minutes. From the stillness and darkness around him, he guessed it to be around three a.m, although it was in fact just five past midnight.

He was asleep again in moments, but he woke every fifteen minutes, disrupted either from anticipation that the dreadful cat would return, or from the tickle in his throat that caused him to cough. It was a fitful, not restful sleep, and the cough did get worse.

Eventually he had to sit up to alleviate it. It didn't do the trick. It was then that he noticed how sore and swollen his throat was, and how hard it was for him to swallow. His ears were plugged as well. He was still dizzy. He felt feverish, both chilled and hot at the same time.

Garrett remained seated on the cold ground and coughed several more times. This turned out to be a good thing, because it drew the attention of the two young couples who were in the middle of the road. They were rowdy and no doubt high. The young men were the first to run up to the bush and spot him, their intentions weren't good. However, before they could show off for the girls and harass the drunken bum in the bushes, one of the ladies recognized him and demanded that the others step aside.

"You are guest at Hibiscus. Why are you heres in cold with little clothes? You've been out all nights you bad boy, no?" She and the young men laughed.

He knew she was one of the Hibiscus Inn's staff. It was Sonia.

The other woman, Lizavetta, moved up to Garrett and felt his forehead. She spoke in Russian that he had a fever. Sonia interpreted for the young men what Liza had said and one of them flipped it off, "Let him rot out here. What's he to us?"

Liza grabbed Garrett under the armpit, steadied him to his feet, and with Sonia on his other side, they started to walk him towards the Inn. Sonia turned back to the fellows and said, "Igor and Henry its bees very lates. Thanks for fun. We takes him to bed. See you tomorrow nights, no?"

Henry pleaded, "What. It's three thirty, the night's young."

Sonia giggled, then waved goodbye and concentrated, along with Liza, on getting Garrett back to Martha's Inn. Garrett mumbled a few words between coughs and wasn't aware of how lucky he was that they had showed up when they had.

Just five minutes later they were back outside the Hibiscus Inn. Sean had dropped him off just an eighth of a mile away, but it may as well have been twenty. He could have been safe and sound hours ago.

It took quite an effort to get him up the stairs and inside the build-ing without causing a stir for Martha or any of her guests. And once they got him into his room, both ladies worked in unison to get his soiled clothes off of him. When his driver's license fell on the floor, without looking at it, Liza picked it up and put it his pocket. Then she helped him put on his lone pair of pajamas. He shook so, that Liza went out of the room for a minute and returned with an extra heavy blanket. Sonia had gone into his bathroom and brought back a wash cloth, a glassful of water and his toothpaste and tooth brush. She sat him up and brushed his teeth for him, then wiped the dried vomit from around his face and neck. When she had finished, she lowered him down onto the two large pillows that Liza had just positioned behind him, to help prop him up so that his cough might subside. Sonia then went back to the bathroom to put the dirty towels in the bathtub.

She was surprised to see Garrett's attaché case sitting there. High, she didn't think it was that unusual, so she picked it up and carried it over to the closet and set it down on the floor, where she had seen it before.

They stood over him for another minute at most and decided that he didn't need their attention any longer. Sonia gave him a hard candy to soothe his throat and went over to the bathroom and turned on the dimmer light to low, for guidance in case Garrett awoke in the night. What else could they do? They both exited his room.

Liza listened outside his door for another thirty seconds. She heard an occasional muted cough and decided to leave as she would have to be up in a couple of hours. She felt uneasy and quite certain that she'd find a very sick man the next morning.

16

Sean Garland was up at the crack of dawn on Friday. He felt no ill effects from the excessive alcohol he had drunk the night before. His body was a well-conditioned machine that rid itself of toxins posthaste. In concise military fashion, he stretched, exercised, showered and shaved. He drove to the Eatery around seven thirty.

He was still pumped up from his confrontation with Garrett and he was anxious to share the details with the *Round Table Group*. Of course, with a day left before their wedding and two days before he shipped off, he wanted to see his love Caroline as well.

When he arrived, all the regulars were there, except for Doc. Caroline brought him a cup of black coffee and they gave each other a kiss on the cheek.

After the usual salutations Sean said, "Have I got some shit to share with you guys about our stranger boy."

He went on to describe, almost without prejudice, the details of their encounter the previous night. The part he left out was when he had punched Garrett out of his truck. He told them that he had warned the draft dodger to stay away from Caroline or there would be hell to pay.

Gilbert Andrade said, "The Chief just told us about Garrett's curious behavior at the Country Club. He accused Doc of cheating and later he told a strange parable about a man whose daughter had drown in a pond. Very peculiar and a little coincidental ya think?" To which everyone at the table agreed.

Sean said, "I know I heard all about it from Doc. Is there any doubt that Bob's right, that this twerp did away with Carrie?"

"Now, now gentlemen. I know the circumstances all point to the bullseye on Garrett's forehead, but we have no evidence that places him at the crime scene.. **yet**," the Chief emphasized.

"Why don't you tell them some of what Scotty found Chief?" Maxwell asked.

"I don't know."

They begged him not to tease them. They all said they could be trusted to keep quiet and that it all was off the record of course. Stuart reminded the Chief that they'd all sworn a confidential oath in order to join the *Group* in the first place.

"Well, since it isn't an official police matter as we speak, just good friends speculating, I guess I could share, in secrecy of course, a few of the details that might undo the plans of our future suspect."

He waived Caroline over, and when she approached the table the Chief said, "Darling I'll have a couple of English muffins and please tell Hank that it won't drive up his electric bill if he toasts the damned muffins 'til they're burnt. The cheapskate would serve them right out of the package if you didn't tell him otherwise. Thanks honey."

The rest of the group placed their orders, and when Caroline had left, the Chief shared his confidence. "I won't tell you how we came across the information, but I'll tell you that Scotty found a lead to where we think this chap is from. If the lead proves to be rock solid I suspect it will reveal a whole lot more about this strange bird."

He held up his hand to stop their questions, and said, "All I can tell you is that he's from a Western state."

"Do you plan to send someone out there to investigate Carl?" Bill Dimmock asked.

"Hell no Bill. I've already said that we haven't any evidence. Our hands are tied until we have proof, or something close to proof. We're working on that as we speak."

"So just because the police can't investigate him yet, what about us digging up his past? I say send my brother Tip to wherever the hell this *Bozo* is from and let him dig in, as a newsman who's after a story," Sean said.

"Great idea." Bill said.

The Chief then spoke in a detached tone. "Well I guess that if a journalist was on vacation out West and just happened to look up an old friend named Garrett, whom he knew from years past, what harm could it do? Of course the police here wouldn't even know he was out there. I hear the weather is still pretty warm this time of year in Arizona. Better tell Tip to take lots of sunblock. My guess is that Sean and his brother will plan a vacation trip to the West, a.s.a.p. Have him contact me for the details."

" So he's from Arizona heh?" Stuart added.

"Perhaps," said the Chief.

The good soldier Sean stood up and said goodbye to the group, an indication that he would carry out the Chief's offhanded order. They all congratulated him one last time for his wedding tomorrow night.

The Chief smiled at Sean's sense of urgency. He admired him for the professional whom he was. He knew that the plan would be carried out without a hitch.

Later, when Caroline came back to the table with a huge tray with their breakfast orders, she asked no one in particular, "Where's Sean?"

Andrade lied, "He got a call from Tip and said he'd be back later."

Once Caroline had served them and was back behind the counter, the ever thorough Stuart Holmes spoke up. "Carl you said there were more details, but you just shared the one that he's from somewhere in Arizona. What else can you spill?"

The Chief's mouth was full of English Muffins, so the afore silent Bob Maxwell took the stage and to no one's great surprise, he weaved an intricate web of treachery and deceit.

"We know (as if he were part of the investigation) that he's obsessed with Carrie and is the only one, outside of the immediate family, and the police, well, and us now, who knew that Carrie had her bicycle with her when he killed her. We believe that Garrett has set up Amelia, he wants to position her to take the rap for Carrie's death and any untoward deeds he's done, and still might want to accomplish. She's so naive and in awe of him, and with the attention he has lavished upon her, there's no way a woman of her low mental capacity could see through his scheme. Poor Amelia doesn't deserve his lies. But that's what lowlife criminals are, professional liars. The evidence, not coincidences, point to him as the murderer of Carrie. I bet he figures that he'll provide money for a top Boston attorney and that Amelia would get off on a plea of insanity. This is a clever, evil man we're up against. And by the way, we know he has an enormous amount of cash with him too, fifty thousand dollars," he exaggerated. "For what villainous purposes he'll use it we must discover before it's too late!"

He let it sink in for a moment.

"So, to protect Amelia from his diabolical plan, we thought it best that we find out what she knows about the man and Carrie first, before we alert her. Mind you, Amelia in all likelihood wouldn't comprehend it anyway. She refuses to talk to the police again, so the Chief had the brilliant idea to have Doc talk with her. That's why he isn't here with us now. This very minute he's with Amelia, under the guise that she should have a medical checkup. He'll get her relaxed, then he'll sneak a few questions in on her that shouldn't arouse her suspicions. I helped him craft a few *trap setters*."

The others were exhilarated to be part of all the intrigue.

At the same time on the other side of town, Doc Nickerson had parked his car just off of the pathway near Amelia's house. He had great reservations about meeting with her. Their past weighed heavy on his mind. He knew this was good for the community, as well as for Amelia, but he hesitated before he got out of the car, because he wanted to rehearse just how he would start the conversation.

But their encounter would turn out to be as far from his present anxiety and expectations as he might have ever imagined. It would have profound psychological and emotional impact on them both.

Doc knocked on Amelia's front door and asked if he could have a brief chat with her. Amelia was suspicious of his intent, but nonetheless agreed, and told him to meet her down below on one of the park benches. No one beside her son had ever set foot inside her cluttered home.

He had to wait several minutes before Amelia descended her steps, walked over to the bench and sat down next to him, to begin their awkward conversation. And at first, it was very awkward.

But within a few moments of self-conscious small talk, out of nowhere, he couldn't articulate later what had prompted him, he felt the urge to put his arms around her and give her a genuine hug. She didn't find his action strange in the least and accepted his warm advance. At one point she pulled his head to her shoulder, like when he was a toddler, and it rested there for a short time. They both wept.

The emotional moment overtook him and Doc told her that it was now time to make amends to her for all the years that he and the others had shunned her. He thought of Garrett's exact words from the yesterday, "You have taken Amelia's privileges and have abused her and ostracized her from your precious society."

He thought about how this eccentric man, with all his faults, had made complete sense with this statement. A statement that had hit home hard.

Her brother then told her that when he saw her so happy the other night at the *Church Bazaar*, it had changed his and Martha's perceptions forever. Amelia was their sister. They would never hide that fact, ever again. She had cared for them when no one cared for her. She was abused, but never abandoned her duty to watch over the children when she was thrust into the role of surrogate mother, when their own mother had died. Amelia was a mere adolescent, yet had the weight of the world hoisted upon her shoulders, thanks to their detestable father. She accepted her fate at the cost of her own good. The kids were never made aware of her ordeal. And although Doc was a toddler when their father remarried and had banished Amelia and her unborn son from their home, Doc could no longer excuse himself for his gross denial of her existence as a Nickerson.

He asked her point blank, "Amelia, my dear sister, could you ever find forgiveness in your heart for me, Martha and Eileen, for all these years that we've not been there for you?"

Amelia could see her own reflection in her brother's tears and she didn't hesitate, in her unconditional manner, to tell him that she always had love in her heart for all of her family. She told him that she understood why they had to isolate her and make better lives for themselves.

He so admired her honesty and incredible character, and too, he was so relieved from the burden of the years of guilt that had just been lifted from his soul. He knew this wasn't the time to ask Amelia questions about Garrett, nor did he even care to. Calvert wished to bask in the warmth of this incredible reunion with his sister. He'd talk with her about Garrett the next time they were together. Perhaps he and Helen would have Amelia over for dinner soon.

Although his head now rested once again on her shoulder for support, he vowed to be protective of her from this day forward. If Garrett even dared try to *set Amelia up* so that he could carry out his unknown awful deeds, "He'll have to pass over my dead body first before he causes my sister any harm."

Doc felt that he owed her so much. He couldn't wait to make up for lost time. The two reunited siblings remained seated on the bench embraced in a happy silence...

Doc was anxious to tell Martha and Eileen the good news about his reconciliation with Amelia. So, on his way back to the office, he called Martha on his cell phone.

As excited as Martha was to hear the wonderful account of their get together, she was too distracted with Garrett's poor health.

Martha said, "Calvert, I am sorry to interrupt, but I have an urgent favor to ask of you. Would you be so kind to come by the Inn right away to tend to Garrett? He is in a dreadful state." She went on to tell him of Garrett's travails the night before and how the girls had returned him to his bed in the wee hours.

Her brother agreed. He'd just needed to swing by his office to pick up his medical bag. He told her he'd call Eileen and tell her the good news about his visit with Amelia.

When Doc entered Garrett's room it was easy to see that the odd patient was delirious. Garrett hallucinated and a couple of times yelled out for the others to avoid being trampled by pink elephants and other improbable Cape stampeders.

Doc had taken Garrett's vitals, heard his congested chest, felt his forehead and witnessed his incessant coughing, and concluded, without a doubt, that Garrett had viral pneumonia and was also dehydrated. His fever was very high at a hundred and three.

Garrett had refused to go to the hospital when asked and since Doc knew that the man had no identification or credit cards with him, and wouldn't be able to pay for a hospital stay, he agreed to treat him right there. With Martha and her staff looking after him, he would get just as good care, if not better, at the Hibiscus Inn. So Doc called in an order for an IV to be delivered to Garrett's room.

Doc told Garrett that he should drink plenty of liquids and wanted him to take a couple of aspirins, some viral medication, and a sleeping pill, but the patient didn't respond.

So with Martha and Sonia's assistance, he attempted to pry open Garrett's jaws and force the pills in one by one. But Garrett was adamant and shook his head and said, "No pills. No hospitals. Take what Allah has given, why prolong."

Martha was stunned, and said as she looked at her brother, "Allah? He is a Muslim?"

Garrett again rattled out, "Kassim's a wise man, no drugs."

"This is incredible! What is this man up to? the Doctor asked.

He handed Martha the pills, "I'll pull his jaws open as wide as this room if I have to. Throw these down as soon as I say go."

He placed his hands in Garrett's mouth and with all of his strength, he managed to pry open his jaws just enough. He commanded Martha, "Go!" The pills were inside Garrett's mouth in a flash and Doc closed his jaws and had Martha rub his neck, which caused him to swallow. They'd succeeded.

In time Garrett fell off to his delirious fantasy land.

Doc told Sonia to check in on him every thirty minutes or so and to report to Martha if he appeared worse. He told Martha to give Garrett the viral medication per the instructions on the label, and if she and the girls couldn't manage to get him to take them, he'd come back and inject him with some sort of sedative. He also left a vial of pain pills to give to Garret, should the cough cause him agony.

Before he left, he kissed Martha on the cheek and told her that he wanted to invite Amelia to his home for dinner soon. He asked Martha if she and Eileen would join them as well. She told him she would be delighted. They said goodbye and Martha thanked him for coming to Garrett's aid.

Doc turned to his sister as he exited the room, "If I weren't so respectful of the sworn oaths I've taken, I'd have the mind to let his health deteriorate. He's in bad shape you know."

17

Martha phoned Annie Temple on Friday and told her, among other things, that Garrett was in no condition to have visitors. Annie called Martha every day thereafter to check on his status.

It wasn't until Tuesday that Martha encouraged Annie and Nick to stop by. She said that Garrett was progressing a wee bit and had been having long spells of consciousness the last two days. His cough had subsided somewhat as well. She thought he would be up for a conversation.

When the Temples arrived it was obvious to Nick that Garrett was drugged big time. He knew that the drugs must be masking Garrett's illness, because, although he looked so frail, his spirits seemed sky high. He was ecstatic to see the Temples. He asked if they had some time to spend with him and they both said that they had a couple of hours to spare. If Garrett could summon the energy, Nick and Annie would be happy to listen. They both figured that there must be a lot on his mind that he wished to convey.

Garrett walked over to an arm chair and sat down. "I feel the need to bare my soul. I've not looked inside for quite sometime and I know from my work experience, that when you just look outside yourself there is so much that can be misperceived and lost. Isn't that so true? Almost profound," he self deprecated with a smile.

"Why tell us?" asked Annie, who, along with her son, had sat down on the edge of the bed.

"Because you're both real. You're not the usual phonies who hide behind money or fantasy tales of gods and heavens. I can sense that you have a passion for life and for others as well. I haven't seen those qualities in many others, none whom I've met here anyway, well, except for Caroline. Your approach is positive, that's what I admire."

He said, "Nick, you're well respected. I feel somehow we are soul-mates, strangers amongst the throng in this negative world. You have a kindness and gentle aura that attracts others to you. You get that from your mother no doubt. Others feel safe and alive in your presence. Just as many people used to feel with me. Until their trust was broken.

"I've been weak from the burden I carry, weak in character and too weak to end the misery that I was, I'm now happy to say. I'm no longer a ventriloquist's dummy. I'm the ventriloquist once again."

"Garrett we're happy and humbled that you would want us to lend an ear, but if you speak in defeatist riddles, which we couldn't even begin to decipher, I'm afraid you will just be in your own echo chamber and will hear the same monologues that you've wrestled with for a very long time," Annie said.

"Bravo! You're on to me, more so than I'm on to myself. Yes my thoughts wander. It's sometimes hard for me to know what is real from that which I have just dreamt, or have imagined. Because my ego conjures up things to distract me.

"So please my friends, help me pierce the illusions and help me differentiate my nightmares from my realities. I would be elated to find out that this is all a charade."

He appeared very weak and his voice was almost inaudible at times. But it didn't stop him from continuing. He babbled on in a somewhat feverish rant. He became more animated, with a tinge of delirium sprinkled in. At times he acted as if no one else was in the room with him.

"I know that the ego is a tape recorder. It doesn't fool me. It digs up past fears for its own protection and then throws up barriers that are meant to preserve it. But in essence it debilitates and entraps the very mind that it lives within. How foolish of it."

Nick spoke, "If you know, and I agree, that your troubles are ego based, then you must let go. I think then you'll be able to see the abundance of the present and the beauty of what might lie ahead for you.

"Not to sound too pious or pretentious, but relax your mind and release whatever has held you back Garrett and made you ill, both mentally and physically. Tell us what you need to, because you alone can rid yourself of your burdens. We'll listen," Nick said.

It was unclear to the Temples if Garrett had heard Nick when he said, "Let me get a grip on how I can tell you of these dreams, or facts, that have possessed me for these long months. Maybe then I'll be able to be at peace with myself and my spirituality.

"When I first arrived here I was not in a good state of mind. I'm sure you detected that. I tried to get as faraway from myself as possible. But all of a sudden I've got it. I see how focused I've been on the negatives that I've created and that I let others ensnare me with. My present had morphed into my past and left my future uncertain. But now I've found the strength to not feel sorry for myself, thanks to Lupita. She's my assistant and the one person who has loved me without judgment. I see how blind I have been not to recognize that I love her too. I feel renewed.

"Oh! By the way, Garrett is my name. I mean it's my middle name. What I mean to say, my name is Archie G. Moon, Archimedes is my formal name. Look, I'm aware that I'm all over the place, but it's from my excitement for my revival, not from the drugs that run through my brain, I think.

"So please listen to what I am about to tell you and weave your way through what is real and what is fiction. Be my detectives for hire. I hope that this time it's not a dream. Help me find out."

He took a sip of water and, with a noticeable shaky hand, he set the glass back down on the end table. He looked like he had forgotten that he was about to tell them his story, warts and all. Then all of a sudden, with no indication that he was tired, he nodded off to sleep.

The Temples looked at each other in bemusement and Nick shrugged his shoulders.

"Let him sleep. We can come back another time," his mother said.

But as they were about to exit the room, Archie woke and said, "You're not leaving? Come, please sit down."

Archie appeared straight as an arrow all of a sudden.

The Temples sat back down.

"You were saying?" Nick asked.

Archie didn't speak.

"You were going to tell us about your past. Your true identity Archie," Nick said.

Archie got in rhythm and seemed to be clearheaded all of a sudden. The Temples were both quite surprised by the change, from a disjointed monologue to a precise account of his life.

"I'll try to be modest and as brief as possible, but I will be combing over all thirty-seven years of my life, so I hope you have the time and patience. I may jump around a bit too, but I just want to be sure to tell you what I think may have affected my life up to the present. Pardon me if I sound too full of myself.

"I was born in the Mass General Hospital, in Boston, 1979. I was Charles and Athena Moon's *miracle child*, (my parents, both in their forties, had been told that my mother would never conceive). I was the beneficiary of admirable bloodlines, inheriting a fine mix of English, Greek and French genes. It's pretty much a sound lineage, except for the strain of insanity that is rooted in my father's ancestral tree, that exhibited itself every third generation or so, and that many family members felt was long overdue.

"For the record, I know I wasn't born with the *madness*, because it wasn't recorded anywhere on my birth certificate, ha! ha! And there was no mention that I was a born murderer either (a poor attempt at humor here). Although, there are many people as you well know, authorities included, who are convinced that these negative traits are well embedded in my DNA.

"As soon as I was able to speak, my mother told me that I demonstrated an above average intellect and a strong commonsense logic. I was an advanced problem solver she told me, and I excelled in communication skills, able to describe, in perfect chronological order, a movie storyline or a day's lessons at pre-school, all at the young age of two. I of course don't remember anything from that time.

"In concert with these strengths, as I aged, I'd say that I had a more purpose driven childhood than a happiness driven one, because of my ferocious desire to learn and succeed. I gravitated toward the company of adults more so than to my immature classmates and friends. I know I was a very serious and intense kid too, because my father had said that I was seldom prone to a good laugh. I believe I do have a fine sense of humor but I guess I didn't display it early on. Playtime for me meant reading another science journal.

"I wasn't a hyperactive kid by any stretch, although I always seemed to be in a hurry. I think that's because I was confident and my competitive spirit and creative imagination drove me. I've always felt driven by what's inside me. One of my noticeable short- comings I have to admit, was that I did demonstrate an air of mental superiority, perhaps because I always surpassed my goals at a much earlier age than the norm. It wasn't my fault that I was wired this way, but it said a lot about why I have always been somewhat of a loner. Many of my schoolmates couldn't compete with me and several others thought I was, quote, *different*, so they chose not to hang out with me. Again, this account of my young life is from what I remember or what my mother either told to me or wrote in letters. Whatever, the fact is I was so motivated and focused on my own performance, that except for an occasional run in with a bully, I don't think I ever noticed or cared whether I was liked or not.

"Don't get me wrong, I wasn't shy, yet socializing never made it to the top of my to-do list. For the most part I much more enjoyed my own company, although I would engage with others once in a while, when I wished to. On those occasions I seemed to be drawn to kids who were the underdogs, the least fortunate. I wanted to befriend them and be there for them if they wished. My entire life has been centered around giving to others. The greed of the nineteen eighties didn't effect me I'm happy to say.

"Like most everyone else, my character was sculpted from a handful of traumatic events. A few of mine took place in the waters of the Atlantic. The first such incident happened when I was just a little shit of seven years old. I remember it as if it were yesterday. It was prophetic that on that day of destiny, at such a tender age, I would hear my calling.

"Every August we Moons summered here on Cape Cod. My father's brother, uncle Ray, my auntie Maggie, and their twin sons would accompany us. We often rented a magnificent farmhouse in East Falmouth that was built in 1792, *Hunky Dory Farm*.

"Most every day our extended family would cram into uncle Ray's station wagon and drive to a beach we'd never been to before. After they had staked out their substantial space requirements with their beach chairs, blankets and coolers along the perimeter, both men would spend the majority of their time in the water. They played various ball games with Ray's sons, James and Ray jr.. At the time I was four or five years younger than the twins and they never considered me their playmate. But I didn't care to play by myself on the beach either, so I would go in the water when they did. Instead of ball games though, I would choose to swim, or dive for imaginary treasures nearby.

"My father never paid attention to me on those holidays. Not that Charlie didn't love me, I know my father did. It was just that we were from such different mindsets. I was scholarly and my mother thought me to be gifted, while Papa, a solid, middle class guy, a manager at Stop and Shop, would have preferred that I excelled in sports. I was athletic, and I'd become an accomplished swimmer and golfer later on, but I just wasn't into to their games as a youngster. Though I did yearn for my father's attention nonetheless.

"This particular day was quite calm, which was unusual for the always breezy Cape, as you well know. We were at beautiful Old Silver Beach down the way from here. In a shallow part of the ocean both my father, uncle and the boys had their backs to me the entire time. Dodgeball was the game that they played.

147

"At some point I became bored and jealous of my cousins getting all the attention, so I called out several times, "Daddy look at the shell I just found; or "Papa watch me do a back flip under water."

But never once did my father or uncle Ray turn my way. It seemed intentional.

"This made me crave even more for my father to look at me. So I concocted a plan to get noticed. I swam closer to the men and when I was no more than ten feet away, in fake desperation I cried out for help. Then I dove under the sea's surface and pretended that I was drowning. I held my breath for many seconds and floated to the surface face down in a *dead man's pose*. I fantasized how my father would come to my rescue and hold me in his arms, afraid that he had almost lost his precious son. But to my deep sorrow no one came to my aid. I felt invisible.

"My lungs felt like they were about to burst. I gasped for breath and flailed my arms in panic and managed to resurface. My mild hoax had almost become fatal.

"I knelt on a nearby sandbar and tried to gather my senses. With the salt water still stinging in my eyes, with bleary vision I was demoralized when I saw the backs of my father, uncle Ray and my cousins, as they exited the ocean fifty feet away. They had their arms wrapped around one another and I could hear their laughter from my sorry position.

"A sudden shudder shot through me and it frightened me. It wasn't caused by the Atlantic's icy waters though. I quivered because it felt like I had been gutted by the onslaught of abandonment. I get queasy just talking about it. Little did I know that loneliness would be my life long companion. I cried with self pity. They didn't know, or care that I existed, or so I thought.

"But somehow, out of this emotional devastation rose a spirit of defiance and confidence within me, that until that moment I'd never exhibited. It scared me. I felt possessed. For right then and there I had a clear vision and believed that I saw my purpose in life. Imagine, I was just a child. I knew that some way I would devote my energy to helping others. If I had any say in the matter, no one would ever feel left out, alone, or crushed by rejection, like I did that day.

"So as I sloshed my way through the seawater back to shore, I determined, as much as a seven year old mind could fathom, that I would become a psychologist. Not that I knew of the profession at such a ripe age of course, but that day's event would someday guide me to a career in the head-mending business. Imagine that.

"Over the years my conviction and focus never wavered, and driven by my mother's faith in me and her support (she was a cold woman, never demonstrated her love, but did want the best for me always) I graduated with honors from Boston Latin High School at age sixteen. I was flattered when they created a new category in their year-book just for me, *Most likely to Exceed.*

"I was accepted into Stanford's undergraduate program in Psychology and was very excited to get my first taste of the West. You know it's funny, it seemed that the further I got away from my Boston roots, the more comfortable I became. I didn't experience loneliness in the least. I had hardened to it. In fact, I reveled in the anonymity. I liked the role of the stranger. All was new to me and I was new to it.

"To fast forward my bio, I had a typical college life even though I was younger than the majority of my classmates. I partook in all the vices that a young man should. The ladies, all older than me, took me into their care. I'm happy to say I received a fine education in much more than psychology. Although the way things have gone I'm not sure that I retained much of that knowledge.

"I graduated with honors and wished to pursue a doctorate in clinical psychology, which was not offered at Stanford. I wanted to stay in Northern California and applied, and was accepted into the six-year *Doctor of Psychology* program at the University of San Francisco. The reason that I didn't wish to pursue a PhD in Psychiatry is that I was, and am, opposed to medication therapy. Ironic, with all the pills I've popped of late.

"I loved the research and patient work the most and didn't much care for the compulsory assignments, which required me to teach and to grade term papers and essay exams. But all in all it was a very positive experience.

"The years peeled off the calendar and in my final months I interned full time at UCSF Hospital and worked at the clinic as the doctorate program required. Somehow, one night a week, driven by my ambition, I also managed to help out at a psychologist's practice in downtown San Francisco as well. That proved beneficial, because it highlighted just how much I wanted to open a private practice in the profession."

Archie stopped speaking and took a long drink of water. "Are you bored rigid yet?" he asked them. Annie waved him on.

"Thanks. After I graduated three months ahead of schedule, I needed a break, so I rewarded myself with a return trip to the East Coast. I had arranged to work as a bartender at Dylan's that summer in Falmouth. I was twenty six. So you see I have a lot of memories of the Cape.

"During that summer further refinements to my character would be chiseled out by a second major event in my life. It further shaped the person I was preordained to become, I believe.

"One week in late June, I was happy to get two consecutive days off from work and I was invited by my roommate, Hank, to spend the time on Martha's Vineyard. We took the beautiful *Island Queen Ferry* over to Oak Bluffs, then the bus to Chilmark, and stayed at Hanks parent's house. What a fine place that was. Hank's girlfriend and two of her college roommates met us there, and since Hank's parents were away, it made for a fun time. I had the hots for one of the girls, a pretty dark haired girl named Jane, and I could tell that she had designs on me as well.

"On the afternoon of our arrival we went to the magnificent Lucy Vincent Beach and walked quite a while on the powdery sand, lugging coolers and beach chairs, just so we could reach the nude section. My first time in the raw on a beach. You ever go there? Gorgeous.

"We swam and bodyboarded for about fifteen minutes but the waves grew higher and the riptide became quite dangerous, so we decided to come ashore. That is, except for Jane and Katherine, her rather homely best friend, who dyed her hair a terrible bright orange color in an attempt to distract from her obesity I guessed. The two ladies continued to ride the hazardous surf.

"Neither of the women had gone out too far in the water, but I still kept a close watch on Jane, because I became concerned with how the powerful waves were thrashing her about. My caution was justified because in a very short time, another large wave pummeled both of them and they were flipped over and the tide ripped them out to sea.

"I laced up my swim trunks, I didn't want my family jewels to get hammered around, and sprinted towards the water. Even though I was an excellent swimmer, I knew that my life would be in jeopardy too. Except for a lifeguard who was alerted to the problem and was a good three hundred yards away from either of them, as she paddled on her board, no one else felt comfortable, heroic, or foolish enough to dive in.

"I managed to reach the panicky Katherine first (her screams still echo in my ears) however, I swam right past her towards Jane. Fortunately, I was able to calm Jane down and get a tight grip on her and after a tiresome ten, twelve minutes or so, I managed to get her back to shore, where several others stood by to help. I never felt so exhausted. I collapsed on my back on the beach. I was spent, but ecstatic that Jane was fine.

"But for Katherine the outcome was tragic. The lifeguard hadn't been able to reach her in time.

"This is a humiliating admission, but I had never once considered saving Katherine.

"As a fog of guilt folded over me, I wondered then, and still do so today, was it because she was so unattractive to me that I had chosen not to pay attention to her cries? Many times I would over analyze the episode and conclude that I was a shallow, self-centered, horny asshole back then. Perhaps Jane could have stayed afloat and been rescued by the lifeguard? And even worse than that, I realized that if Jane hadn't been in any danger, I wouldn't have given a thought to challenging the treacherous ocean in order to save Katherine. I saw the palpable irony in all of this. Katherine was me when I was a young boy at Old Silver Beach, when I had clamored for my father's attention. But this time I was the one who didn't hear. As if she didn't exist."

Archie went silent for a minute as he tried to shake himself from the memory.

"Despite Katherine's tragedy, I did get the ultimate prize for my efforts. Jane took a seasonal job in Falmouth so that she could be near me. We were locked in love. It was wonderful.

"After her friend's funeral, we both had a blast the remainder of the summer, we never again spoke of Katherine's tragedy.

"I made the obligatory visit to see my parents in Boston just once that summer and I pretty much followed the independent path that I had blazed over the past few years. Too bad I didn't know that it would be the last time that I would see my father alive, because, depressed at age seventy-nine, he hung himself on his birthday seven months later. I felt sad for him. I wished we had a more connected relationship. I regretted that I had never known my father and that he never took the time to understand me.

"At the end of that summer I returned to the West to take a pre-arranged junior position at a practice in L.A. and Jane joined me. Soon we planned our engagement, at least I thought she was into it.

But it wasn't many months later that our relationship soured. Jane told me that she realized all that we had in common were our mutual friends from those days at Lucy Vincent Beach. She told me that it was her sense of guilt that made her stay with me. Ouch! I had saved her life and she felt obligated to me. But she told me that she didn't love me and never had.

"The last words Jane said to me were, "Why didn't you even try to save Katherine?"

"It took me a very long time to recover from our breakup. I was down. What got me through this rough patch though were my dedication to my work and the trip back East when I attended my father's funeral. I also took the responsibility to make sure that my widowed mother was well situated.

"I spent the next several years buried in my work. I seldom socialized, choosing instead to toil away on many fifteen hour days, my pattern.

"My mentor was quite a brilliant man, but this attribute was far overshadowed by his poor attitude, laziness and propensity for disorganization. His name was Urs Gelber and he was the model of the *Euro Trash* stereotype: unclean, with pungent body odor; filthy fingernails; shirt pulled out of his pants; he wore the same clothes for days; bad, alcoholic breath; unkempt hair, thick flakes of dandruff on his always black stained silk shirt, and very self involved. What a piece of work.. When I had my one interview with him, Urs asked no questions of me, the applicant. Instead he rapid-fired a *me, me, me,* monologue. He bragged that he was worth a hundred million dollars; that he was the only Swiss born citizen on the Modern Museum's board; that he was a trustee for the Los Angeles Symphony; that his son rode motorcycles with Dennis Hopper; and several other inane boasts. I was certain that this was psychology 101, and diagnosed Urs to be an insecure, alcoholic, windbag.

"Many of my colleagues were surprised when I accepted Urs' offer to work under him. But I saw the opportunity to be involved in the business, to implement my organizational skills and to make a considerable difference in his rat's nest. I wasn't looking for just a job, I wanted to be engaged.

"My perceptions were prescient, because right from the start I was forced to take on much more responsibility than normal for my position. I ran the place. I learned as I went along. The good news, as I had calculated, was that it sped up my learning curve, always my goal, and fulfilled my needs to stay busy and to grow.

"It served me well, because one of Ur's associates from his faculty days at Berkley, who had a successful private practice in Sedona, was impressed with my work ethic and knowledge. He offered me an equal partnership in his lucrative Arizona practice. He told me that he planned to retire within three years and that if I chose, I could buy him out then. I was so tired of the LA scene (which I admit I didn't participate in) and the traffic and over population. I had hoped for a small-town environment. What a wonderful opportunity!

"My new mentor in Sedona was the exact opposite of Urs. Mr. Hargrove, Harry, was the consummate professional. He took me under his guidance and into his spotless and efficient practice in his in-home office on Last Wagon Trail. His wife Dorothy cared for us both as we worked our asses off. I was the son they never had and Harry and Dorothy became the attentive parents I always craved. It was ideal. I learned so much from Harry.

"The property had four bedrooms and baths for the owners' quarters and two large meeting rooms and a small quiet room for the patients. As soon as I was able to buy out Harry, I transformed the interior to the more mid-century modern decor that exists now, not the western theme that Harry and Dorothy so enjoyed. I downsized the bedroom quarters to one large master suite with bath. The other bedrooms I converted into additional patient rooms. I even had a one-way mirror installed in one of the rooms, for observations.

"I was thirty-one years old, owned a fantastic practice and resided in one of the most desirable locations on the planet. What more could I ask for?

"Once the practice was my baby, I put every waking hour into my patients' concerns. I had built up a strong client roster while I was Harry's partner and a fair amount of his patients switched over to me when he retired, so it was a tremendous way to start off on my own. Also I was blessed that the very competent Lupita, Hargrove's assistant, decided to remain on with me. So my business didn't skip a beat.

"My energy knew no bounds. I was determined to apply my unique insights (I thought them to be unique, praise addiction perhaps?) in order to help others and to fulfill my destiny. Not for ego gratification or a financial windfall, but because I felt driven to dedicate my talents to others day and night.

"I was energized. I was unstoppable. I loved life.

"Too bad I was oblivious to the painful times ahead."

18

Archie took a few deep breaths and continued his monologue.

"Sedona is a very small town and its people, to a fault, are eager to latch on to new ways and new ideas. It's the nature and the power of the *vortex* that they live amidst. They were very receptive to my approach. The word had spread that I was someone to see. I was a man who listened and wasn't afraid to give unpopular advice. I always offered solutions. They could see that I was a person who cared for my patients and who stayed current in my field so that I could offer them the very best guidance. They knew that I had a genuine compassion for others. I tried to offer a more spiritual, connected and holistic approach. I wanted to untangle the pain in the brain and felt that the mind controlled the body and its health. Its complexity was the challenge and I was more than ready to take it on.

"And my patients knew that I was the real deal since I wasn't just about money. Even though I could've charged them a hefty fee, many were affluent, I encouraged them to pay what they thought each visit was worth. There was no set rate. No pressure to sign on for twenty more sessions. It was my way of giving them back control and encouraging them to take responsibility for their participation. I never acted as their guru who was above them. They were my equal, although many would've loved for me to make their decisions for them. First and foremost, they knew that I would keep their secrets private and never disclose their vulnerabilities. Oh how I would fail them!

"The business grew, it was nuts. Lupita urged me to take on a junior partner, but I decided to go it alone. After all I reasoned, they wished to share their concerns with me. There was a continuity that needed to be maintained. How could I pawn them off on an amateur associate? I cared that much for them.

"People can debate what normal is and I could tell you that the majority of my patients were not. I had an eclectic bunch of *New Agers*, *conspiracy peddlers*, *crystal worshipers*, *UFO believers*, and *insecure gun nuts*, who were possessed by every malady known to man and womankind. They always kept my interest acute and my passion vigorous. I was the consummate idealist and I felt that my patients loved me, as I did them.

"The months flew by as if they were in a time-lapse video. I was so consumed with my work, that I hadn't noticed that I would soon turn thirty-four. It was Lupita who pointed it out. She urged me to take a few days off to enjoy my birthday. She said something like, "You look so pale and stressed. It's not healthy that you work eighteen hours a day on other people's problems. You're too focused on their negative stuff. You need a few distractions. Treat yourself. Go away from the office, take a vacation, climb *Coffee Pot*, explore like you used to before your practice grew so large. Have some fun for a change. It can't always be about them. You deserve it."

"At the time I paid little attention to her prudent advice. My patients depended upon me. How could I let them down and not be there for them for even a day?"

Archie stopped his monologue and asked, "How's our time?"

"We're fine. Please continue," Nick said.

"As fate would have it, a couple of days after Lupita had encouraged me to chill, a woman had canceled her appointment and I found myself with some time on my hands. On a typical afternoon I would fill the welcome void with research, paperwork, phone calls, whatever. Instead, on this particular day, since Lupita's words still lingered in my mind, I decided to heed her good counsel and do an unfamiliar task, have fun, look after myself.

"But before the fun part (typical of me I know) I thought it would be wise to have a self session, to critique my first three years of ownership and to focus on where I was at. It was always about others, I wanted to explore my inner self for a change.

"I have to say that I was taken aback to realize that I hadn't looked within since I had become the sole owner. My workaholic routine wasn't super healthy I knew, so there were bound to be a few patterns I'd see that I'd have to break, then afterwards, if there was time, I'd go for a hike or jog somewhere.

"What an epiphany that session turned out to be.

"If I had viewed my life as if it were one of my patient's, I would've determined that I had no life. I took an honest and brutal look at myself and understood that I wasn't who I thought I was.

"I recognized that I had lost my identity. I had become them and their problems. Lupita knew. I'd become a human sponge. I was so focused on patients' needs, that theirs had become mine. Hell, I didn't even know what my needs were. Can you imagine if you had that self revelation? I wasn't the beneficiary of my own expertise. The sound advice I had prescribed to others I hadn't prescribed for myself, because I was too blind to even know that I needed it.

"I realized that my clients controlled me, not vice versa. I saw that I needed them maybe more than they did me, in order to validate my worth. The shock was, that I then and there saw that I'd become a prisoner to what I knew and what I thought I knew.

"What startled me most on that crucial day of self-analysis, was that I saw that I'd withdrawn from life on a steady downward spiral. As I said I had no life. This was some sort of subconscious survival mechanism that I used to wean myself from socializing in that claustrophobic town. Out of necessity, I grew more antisocial. Imagine, an antisocial shrink!

"In the past I used to attend conferences and all the local events. I even threw my patients an appreciation party once a year. I was happy, to a great degree. Then something happened. At some point I began to feel closed in on by them and their *problems*. Because no matter where I went in public I couldn't relax and enjoy the company of friends or new acquaintances. There were always those patients who would hound me for advice. They could care less if they invaded my space. They had to tell me how their lives had progressed since their last session, or how my suggestions did or didn't work out for them. Me, Me, Me. It made me very uneasy. I began to feel smothered by them and the small-town mentality.

"Worse than that, I felt even more uptight in social settings when certain patients would scatter from my presence as soon as they spotted me, as if I were a leper. They were paranoid. They knew that I held their secrets and that I could blow their cover at any moment. Many avoided me because they were embarrassed by their flaws and the fact that I knew them. And for me it had become so instinctual, that I shied from them as well. It was a very strained situation and I felt pressured to act nonchalant. I wasn't being myself. I was an actor just so that they'd feel at ease, even though it made me edgy. I knew of their peculiarities and didn't want to make them more uncomfortable. They and their trite bourgeoisie *issues*. Who was fucking whose wife; (pardon my language); who still wets the bed at age fifty; who abused children; and the uber absurd fears some voiced that they would be abducted by aliens, or die in a dirigible crash. Good God what I put up with!

"I didn't feel it appropriate to discuss their troubles outside of the office, so couldn't they just leave me alone and let me enjoy myself? They needed to figure out how to cope on their own and not use me as their crutch. Just once could I get a break from this crap and have a mindless night out. Sorry, I'm getting all worked up just talking about them.

"I saw how annoyed I'd become with many patients whom I thought had progressed well in sessions, but had in fact drifted backwards. Not able to self-correct, they relived their past difficulties and didn't view life through the prism of *now*. I felt that so many had approached therapy as if it were just another self-improvement game. Most, I knew, had lives of financial leisure and had come to see me more for social reasons than conscious raising ones. I needed to hide from these *crazy makers*.

"I'd considered how they felt but hadn't evaluated the toll it had taken on me. It became clear that I didn't even know what I felt anymore. I mean it. I worried that I'd caught my ancestor's *Half Moon Madness*. I'm half joking.

"Except for all the appointments at my office sanctuary, out of necessity I'd become a social recluse. Wise Lupita knew. I seldom left my hermitage, except on those rare occasions when I'd take a trip to Phoenix where I could be anonymous. With all the beauty that surrounded me, the great trails and vistas, I instead hunkered down in my home office bunker. Lupita ordered all my food and supplies and she cooked three meals a day for me.

"I'd become an island. I felt like a boat pulled out of the harbor for the winter, shrink-wrapped, put in storage. I'd caught that dreaded disease once again, loneliness. Hell, I didn't catch it, I created it. Until that day I'd denied that it had always resided within me.

"I go inside myself whenever I hurt, I always did since I was a kid. It's my talent to go deep, to analyze, conclude and build a defense. However, on that particular day I was dumbstruck to admit that my life had been braided with self-denial and fear of my own irrelevance. I'd buried my head in my practice on purpose, that was my biggest revelation, forget all that other stuff. I had enhanced the lives of others so that I wouldn't have to look at myself. I'd kept busy all my adult life because I didn't want to be exposed. I'd built a self-fortress and the more I looked back that day at the pattern my life had sketched, the more I understood that this protective behavior had made me bitter.

"Holding on to anger is like grasping a hot coal with the intention of throwing it at someone else; you are the one who gets burned." Buddha had it right. I was the loser.

"Had I just been going through the motions all these years I wondered? I was very hard on myself. I saw that my ideal profession had been a hoax. The practice that was once my lifeblood, my sole purpose to exist, had become a dungeon and pathetically, I'd become both the captive and captor.

"What I recognized that fateful day of self-analysis is that I 'd been shrinking… from society, from life, and from myself."

19

Liza interrupted Archie's soliloquy and brought he and his guests a pot of tea, as well as a plate of tomato and cucumber sandwiches. She gave him a new pitcher of ice water and a cough drop for his dry throat. She bowed to them all and left in a hurry.

After they had thanked her, Archie said, "It blew me away to see that what I'd dedicated my entire thirty-four years to, appeared to be a bluff. The madness I saw in my reflection that blackened day was, that like so many of my patients, I had become just another ego tethered to a mirage.

"I didn't know what I should do. I knew I couldn't continue working with my patients if I felt so negative and confused about myself, and them. It wouldn't be fair to them or me. Yet I had no other skills, this was my life's purpose, or so I once thought.

"I needed some time to think.

"I had Lupita cancel the rest of the week's appointments and I fell into a blue funk. I didn't seem to be able to muster up the confidence, nor the energy that were my signature strengths. My perspective on life had changed. All that I once believed to be true seemed like one big lie. I needed to search my mind for answers.

"But to my surprise, in a remarkable twist of fate, my life would do a complete three sixty in just a short week's time. Because, as if the gods had listened to Lupita's plea for my happiness, I was sent an incredible birthday gift. One that I would cherish forever, but would never feel worthy of.

"For on the very night of my thirty fourth birthday, back at work in the office as usual, at eight o'clock or so, I was distracted by a noise that came from the small room next to mine. I listened to see if it was just my imagination, but when I walked over and saw through the cracks that a light was on, I threw open the door. What a glorious sight! There seated crossed legged on top of the lone cherry wood desk in the room, was the most beautiful, sensual woman I'd ever laid eyes upon. That statement is true even to this very day. She wore a full length brown fur coat (*PETA* would gag) with its collar turned up against her natural long ash blond hair. She looked so young and vibrant. I was awestruck in her presence, and I realize that in hindsight I was so vulnerable. Her name was Marlie.

"She fixed her eyes on me and unfolded her legs. She wet her lips and opened up her fur coat to reveal her perfect, naked bronzed body.

"Then Marlie motioned for me to come over to her and she enveloped me within her coat. I was in fantasyland, too much information I know.

"We retreated to my bedroom and made love all night. We spoke very little. About three a.m. she got up and dressed. Marlie said in the most sensual voice, "I hope all of our sessions will be as frisky as this one. See you next Thursday night cutie? Or do I need to make an appointment Doctor?"

"I told her she should come every night, Doctor's orders!

"After she had left I remained awake for hours. I couldn't comprehend how such great fortune had befallen me, since I'd been in such a terrible state of mind. I thought that the *Secret* was to think positive thoughts to attract? Ha! I felt so alive again."

Archie said to Annie and Nick, "This is great therapy for me, but I feel self-conscious to be rapping on and on. Thank you both.

"Marlie and I were so enthralled with one another that soon we were together every night as I had prescribed. We were inseparable and it wasn't just because of the magnificent sex. She was a very smart young lady and quite a charmer too. Marlie had insight. She had an uncanny ability to get right to the point. She was direct and she was loving, a shrink's delight. She fascinated the hell out of me and she took a genuine interest in me and my expertise. I can't figure out to this day why she came to me. She was the sole reason that I bolted out of my solitary confinement. Marlie was a nonstop doer, a whirlwind. And as if

I was trailing after a jet airplane, I was happy to be pulled along by the slipstream of her energy. She was a partier and I was her escort. She fell all over me and I no longer focused my undivided attention on others around me. I was so happy again.

"After three months together, we surprised everyone when we announced our plans to marry. We arranged to have our wedding on spectacular Cathedral Rock the following month. It was the first marriage for both of us. I was thirty four and Marlie was twenty five. Marlie was adamant that she keep her maiden name, Stone, and I agreed, because that's who she was after all. Like me, she was an only child of older parents. But that's where the comparisons stopped. She could've been the poster girl for what an only child acted like: Daddy's girl, confident, cocky, selfish. The world revolved around her, or so she thought and I believed it did as well.

"Marlie was from a prominent family in La Jolla, California. Both her parents were lawyers, and she graduated from UCLA with a degree in business administration. Besides her natural beauty, I was in awe of her boundless energy and her innate curiosity. She was almost ten years my junior and so full of life, that I found it hard to keep up with her. I would return after a long day's sessions and she would have all sorts of activities planned with others, or for just the two of us. It was sensational.

"I didn't think my business suffered much at those times either. In fact, I may not have put in as many hours with my patients, but what I did give them was more quality time. I was, for the first time ever, so happy in my life, because of this wonderful woman, that I once again looked forward to working on my patients' personal problems. I was now a much stronger and more centered person, so my patients benefitted from my new outlook. I was engaged in their stories once again. I had a love distraction. As corny as it sounds, my after-hours focus was now on love, not on my patient's disorders.

"So that we didn't put any undo stress on our relationship, we agreed that we would play three nights a week and one day a week, at her insistence, we would discuss some of my patients' concerns, in confidence. She wanted to feel part of our business and perhaps, who knew, she might be able to offer a female intuition and perspective that I wouldn't have had the experience to even consider. Of course I wouldn't name names, just their quirky ailments and the solutions that I had encouraged them to uncover for themselves.

"To my delight, Marlie was very interested in the activity and many times offered insightful advice that I implemented. She had excellent instincts as to what motivated people, both male and female. She enjoyed it so, that soon she asked to add a second night of patient reviews. She pleaded with me to let her be my assistant.

"Better judgment aside, I suggested that she monitor a group session the next afternoon. She could sit behind the one-way mirror to see if she liked it and if she could be of benefit to my patients and me. Of course my clients had no knowledge of her presence.

"Marlie was ecstatic with the assignment, and with all her enthusiasm and manic energy she became a regular group therapy spy.

"I just saw you cringe," Archie said to Annie Temple..

"At this point did I feel guilty that I was betraying my clients' trust and confidentiality? Yes and no. I was so in love, that somehow it felt right to me at the time. Poor conclusion on my part I know. But the clouds of love blocked the light rays of better judgment. I rationalized that the patients got what they wished and so did Marlie and me. Strange as it sounds, to me it seemed rather an idyllic arrangement.

"However, after six months into our marriage the spontaneity that she had thrived upon had waned and her assistance in the practice became more routine and too mundane for Marlie. She was more inclined for action and found that this had become anything but. So we agreed that she would drop one of the days of patient reviews and replace it with two more nights out on the town.

"This proved way too much for me. It didn't take long for me to wear down. The demands of my practice weighed heavy enough and coupled with all the parties, it was difficult for me to keep pace with her, and to be honest, I wasn't all that interested in socializing.

"Once in a while I could handle the parties, but several nights a week, forget it. It was just not in my makeup. When you added to my disinterest the fact that she no longer hung out with me very long at parties, I saw very little incentive to make an appearance. Marlie would slip off with one of her friends and leave me all alone. I'd become uncomfortable and it irked me that my needy, clever and selfish patients were able to wedge their way into my space again. They leapt at the opportunity to get my attention and solicit my advice. It was deja vu. Wherever I went my clients felt it was their right to as much of my time as they wished.

"When I first told Marlie that I wasn't as enthused as she to attend parties, she became upset with me and scolded me saying that I was old beyond my years. She condescended that I was past my prime and that I had the libido of a corpse.

"But it was fortunate for both of us that her best friend Boris, her hairstylist, had hung around with her of late and he more than filled my place by her side. So, to my great pleasure, Marlie gave me permission to stay home on many occasions, and since Boris was gay and all, their gallivanting gave me no need for jealous concerns.

"I did join them once a month, but it became very evident to me that the pleasure of Boris' company was far more her choice. I knew I was a bore by her standards and I was fine with that.

"However, it didn't take me long to find myself back in the same deep dark antisocial rut that I'd been in prior to meeting Marlie. When I would go to a party with her, Boris and his lover would meet us there. That would be the last I'd see of her. The threesome would laugh and mock the other guests, then they'd slink off to a room, or the garden, to smoke pot or do coke or whatever.

"I'd be stuck with the rest. Some of them were patients, others strangers, and most of them were cautious around me and me around them. Here we go again. I began to feel that I was wasting my time. I felt so out of place and uncomfortable in my own skin.

"It had all came back so fast to haunt me. To repeat the painful past became even more debilitating. This time it wasn't in stages that my withdrawal from society manifested itself. No, I fell right into the depths of my uncertainty, as if in free fall through a bottomless elevator shaft. I wanted to run back to my impenetrable fortress, as far away from these phonies as possible, and work on meaningful stuff.

"I participated less and less in these activities and instead of going out once a month, it became once every two months, and even that started to feel too often to me. But for Marlie, ever the restless one, she was on the exact opposite schedule. She went on a tear.

"I was relieved to be a hermit at those times, so I wasn't too suspicious of her whereabouts. On many occasions she wouldn't return home until the next day, always with the same kind of excuse. "Bo and I had a blast last night at the Corey Ranch party. After we got rid of that drip of a boyfriend of his, we partyeeeeeeed! I had so much to drink and smoke that I didn't dare drive home. I slept in Bo's bed with him. But don't worry honey, even I couldn't turn him into a hetero."

"I didn't worry. I was just happy that she came back to me, go figure.

"It did have an impact on her interest with work though. She couldn't get her ass out of bed until noon most days that followed. At times she seemed debauched to me. No question, the bloom was off the rose. But I believed I loved her, however, I doubted that she felt the same about me.

"Marlie was on the cutting edge of now and once she sensed someone to be past, be played out, she no longer had any use for them. She didn't have a rear-view mirror and I didn't want to chance that she'd leave me behind.

"Boris and she were quite a pair. The word of their escapades spread and I often felt mortified when one of my patients would be excited to relay how much fun my wife was last night. "You should have seen Marlie dancing on top of the bar. All the men howled for her attention. She's a real tease and quite a hoot."

"They were talking about my wife for Christ's sake..the life of the party."

20

Archie continued, "With all my experience and training I should have known that I couldn't hide my head in my practice forever and ignore the obvious. Because one day a patient came to me in a fit of anguish. She told me that Marlie and her husband were having an affair.

"I was jolted by her claim, but acted ever the stoic professional and tried to get to the bottom of her angst, as if this were somehow her responsibility. What bull shit! I knew that it must be true, but wished to believe otherwise. I was in complete denial, or to be more truthful, I worked very hard at fooling myself into being in denial.

"I had seen her flirt several times with various men at parties, but I'd written it off to her exhibitionist needs. You know, to be the center of attention.

"Paranoid, I became more vigilant, but I didn't dare confront her because I feared that she might tell me the truth, and wave goodbye.

So I decided, that despite my strong desire not to go, I'd accompany her to the next social event. When I told her that I'd join her, she gave me a lame excuse why I shouldn't go. "Don't bother, the people are such drips."

"It was a group of Boris' older women clients she told me. Marlie said, "Trust me honey. You would be your regular bored stiff self."

"I saw the lie in her eyes and was hurt, but covered up my reaction so that she didn't notice.

"More lame excuses followed the next few times I offered to come along. But one day I insisted that I join her for the *Festival of Lights* after party at Dahl and Delucas. I'd always enjoyed that particular event and venue. I was surprised when she didn't resist. As a matter of fact, she seemed excited that I wanted to come. I remember thinking how flawed the ego can be. Was it my own lack of self-worth that had me convinced that she was perhaps cheating on me?

"But when we attended the party I got quite a shock.

"Midway through the festivities, higher than a kite, Marlie and Boris interrupted a superficial conversation I was trapped into having with one of my male patients. I could tell by the way that she and he had looked at one another that they'd never met. The rude patient became uncomfortable with Marlie's energy and condescended, "If you wouldn't mind, your husband and I have important matters to discuss, in private."

"His arrogance irked her and she snarled back, "If it's about your impotence, we don't need to hear all the soft and boring details. Come along Bo Bo, let's find a livelier bunch."

"They giggled and went off.

"The man and me were both dumbstruck. He glared at me as if to say how does she know? Have you told her about my problems? How dare you."

"All I could manage to say was, "My wife knows shit Roy. That's just her poor sense of humor with men who don't treat her as an equal, in her mind. She's drunk, I'm sure you could see. She's used that same line on three other guys already tonight. Please."

"Roy appeared to be relieved and to accept my explanation, but I had become very concerned. I shuddered to think what else she might do. I knew that Marlie never filtered her words, whether she was drunk or sober. I feared that this could get nasty. How many other patients' secrets had she divulged or would soon let drop? She'd ruin me!

"A week later another patient told me, point blank, at the end of his session, that, "If you don't put a lid on that wife of yours I'll see to it."

"I figured that she had revealed that the guy was a klepto. I knew she was out of control. I had to confront her. She couldn't shoot her mouth off about other people's sacred bonds with their psychologist, it would be devastating for them and would be my downfall. She had to be corralled.

"So on one of those rare times when we were at home alone, and with Marlie in a mellow mood, I asked her point-blank if she had eavesdropped on my sessions and how much did she know? She was bugged and told me to chill.

She admitted, "Yes, of course at one time I was fascinated with all the drivel and self-pity of your hopeless patients. I looked in through the one-way mirror and rifled through their files. I wanted to help. Don't pretend that you didn't know *Mr. Controller*. But after a while it was easy to see that they didn't want to be cured. They just wanted to whine to you, Dr. Freud, their master. Even you have to admit that they're the paradigm of boredom, just like you.

"I know tons about all of your regular, half-witted patients, but I promise that I won't say another word about them, to anyone. So drop the big inquisition. I don't want to waste my breath. I'm so beyond them and their trivialities. How in the hell do you put up with them? You need to get a life honey."

"I asked her to make sure that that *loose cannon* of a friend of her's, Boris, didn't blast any stuff either. She was pissed that I'd insinuated she would have told him, but I knew that she had. I'm sure they had a few laughs at other people's expense, after all that was their favorite sport.

"After our confrontation, although I wanted to believe that she wouldn't speak out about my patients, I knew I could never trust her again. I felt lousy. I couldn't avoid the truth that if you didn't trust someone, it was over. Our relationship had sunk to its nadir.

"Marlie further distanced herself from me after our talk and on those rare occasions when we did speak, she would laugh and berate me because I hid in my stuffy shell; because I didn't have the drive to keep her satisfied and because I was weak and gave her the permission to run free. "You created it all *Mr. Big Shot* psychologist. How does it taste? You didn't think that I'd find your life of solitude attractive did ya? You want me to stay at home and hibernate with you by the fire?"

"I knew she was right. I was a bore once again and she was so full of curiosity.

"Marlie had Lupita fix a bedroom for her in one of the other offices that I seldom used. She might as well have been on Mars, because in the next three months or more, except when I inhaled her ever present aroma, I never saw her, nor would have known if she had even lived there anymore.

"You'll be happy to know that I'm almost finished Annie and Nick," Archie said with a half-smile.

"It had become quite clear to me that she was with someone else. But I was still powerless to challenge her, for I knew full well that it was over between us. I didn't want to hear the words come from her lips. I didn't think I could take the failure. I played the victim role to the max.

I had become more irrational by the hour. I saw the obvious paradox, that if this were one of my patients who had experienced the same marital erosion, no doubt I would have encouraged him to leave such a destructive relationship. Concede that their relationship was over and look forward to better times.

"I had looked at so many phonies in my life and now the biggest one of all, the ultimate hypocrite, was reflected back at me in the water.

"Then one day my dear, loyal Lupita, who loves me more than any other person, for who I am and with all my defects, begged me to kick Marlie out of the house. At first I blew it off as jealousy, because Lupita and me once had a thing prior to Marlie coming on the scene. But out of character for her she got right in my face and told me that everyone in the town knew of Marlie's affairs.

"Lupita said, "Archie that wife of yours has had dozens of men both young and old, and most of them are your patients."

"Wow did that hurt."

"If that didn't crush me, Lupita told me that Marlie made fun of my patient's problems and that she broadcast them to anyone who'd listen. I felt run over by a bus.

"Lupita cried and said, "Archie you're the laughing stock of the town. It isn't right. You've worked too hard and have cared so much. Marlie is bad, evil. She's destructive. You have get rid of her for good."

"I cried that night too. I felt powerless. I knew what Lupita had related was true and I was grateful that she had the courage to tell me. How could I ever face my patients? Whose secrets had she revealed? This was insane. I went numb for days.

"But one day I determined to put an end to my paralysis. I rallied up some strength and decided that I had to stop the deceit before it destroyed me and my practice completely. That's when I used the well-worn caveat, that unless I had closure and saw her in action with my own two eyes, I would never be rid of the emptiness that had consumed me. I decided I would trail her on a few of her flings.

"I saw her with Boris a couple of those nights and they hung out with a young kid one time and a patient I recognized to be the yoga instructor, Sidhartha (Paul Goldberg was the phony's alias). It became my night's routine to shadow her and I looked forward to it. How sick was that? But I still had no proof that she had slept with anyone, I just saw that she was partying.

"Then one night there was a very strange occurrence that threw me off balance. After I had gotten into bed and turned out the lights, there was a tap at my door. Marlie pushed it open and walked up to the foot of the bed. I thought she knew that I'd been following her and that she was about to lay into me. But instead, she asked if she could lie down next to me.

"She wore just a white tee shirt and slid under the covers and pushed her back up against me. I went weak. I put my arms around her and nuzzled my face into her hair. She sobbed and said, "You must hate me." Neither of us spoke another word.

"Excited with the fact that she had returned to me, I didn't want to fall asleep and awake to find her gone. But that's what in fact happened. For the next several weeks to come I never saw her again. She hadn't come home and I hadn't chosen to play detective and trail her again. I was confused and felt under her complete control. What's new?

"However, weeks later it all became more clear. That horrific Saturday Lupita interrupted a patient visit to tell me that Marlie had just come back. I ended the session and went straight to her room. I was surprised to see that she had packed her suitcase.

"She told me that she was off to visit her aunt in Tucson for the weekend. She said she wanted some time to think. She didn't answer my battery of questions but did say, "Honey, you know that it's best for us that I stop torturing you so."

"That night I lost it. I was bitter. I knew she didn't have a relative in Tucson. Did she think I was that pitiful? Why did she want to harm me and dole out all this pain? All the gossip about her affairs were now obvious to me. And worse, she had ruined my practice when she'd divulged my patients' confidential information. I needed to do something fast. She had never stopped her wanton ways. Even though I'd known for months that she was cheating on me, until that very moment, it was the first time that I acknowledged it. It felt like I was in a head on collision. The reality that it was over between us had finally sunk in. D'oh. Street's smart isn't my strong suit."

He told the Temples that now that he was certain of her betrayal, he was scared and didn't know what to do. He wasn't sure if he could muster the courage to survive the blow. He felt backed into a corner.

"I was distraught, my mind had gone dark. I was too weak without her. I felt like a tarsier," he said. When he saw the blank looks on the Temples' faces he clarified, "Tarsier, that bug-eyed miniature creature in the Philippines, that when it becomes unhappy, feels trapped or enclosed, it kills itself.

"A wave of madness washed over me. I'd become enraged, my anger rushed out of control. I found courage for the first time and knew that I needed to end my nightmare. My mind overflowed with dark ideas. I decided to follow Marlie later on that November night. Not to observe, but to act."

PART Three

1

Tip Garland had arrived in Phoenix at noon on Tuesday October 2nd, on a flight from Providence Rhode Island. He wasn't able to sleep on the plane, plus he was very tired from partying for two days straight at his brother's bachelor party and great wedding bash. Tip just wanted to lay low for the rest of the day, but he knew he couldn't until he completed the two-hour drive north to Sedona.

The weather was hot, high nineties, but it felt just fine to him. It was a dry heat as the locals always reminded you. He didn't see any cowboys, but the vision of the *Wild West* seemed to be front and center. The small mountains surrounding the city gave it a dimension and a solidity that pleased his eyes.

Tip Garland was a tall and lanky six foot four, brown haired twenty eight year old, his stature the total opposite of his older brother Sean's medium, muscular structure. He was much faster on his feet than he was in his head. Inventive and creative thinking weren't considered his strong suits. However, he did have perseverance and street sense, and those perhaps would turn out to be more valuable to him in his quest to the top. They were the essentials that not all reporters possessed.

Tip was bored with the local sports scene that he covered for the Falmouth Enterprise and the occasional assignment to interview an area writer or a celebrity who was vacationing on the Cape, Nantucket or on Martha's Vineyard. So, when his big brother got him this important assignment, he jumped at the opportunity to play in the big leagues.

Tip was an ambitious guy and he looked to parlay the discovery of important evidence there in Arizona, (that would lead to the eventual incarceration of a criminal), with an assignment for the Boston Globe. His stellar reporting would jettison his name in the industry and at the very least open doors and hook him up. He was cocky, no question about it. This was his primary motivation. It would be hard for a man with such high aspirations to view what he was about to uncover with any sense of objectivity. To be clear, he was there to find evidence that would help convict Garrett in the death of Carrie Baker, not to discover his innocence.

On the scenic drive up Route17 he remained in deep thought considering how he would approach the investigation. At first he ran through the small inventory of information he had on the suspect. His name was Garrett or Ian, or Ian Garrett; he had a boatload of cash; he was a confrontational guy; and he had purchased suitcases from Brugman's Luggage and Potpourri in Sedona.

Tip knew that these leads, in and of themselves, were worthless. But there was one good, strong piece of evidence about the stranger, that, thanks to his own brilliance, he had brought with him. It was the picture that Caroline had taken of their foursome at the *Carrie Baker Golf Event*, that Tip had purchased. He brimmed with self-congratulations. This would prove to be of great value.

It took him almost the entire ride to Sedona to figure out his strategy for how to begin the investigation. Since he was a reporter, you'd have thought it would have been his primary idea. He decided that his first tactic would be to visit the local newspaper and inquire there. After all, the village had no more than ten or eleven thousand residents and this guy Garrett seemed to be a wealthy man, so there was an excellent chance he would be known, at least to someone at the paper. He puffed out his chest, once again proud with himself and his awesome deductive powers. Tip wasn't the most modest guy, nor the sharpest tool in the box.

It was at that very instant, elevated some forty-five hundred feet above sea level, that he rounded a bend to witness the most incredible panorama he'd ever seen, *The Red Rock Monuments of Sedona*. He sat up in his car seat and was stunned by the natural beauty. Although, he was a bit uncomfortable because the mountains seemed too close. He would remain in this awestruck state for the next twenty minutes, until he reached the Hyatt Hotel.

Tip checked in, and after he had put his belongings in his room, he went back down to the lobby and asked at the front desk for the name of the local newspaper in Sedona, or if there wasn't one, any in a near-by town. He was told that The Red Rock Daily was a fine community paper.

He spent the remainder of the day sightseeing, to get his bearings, and didn't return to the Hyatt until nightfall. So Tuesday had passed, and our astute, wannabe prize winning reporter, hadn't as much as sniffed a clue.

It wouldn't be until after dinner and drinks at the hotel that reality, and his anxiety, would kick in. He was reminded when he saw the desk calendar that he had less than two days to get answers, Wednesday and part of Thursday..

Tip was up and at 'em at dawn on Wednesday. His body clock was still set on Eastern Standard Time. He put on his sneakers and loose clothes and went outside for a jog. When he returned to the Hyatt around seven, he went straight into the restaurant and ordered a full breakfast. By eight o'clock he was back in his room, showered, shaved and dressed. He packed his bag, and although check out wasn't until eleven, he went down to the front desk to settle up.

There was a young bearded guy behind the desk, clad in the hotel's uniform of white shirt, black tie and burgundy vest. After Tip paid his bill, he asked the man if he would look at a photograph of a distant cousin of his, to see if the young man could identify him. Tip told him they had lost contact with one another for years.

The young man looked at the golf foursome's picture and stroked his beard. He lit up and said, "Yes, I recognize the one on the left, but have no clue who the others are."

Tip sighed as if to say hey stupid, the one on the left is me. But he gathered his manners and told the clerk, "That's me with a golf cap on that you pointed to. I know, I look much different."

The clerk felt embarrassed. "Oh yeah, I see the resemblance now."

Tip pointed to the person on the far right and asked again, "Ever seen this guy around?"

"No" answered the clerk. "But that doesn't mean much, 'cause I just moved here from Yuma three weeks ago."

Tip just shook his head and thought, "Why didn't the asshole say so in the first place?"

He asked one last question, "Can you give me the directions to the "Whatyamacallit? The Red Rock Daily."

The clerk had to look them up on the computer, and was kind enough to print them out. Then he said, "Your reservation was for two nights, we're sorry to see that you've had to depart today."

It was Tip's turn to be embarrassed. He was a bit out of it. "It must be the jet lag, sorry. You're right, I have another night. Can you rebook me in the same room?"

"I'm sure that won't be a problem," the clerk said.

After he put his luggage back in the room, Tip left the hotel and drove up to the *Airport Mesa* to see, what many locals feel, are the best views in Sedona, and to kill some time.

A half hour or so later he followed the clerk's directions and arrived at the Red Rock Daily's office building just before nine o'clock. When he walked up to the front desk there was no one there. Tip cleared his throat, he hoped it would get someone's attention. "Pretty laid back", he thought

He waited a moment before he shouted, "Hello, anyone here?"

He stood waiting for quite awhile before he spotted a middle aged woman who held a cup of coffee in her hand and was walking toward him. She didn't acknowledge his presence until she went around the desk and took her seat on the opposite side. She took a couple of sips from her mug, then changed her demeanor. "May I help you young man?"

Tip identified himself as an ace reporter from the Boston area who was there to follow up on a lead for a local story. He pulled out the golf picture from his attaché and asked her if she recognized the man on the right. She didn't blink an eye, or change the expression on her face, but said in a matter of fact tone, "Yes, I know the jerk."

Her remark got his attention. "What can you tell be about him?"

She didn't look at him as she pushed a button on the elaborate phone system and picked up the receiver. She said to the person on the other end, "Some hot shot Boston guy is here to see you about our *killer boy*."

Tip was confused and the look on his face screamed it out. When the woman hung up the phone she said, "Gracie will be here in two or three minutes. Would you like a cup of coffee or tea?"

"Yes, tea with milk would be great," Tip said.

She added, "Gracie covered the case, she knows a hell of a lot more about the gruesome details then I do."

He was beside himself with excited anticipation. "I've hit the jackpot!" his mind screamed.

It was closer to twenty minutes before the gorgeous red head Gracie Dutton appeared. She looked as confused as Tip, since the receptionist, Greta, had only told her that there was someone here to see her about the murders. She introduced herself and apologized that he had to wait so long. Tip shook her hand and told her that it was fine because it gave him a chance to look over their paper. He told her that as a fellow reporter he knew how time controls you not vice versa.

Gracie relaxed and said, "Sorry but I have a tight deadline for the prelude article on the big *Bikram Yoga Conference* that starts here tomorrow. How can I help you?"

Tip set the picture of the golfers on the top of the reception desk for her to look at. "I heard from the receptionist that you're the one to talk to about Ian Garrett."

Just then the uninterested Greta brought him his tea, she had forgotten to add milk. Tip thanked her and she left them alone.

Gracie scanned the photograph and told him, "His name is Archie (Archimedes) G. Moon. Garrett is his middle name. What is it that you'd like to know?"

Tip went on to tell her that there'd been a few suspicious events on Cape Cod and more than dumb coincidences, they'd happened since Garrett, Archie had arrived. He told her how the Chief and the town dignitaries had called upon him to conduct a thorough investigation. Tip mentioned that Archie had given them a couple of false names and that he'd refused to divulge any information about his past. So it was by Tip's sheer perseverance that he had dug up a clue.

"Look, I do have to go Tip. If you want all the details, read my articles. I'll have Greta set you up at a computer, she'll give you the disks. Good luck!"

But when she saw that Tip was disappointed, she changed her mind and said, "I'll tell you what. Since you've traveled this far I can spare a half hour, tops, to relay all the details. But then I must get back to my work. I know you know about screaming editors."

"Thanks. Your receptionist told me that Garrett was involved in something gory. Could you tell me what happened and when?"

"Archie's wife Marlie was murdered in November, last year. The trial started in July, the twenty fifth and ended late August. It was quick," she said.

"His wife? So how did he do it, and get away with it?" he asked.

"Now Tip, we reporters shouldn't jump to any conclusions. Let me give you the details. Sorry that I have to be quick though, but I'll lay out the big picture for you," she said.

"Last year in November, Archie's wife, Marlie, and her recent lover, Gideon Grann, a local radio celeb, were slaughtered in a remote cabin that they'd rented up on Oak Creek, a few miles from here. Archie had left a trail of evidence that implicated him, and because he acted so remorseless and admitted he was outside the cabin, with a Bowie knife and with the intention of killing the lovers, it seemed a no brainer that he did it. He of course became the sheriff's lone suspect: the crazed revengeful husband. Everyone in town was certain that he murdered them and the fact that Archie put up no resistance to the accusations was further indication of his guilt.

"However, it seemed to me that the reason he didn't show regret was because he was so blown away by the fact that she was gone. In his own sick way, if he couldn't bring Marlie back to life, he wanted to be punished.

"The sheriff and the city attorney moved at light speed to get him behind bars, and for several months thereafter he was put under house arrest, after he had posted a massive bail. An election year was around the bend so they were able to get their airtight case to trial by late July. Archie was in court just eight months after the murders. It was unprecedented for these parts.

"The prosecution made a compelling case for jealous rage by a deranged and jilted husband, while the defense had just one card to play, the eyewitness testimony of a nine-year-old deaf boy, Cory Nigilski. The boy used sign language to describe what he had seen and he was certain that Archie was not the murderer whom he had watched leaving the cabin that stormy afternoon.

"The child testified that just before one in the afternoon, on Sunday, while he was hidden behind the wood pile, he saw a crazed man exit the cabin. The man had a long knife in his hand, with blood smeared on the blade. The guy looked around, then in the boy's direction. Cory ducked out of the man's sight, but not before he himself had gotten a clear look at the killer's face. The man walked straight up to the woodpile, grabbed the red gas can next to it and ran back to the cabin.

"The boy watched the man pour the liquid all around the perimeter of the building until he had emptied the can. He then came back to the wood pile and picked up three logs and went back inside the cabin. The boy wasn't sure if Marlie was alright. He saw no trace of anyone, other than this dude. So he decided to creep up the steps and peek inside, since the man had left the door wide open.

"When the boy looked in he didn't see Marlie, but he watched as the man set the three logs on the active fire in the fireplace. In a few moments, when the flames roared, the man tipped the logs out onto the wooden floor with an iron poker. He added the bedspread and a lot of newspapers to the fire, so that it could gather strength.

"Terrified, Cory tipped toed down the steps and ran towards his home, to enlist his father's help. Just before he went inside his house, he turned to look back and saw the man light several stick matches and throw them on the ground. He watched as the gasoline ignited. The *tongues of fire* licked the sides of the cabin's walls, as if sampling whether or not it was suitable to digest. My embellishment, I'm thinking of writing a book about it.

"The boy further testified that when he and Big Bull, his father, a gentle giant, rushed back toward the cabin, the murderer spotted them in the distance, turned from the inferno and ran in the opposite direction.

"By the time Cory and his daddy had reached the cabin it was engulfed in a violent firestorm. Big Bull frantically looked around for a hose or a bucket of water. There were none. He couldn't get inside the main door because the flames were too dangerous. So he went around to the other side, that wasn't yet in total flames, the kitchen door, and attempted to douse out the flames with his coat. He succeeded somewhat, and when he felt safe enough to try to go inside, he was unable to because the door was bolted. The boy said he could see his father scream in anguish as he rammed his massive body against the door time and again as he tried to break it down. No luck. It was then that Big Bull turned to go back to the front door, but he didn't know what hit him. Because, out of nowhere, the murderer had returned and with great force he clubbed Big Bull on the head with a thick log. The boy saw his father's legs buckle and watched in horror as he fell to the earth with such force that even the rain soaked leaves leapt off the ground. The man pummeled Big Bull over and over with the log, even as he lie still. His blood spurted out from his head as if from a fountain. I know I'm getting carried away a little. It's the amateur novelist in me.

"The murderer then spotted Cory and his evil stare froze the kid in place. He rushed towards Little Bull, but he must have heard the sound of sirens from the fire trucks in the distance (I say must have because the deaf boy of course couldn't hear them) and he turned in panic and ran away. The cabin was now overcome.

"Imagine how horrible it must have been for that poor little boy to see his father killed and to have he and his three sisters now orphaned.

"It was fortunate that the fire volunteers got there fast enough to salvage enough evidence so that the coroner could identify the semi-charred bodies. He determined that the victims were at first bound and gagged, then bludgeoned and knifed and dragged into the kitchen area. Gideon was stabbed at least a dozen times more than Marlie. No murder weapon was found."

Gracie looked at her watch and proceed to talk faster than before.

"Hours later credible witnesses came forward. Two young men testified that they had seen Archie throwing a car battery into a dumpster in Jerome around one thirty in the morning on Sunday. Jerome's a nearby hilltop artist town, it was formerly an historic mining town. An old woman said she spotted him asleep in his car on Sunday morning around ten, near the crime scene. Another guy said Archie's truck had cut him off when Archie had made a wild turn on Rte. 89 near the cabin. But the most incriminating testimony came from a patient of Archie's when he described how he had seen Archie at two thirty a.m. at the local diner. He said that Archie seemed insane, reeked of gasoline, and appeared to have been in a fight. Archie's face and shirt had blood stains on them and he had a blood-soaked napkin wrapped around his right hand, to stop the bleeding. When the man asked Archie if he needed any help, Archie barked at him, "Won't anyone leave me alone. When will I ever have peace from you fools?"

"These strong accounts contradicted the boy's assertion that another man had murdered the lovers later that afternoon. The sheriff and the prosecutors theorized that the couple had been killed around one thirty a.m. Sunday. They argued that Archie panicked and took off on an aimless, drunken journey to Jerome and back to Sedona. He must have thrown away the murder weapon somewhere en route, because it's never been found. He made his way back to the Oak Creek area and fell asleep in his truck. When he woke up around noon or so, he went back to the crime scene and doused the cabin with gasoline, as the little boy had testified, and then burnt down the cabin to cover up his tracks and destroy any evidence. They said Archie must have worn a disguise and that's why Cory couldn't identify him.

"The jury watched in disbelief at Archie's lack of reaction to the vivid descriptions and the accusations hurled his way. He sat still and stared the entire trial. I think that's because he was so numb from the death of his wife and from the fact that he wanted to murder them. Of course, with Marlie's multiple affairs being dragged around in public throughout the trial, it was like an overdose to his system. He appeared one hundred percent guilty. His attorney didn't risk calling him to the stand because he was catatonic and wouldn't have made a strong witness on his own behalf, that's for sure.

"The defense lawyer, prominent Scottsdale attorney Brady Seiss, knew that they didn't have much of a choice, so he admitted that Archie had been at the cabin that night. He put forth that Archie's sole purpose was to scare the hell out of the cheaters, it was to be his closure therapy Seiss said. He claimed that Archie had become frightened when he was spotted by Marlie, panicked and fled through the woods. Seiss tried to explain away the blood stains on his clothes and body, saying that all of Archie's lacerations and bruises were caused by the thorns on the low hanging branches that Archie had run through on his retreat to his truck.

"The majority of the evidence and hearsay brought forth by the defense focused on Marlie's character flaws and her promiscuity. Seiss tried to get the jury to believe that she'd had at least ten affairs since she'd been married to Archie. His strategy was to convince the jurors that anyone of her scorned lovers could have done it. Seiss laid his bet on the table that the deaf boy had seen another man commit the atrocity, not Archie. Seiss acted so confident in fact, that although he talked about her affairs ad nauseam, he never called an ex-lover to the stand. I'm sure more than a few of Marlie's lovers were grateful not to have been exposed.

"All said and done, besides the boy's strong evidence, the circumstances pointed to Archie as the murderer, and the community at large was already biased against him, they wanted justice. Marlie was very popular in town. She walked among them. Archie did not.

They saw Archie as a traitor of sorts. He once had respected them and socialized with them, but for the past couple of years he had distanced himself and they felt this was his way of showing them his utter disdain for their problems. Which I don't believe to be true. He had become an arrogant jerk to many of them; an over privileged, wealthy and unhappy man. Most of the villagers liked Marlie very much. She was a source of entertainment and fun. They viewed her as free spirited and Archie as an uptight workaholic and guarded man. Again, with his remorseless attitude, seated in the courtroom without one show of emotion for the jurors to see, everyone thought that the verdict would be nothing but guilty. They would be more than happy to see him put away forever..

"As I mentioned earlier, the prosecution believed that Archie wore a disguise that day and that Cory imagined him to be someone else. In his summation, the prosecutor asserted that the mute boy had panicked and that since he had just seen his father killed in cold blood, it had further exacerbated his mental handicap and thus his ability to think and see clearly.

"However, the jury didn't agree. They took a mere two hours to deliberate. They felt they had no choice but to believe the poor orphaned mute's rendition. They delivered the stunning unanimous verdict of not guilty!

"When they announced his innocence the audience sighed and groaned. Some hissed and booed. Others shouted out obscenities at Archie and had to be restrained by officers of the court.

"But it was very weird to see that Archie wasn't excited, or at the very least relieved by his acquittal. I think he wanted to die. He'd been so distraught over Marlie's loss and he was humiliated by what the trial had uncovered about her shenanigans. Furthermore, his business, that he had dedicated his entire life to, was in near ruin because of her public disclosures of his patient's confidential information. I think he loved her so much and didn't want to go on any longer, at least not in this small town where everyone mistrusted him.

"I had interviewed all the jurors after the trial and not one of them thought he didn't do it. But they felt that the prosecution had done a woeful job, that it was very lax in its aggression. A few even speculated that the lead prosecutor had had an affair with Marlie, and that he in no way wanted to incriminate himself. I looked into that accusation and found zilch. Bottom line is Cory's testimony was solid and it created reasonable doubt in their minds, so they had to set Archie free.

"As far as I know, me and Lupita, Archie's loyal assistant, are the only people in Sedona who believe he's innocent.

"Full disclosure, Marlie even had an affair with my fiancé and he was mad about her, like all the men in this town were. It could have been a handful of them who did it. But Archie was at the scene, so maybe I'm in denial."

"You said he had patients. What did he do?" Tip asked.

"He's a psychologist," Gracie said.

"A shrink heh. That makes more sense. So he got away with it. He's a crafty son of a bitch" Tip said.

Gracie answered, "The townies and the sheriff were pissed off with the not guilty verdict because they were sure Archie got away with murder. They demonstrated their contempt in vicious ways towards him. Rocks were thrown through his office windows; hate mail came by the buckets full every day; they even defaced his property and picketed outside his office. And the serious death threats he received were the most disturbing of all.

"Of course his business came to a standstill. Sheriff Alvarez wouldn't even consider that someone else had murdered Marlie. The evidence was that concrete. The sheriff was so incensed with the acquittal, that he chose to turn his back on the vandalism. He never once investigated the anonymous death threats."

Gracie put her iPhone on the table and pulled up a recorder app on the screen.

"Listen to this tape. It's a short interview I had with the sheriff."

"Sheriff, what happened when you first confronted Archie?"

"Looked like he'd been in a knife fight, an lost! I says are ya gonna tell me you shave up there by yer eyeballs boy? That's a pretty nasty lookin' face ya've got there son."

"Archie was mute, like the lil' 'tard boy. So I had my associate Sammy read him his rights. Then I says to Arch, "Cat got yur tongue son? Well then let me git right ta the point since ya ain't sayin' much. That's yur right, but I think ya'd be better off talkin' an savin' the county all the money of prosecutin' ya. We know ya was out an about late last night an jus so happen ta be in the Oak Creek area. Ain't that so?"

"I was surprised when Archie says, "yes"

"Round one in the mornin' correct?" I ask.

"I guess", he says.

"Look here Arch, let's not beat around the cactus. Ya was seen at Oak Creek, ya was spotted in Jerome dumpin' their car battery, an we got a call from the diner that ya was there actin' strange and all, hasslein' the patrons, an with blood all over ya, an the smell a gas so thick that they was afraid ta light a match within a hundred yards a ya. An some old lady said she saw ya asleep in yur truck aroun' ten this mornin' on a dirt road off 89. A trucker saw ya parked somewhere in the woods after noon. And if this ain't a wild an crazy coincidence, yur gallavantin' wife Marlie an her lover Grann were found butchered and burned at their love shack up there on the creek about an eighth of a mile away. He was a patient a yurs wasn't he son? So this begs the obvious question, why'd ya kill them boy?"

"Arch says, "I don't think I did. No. I'm sure I didn't.""

"Well, I says, how in God's name could ya be unsure son? Tell me please, this is goin' ta be a good tale sure as shit."

"He says, "I mean, I wanted ta kill my pain. I wanted ta kill her and that jerk. I had the knife, I had the plan, so in that way, in my mind yes I did it. But I couldn't do it. Was there any doubt that I wouldn't ? I don't know what come over me.""

"It was incredible, so I says, "You been listenin' ta all yur weirdo client's trumped up problems fer too long Archie, that's what come over ya. Yur crazy like them. Can't be healthy, no wonder ya snapped, ha. ha.""

"What'd ya do with the knife Arch? I says.

"I don't remember" he says."

"That's when I tol Sammy ta take him ta his bathrum ta get him cleaned up and dressed. But I tol Sammy don't go lettin' him near a razor cause he might jus wanna slit his throat so it matches the rest a his face, ha.ha"...

Gracie turned off the recorder and said, "Sheriff Pedro is quite the character as you just heard. Anyway, the situation became very dangerous for Archie, but he seemed too numb to be aware of that fact. Ten days after the acquittal it was Lupita who convinced him to leave for awhile and hide out with her and her brother at their Cottonwood home, until the anger subsided. He acquiesced.

"While Archie laid low at her home, Lupita went to the office every day to check on stuff. At least that's what Archie believed she did. But what she and her brother Javier hadn't told him, was that they had set in motion their own investigation into Marlie's murder. Javier worked at the Post Office by day and would do his sleuthing at night.

"Despite all their good intentions, it didn't take long for the amateur detectives to hit a roadblock. So Lupita decided to have a conversation with me. As far as Lupita knew, I believed in Archie's innocence and I'd be impartial and cooperative.

"After we had a first meeting I left many files for them to peruse..

"Lupita later told me that Archie started to come around a bit. He was getting to be more of himself. She said he was tired of feeling hapless, he wanted to do his own investigating. So one day, without divulging his intentions, once Javier and his sister were out of the house at eight o'clock, he decided to go back to his office to survey the property. He also wanted to gather a few confidential files from the safe and take them back to Lupita's to comb over them for any client clues. He had learned the painful truths at the trial that Marlie had dated a lot of his patients and he could now face those facts.

"He took Javier's Corolla, that was at his disposal, and drove to his place. I imagine Archie was broken hearted when he saw his once pristine property vandalized. Lupita had attempted to clean the premises but, although now dulled, profane graffiti covered the street side of the building and is quite readable still.

"He later told me that when he went into his main office he thought he heard footsteps in the house. He figured it was Lupita. When he called her name and got no response, Archie thought that maybe the sound of the door creaking was what he had heard. He remained alert and defensive as he started to read over his files. He grabbed a number of folders and left the office.

"But as he passed the reception desk, out of the shadows from behind him someone leapt onto his back and grabbed him around the throat. Archie struggled to loosen the man's hold and elbowed him in the gut. He spun the intruder around in circles as he tried to loosen the man's grip. But before he could succeed, Archie's world went black when another trespasser delivered a tremendous blow to the side of his skull..

"An hour or so later, after she had gone home and seen that Archie wasn't there, Lupita sped over to his office on Last Wagon Trial.

"Lupita rushed into the house and was frightened when she saw Archie lying face down in a pool of his own blood. She was also startled to see the sign that was written in red lipstick on a piece of paper, and was taped to his back, *Archie is a Very Bad Murderer*.

"Lupita revived him and cleaned him up. She wanted to take him to the emergency room, but he insisted that they go back to her place and regroup.

"It took a good hour before Archie gained his balance. When he had, she gathered all the appropriate folders and put them into the attaché and got him into her car and headed back to her Cottonwood home. He was still feeling disoriented from the head trauma she said. Archie did tell her that he had no idea who the two men were.

"This latest episode was too scary for Archie to ignore. He feared more for Lupita's safety, than his own, not certain what his enemies' anger might morph into.

"But Lupita assured him that she'd be fine. However, she begged him that he should escape their wrath and go faraway from Sedona for a short while, get himself together, reboot. She assured him that she could handle the locals and take care of the property for him. They wanted his skin, not hers, she reminded him.

"She wanted so much to clear his name. It'd be much easier for her to snoop around once the word got out that Archie had fled to an unknown destination. With Javier's assistance, and mine, she felt we could unmask the real culprit who murdered Marlie. In a month or two when it had quieted down, Archie could return, and with a little luck, the real murderer would be in jail

"Archie was reluctant at first, but agreed to Lupita's plan. So three days later, after he had removed tons of cash from his home safe, on September 19th, in disguise (he wore an atrocious, cheap blond wig that Lupita bought at a thrift shop for him) Javier drove him out of Sedona down the mountain to Phoenix. Not even Lupita knew where he was off to. Now I know that he went to your area on Cape Cod.

"Archie hoped that this journey would rebuild his damaged psyche and not be a sad farewell trip. At that point the odds were fifty-fifty."

Tip said, "So he did it and got away with it. I don't see why his picture wasn't sent all over the Internet? Someone on the Cape would have recognized him."

Gracie said, "He was innocent. He hadn't escaped the law, just the vigilantes."

When Gracie had finished her account she looked at her watch once again and stood up to leave, she told Tip, "Why don't you ask Greta for Archie's address and if you can stomach a pro Archie point of view you can talk with Lupita. Have Greta give you Marlie's best friend, Boris' address and Sheriff Pedro Alvarez's as well. You'll get the whole picture."

Tip was so wound up from the thrill of the score that he had to take several short breaths to calm himself down. He was taken off guard. He had gotten such weighty information on his first attempt that it scared him a bit. He realized this would be big, real big.

He decided to email the Chief and copied in his brother Sean, who was, who knew where in the Middle East.

"You have a murderer on your hands and a false acquittal. Murderer here that is, his wife. I'll know much more later and will fill you in on the details. Just know that I've hit pay dirt. I'm all over it!"

2

Tip didn't feel the need to interview Lupita because she'd be bias, as if he weren't. But he did take Gracie's advice and at noon he arrived at the Just Sit Down hair salon in hopes of having a talk with Marlie's best friend Boris.

He entered the salon to the sound of very loud classical music that was being played for the elderly female patrons, who were getting their perms, cuts and colors. There was one man in the shop, mid-thirties in age, who Tip watched in amazement as he flitted back and forth between clients. The man ordered, "Maggie you old goat, how many times do I have to tell you to not turn your head?" And he scolded another who had just squirmed when he had rinsed her head with ice cold water, "Don't be such a chicken shit Helen, loosen up."

The hairstylist was always busy with a shop full of silver hairs, his target customer base, and the more rude he treated them, the more they giggled at his act. It was pure grade B theater.

The man hadn't seen him enter, so Tip decided to take one of the seven seats just left of the entry door and wait to get the man's attention. Meanwhile, he scanned several dated hairstyle magazines that were stacked on the table next to him. None catered to males.

In another minute or two Boris spotted Tip and pranced over to him. Before he spoke, he turned back to one of the ladies and shouted, "Sophie you old bitch, I told you to stay under the hood for another three minutes. Do I have to come over there and spank your tush?"

Tip was self-conscious, he fumbled his words as he stood up to introduce himself. But before he could form a sentence Boris said, "You must be from *unrulymop.com*. You here for a cut or a trick?"

Tip was thrown off balance by the sexual remark, he blushed.

"Cat got your tongue tallboy? Relax. What can I do you for?" Boris asked.

"I...I. Can I ask you a few questions about Garret, Archie Moon I mean," Tip stuttered.

Boris seemed miffed, "What could I possibly tell you that hasn't already been dredged up a thousand times?"

He turned and started to walk back towards his clients but Tip implored, "Wait, please. We want to stop Archie from murdering again. We want to put him behind bars where he belongs. We think that he drowned a little girl on Cape Cod. I'm a reporter from the Cape, and Gracie at the Red Rock Daily suggested that I hear your side of the story."

Boris stopped in his tracks as Tip's appeal had gotten his attention. He pointed towards the door with an affected loose left wrist and said, "Go out to the parking lot. I'll come talk with you on my cigarette break."

Tip didn't have to wait very long, as Boris came parading out the door minutes later. He wore a long sleeve, purple satin shirt and a solid grey colored silk scarf that draped with a certain theatrical flare around his neck. He appeared to Tip to be the quintessential *queen*, a real caricature.

Boris gestured, with a yank of his greying head, for Tip to follow him around to the side of the shop, where they would be out of his customers' sight.

Boris stopped and pulled out a pack of American Spirit cigarettes and a book of matches and lit up. He took a pleasurable drag on the stick, held it in for a couple of seconds and exhaled a satisfied puff of smoke through his nostrils. He removed the scarf from around his neck, as if it were a complete nuisance to him, and spoke to Tip in a much deeper voice than the one he had heard in the salon. "This drag queen act is ancient. My prehistoric clients expect the stereotypical fagot hairstylist, so I accommodate their prejudices. I'm too old for this shit! Shoot your questions, you have me until this burns down to the filter," he held up the cigarette in front of him.

Tip fired a number of questions and Boris answered them all with anti-Archie sentiment.

Boris was emphatic, "That low life of a mental case, Archimedes Moon, killed the sweetest girl in the world, Marlie, in a sheer jealous rage. No doubt about it. Everyone knows he stalked her. He plotted for ages, the prick. He was way out of her league. For the life of me I don't know what Marlie saw in him. He was a drag on her energy and dulled her aura. I mean, talk about a bore. And he's such a wimp. Did he think that someone as alive as our dear Marlie would find his reclusiveness attractive? He was her gravity. But there was no way he could hold her down. She knew it and so did he. He knew she planned to leave him. He was such a mess and needed her to give him what little confidence he had.

"She told me that he had often followed her on her nights out. I warned her that she might be in danger, but she just laughed at me. She said he didn't have a violent bone in his body and that there was no cause for worry. But still, I didn't trust what a wounded lover, in a blind rage, might do. Anybody's capable of bad shit. So I was able to convince her that when she went out with another man, she'd meet me first, so that I could be her decoy and lead Archie off the scent. It worked fine for a while, but she got lax and fell back into her old routine. She met her lovers without a *beard*, she didn't care if he was on her tail or not.

"She said one day, "Archie loves me too much. He'd never hurt me, no matter how angry he might get or how much I hurt him. He knows I have needs."

"I should've never allowed her to let her guard down.

"How do I know that he murdered Marlie and that apeman Gideon Grann? The proof is in one's appearance I always say. That's where you find your absolute evidence. It's the natural lie detector. Look at the man. He's always disheveled. Anytime I was around him I wanted to get out my scissors and attack that awful mop of his. He has no vim or vigor for life whatsoever. He's let himself go and he's always very pasty and pale. He needs vitamin D, sunlight. The bastard is in his late thirties but looks older than Christ. He carries the guilt of his inadequacies, and of their murders, all over that pathetic face of his.

"And can you imagine this is the same clown who people went to for advice? The pathetic shrink couldn't help himself, so you tell me how he was supposed to help others?"

"Strange isn't it? The one person who was so full of life and love is gone, while the miserable, self-loathing hermit is very much alive, but dead, inside"

Boris went on with the same angry diatribe for another few minutes and ended with, "I am very surprised that no one has killed that fuck yet. There are so many people in this town who were outraged with the jury's verdict, the sheriff included. Not that he's any Columbo mind you, but Sheriff Pedro did put together an airtight case. That bad actor of a shrink and his Marx brother lawyer, dragged Marlie's reputation through the mud so many times in the trial that they confused the idiots on the jury. You say something enough times most fools will believe it.

"The sheriff, and everyone else in this *cowpoke* town, drove the bastard away. If he hadn't slithered out in the dead of night he wouldn't have survived here another week, I guarantee it. Hell, everybody wants a shot at him, when and if he returns. Maybe you should give me his Cape Cod address and I'll have a few of our cowboys visit him. 'Cause my bet is that the wimp will never have the guts to show his face here ever again. He'll take the easy way out and commit suicide, if I know him. Good riddance. But it still won't bring my beloved Marlie back to life."

Tip jotted down notes as fast as he could, pissed that he had left the cell phone with its tape recorder app in the car. He hadn't noticed that Boris's cigarette was down to the filter. Boris threw the butt down and ground it into the pavement with the sole of his boot.

Back in character, he flung the scarf around his neck once again and messed up his hair to get the right flaming affect for his customers. "Gotta go Jimmy Olsen. Give me a holler the next time you're in town. I'll be your Superman. Ta-ta."

Tip was ecstatic. He believed Boris one hundred percent. Pumped up from the anti-Archie rhetoric, he hoped to share the latest dirt with someone, so he drove over to the Red Rock Daily to ask Gracie out for a *thank you* dinner. But another reporter told him that she had left for the day. So instead, Tip drove back to the Hyatt and had dinner there.

After his meal he went up to his room and poured over his notes for several minutes. When he had finished, he edited the information to his liking.

Later that evening, Tip sent a cryptic, exaggerated, and of course self-congratulatory email to Chief Nickerson, saying that his persistence was paying off big time.

Tip couldn't believe the good fortune that had come his way on his first day in the *High Country*. He was certain that tomorrow's conversation with the sheriff would gift wrap everything into an award-winning package.

3

Tip arose on Thursday and was anxious to get his work done so that he could drive back down to Phoenix to catch his three p.m. flight to Providence. On the plane he could choreograph the dramatic details of the presentation that he'd be making to the *Round Table Group*.

He had checked out from the Hyatt at eight thirty and arrived at the sheriff's office, where he announced himself to the receptionist. He was told that he was fortunate that Sheriff Alvarez was in, and that he should wait in the coffee room until Mr. Alvarez had finished his staff meeting.

When the receptionist fetched Tip fifteen minutes later, he followed her down a narrow, boring hallway which was enclosed by stark white walls. At the very corner she stopped and motioned for him to enter a large office. It had the most spectacular mountain views, what else did he expect to see in precious Sedona?

Tip was excited when he first spotted the authentic cowboy sheriff, Pedro Alvarez. Sheriff Alvarez was dressed all in white, not the typical brown pants and brown shirt uniform associated with your run of the mill sheriffs. He topped off his appearance with an impressive all white ten gallon Stetson hat. His long jet black dyed mane, tied in a tight ponytail, presented a distinct contrast to his crisp, whiteout look. Sheriff Pedro, as his cronies referred to him, had a long scar that ran down his otherwise smooth left cheek. Local lore claimed he'd acquired it in a fierce knife fight with a California motorcycle gang. But his detractors believed that the disfigurement was self-inflicted, a strategic cut to make Sheriff Pedro appear to be the toughest badass in the West.

Tip fantasized how it must have been back in the *Old West*. He pictured the savage Indians as they spied down from their lofty red rock lookouts and plotted their next raid on the poor unsuspecting settlers. He wondered how the sheriff would have defended them from their inevitable scalpings? What an obnoxious jerk Tip could sometimes be.

Sheriff Pedro had his head down, preoccupied with the pile of paperwork in front of him.

"Excuse me," Tip said.

"What can I do for ya son? I've jus got a couple a minutes," Alvarez spoke with a western drawl that Tip recognized as the voice he had heard on Gracie's recorder.

Tip took a moment to study the sheriff's strong cheekbone features that accentuated his rugged weather-beaten complexion. He appeared more Indian than Mexican.

The ace reporter guessed that the sheriff was in his fifties. Try seventy-five *Mr. Observant.*.

He introduced himself as a big city reporter and told Alvarez that Gracie had recommended he speak with the man most familiar with the details of the case.

"Hell, ain't nobody knows more 'bout that travesty a justice than that pretty l'il gal Gracie. She's puttin' ya on boy. She's way too modest.

"Look here son, here's the truth right between yer peepers. There's no question in my experienced mind that Archie Moon, the poisoned insect, is guilty as original sin. Jealous murderer, plain and simple. Case closed. But shit no!

"Da ya think that those fair minded, crystal lovin' hippies in this town, who sat in that sorry jury box, could see the truth? Why those alternative lovin',tree huggin' sissies wouldn't know a fact from a lie, the truth from a *Baby Ruth*. Damn they're so predictable. I know each and every one of um. Put their punk asses in jail when they were bratty teens, takin' liquor an smokin' dope. But ya know, the people worse than those spoiled, over privileged imps, are their damn snooty parents. They'd bail out little junior every time he screwed up. No sir, no discipline then, no discipline now. They're a bunch a phonies, ya ask me. Just like our killer boy Mr. Moon. So it's l'il wonder that that sorry excuse for a jury took jus two hours ta deliberate the verdict. They were no doubt discussin' some alien abduction when they were sequestered, not the merits a the indisputable case me an the prosecutors put together. Believed the deaf boy's version. Shit! The 'tard had jus witnessed his daddy's murder an all. Don't tell me he weren't traumatized. Those liberal assholes believe anythin' a victim tells them."

He looked at Tip for the first time. "What's this here case got ta do with ya son?"

Tip felt that he was in the presence of a legendary lawman and answered, attempting to mimic the Sheriff's speech, "Yer killer struck again in my village on the East Coast. Ya know about Cape Cod?"

The sheriff gave him a blank look. Fact is he had never been further east than New Mexico, where he was born and raised, and no further west than Utah. Like so many, he had strong opinions about other parts of the States and the world for that matter, though he had never seen them firsthand, just through the lenses of cable news.

Tip said, "Massachusetts, East Coast. We know he killed a little girl there, then made it appear to be an accident. This dude's a clever son of a bitch."

"Hey ya stop that cussin' right there young fella. I may talk some smut in my own office, but not you an that foul mouth a yurs."

"Sorry", Tip slouched.

Tip added, "We think he may have rounded up a bunch of terrorists and they're scheming to knock off the bank or the Post Office, whatever. This little six-year-old girl may have come across them, so Archie did away with her is what we think. We haven't figured out all the details but we're close. Chief Nickerson and the town hired me to investigate a lead I uncovered. That's how I came to be here in Arizona, um.. Sedona."

"Ya said may have son. May is a month in Spring not the concrete evidence like we had on him here boy. Now look, what'd ya say yur name was son? Tip is it? Alvarez asked.

"Yes."

"Well what in the hell kind of a half ass name is that? Tip a my dick? I'll bet ya was teased like mad when ya was a kid. No wonder ya couldn't find a real job."

He saw that Tip acted hurt by his statement, so Sheriff Pedro said, "Now don't go gettin' all girly quiet on me. I was jus funnin' with ya."

"Tip is short for Tipper", he wished he hadn't said that, because he could see that the sheriff had all he could do to hold in his laugh, after he had heard the namby-pamby, *Eastern Liberal* name.

Alvarez took a second to remember what he was about to tell Tip before. "Oh yeah! This here Archie Moon is no doubt a strange bird alright, and when ya have a hot dish of a wife runnin' around with every Tom, Dick and Tip in the town, it's bound ta wake up yer evil side. And believe me, there's an evil side in everyone. Archie's no different. Ta be honest, it musta scared the hell out a him ta see that he had the evil in 'em.

Marlie is a Very Bad Girl. "Yup that's the note that Archie wrote in lipstick, that we found in the garbage can at the scene. Ya know jus 'cause I want him ta be brought ta justice an fried in the chair, don't mean I can't sympathize with him bein' a broken down ex-hubby, with the hottest gal this side a the Rockies. Sure as shit was."

He took a phone call and swiveled his chair around so that he could look out the window, his back faced Tip. He said to the receptionist on the other end, "Thanks Kaye. Have Lance get the car an meet me 'round front. Tell 'em I'll be out there in three, four minutes tops."

He turned back around to Tip, and said in a very dramatic deep whisper, "Archie might be a certified nut, like the rest a his patients, but what the man ain't is a team player. This dude's a loner through and through. Fact! He'd never get involved with a group, other than therapy," he laughed at his own pun. "And it ain't in his profile ta harm a little girl, no way son.

"Now pay close attention here Tit, yer talkin' ta the most decorated sheriff in the history a the West, an that's a mighty fine history I can assure ya. That simpleton Sheriff Joe down in Phoenix, the self-proclaimed *toughest lawman,* can kiss my ass. Arpaio's jus another phony, an with an ego as big as his head. No sir, yer here lookin at the real deal in front a ya son. I know what the hell I'm talkin' about. I've seen it all. So listen up Tit an ya might learn a thing or three." Tip moaned to hear his name being bashed again.

"Come on, follow me out the door, I got ta get checkin' on an illegal."

He stood up and Tip watched in awe as he hoisted his gun belt and adjusted it tighter to his hips and hustled out the door. It was quite the study in opposites, as the lanky Tip couldn't keep up with the quick paced, stocky built sheriff. Man was he ever in fine shape for a seventy five years old.

Sheriff Pedro said over his shoulder, "Ya'd better tell yer folks back home to watch out fer him. Ya jus never know when he'll strike again; an mark my words, they always do. Once they get that taste a power; a taste he never knowed, it's habit forming. He's already killed three, as far as we know that's all, and I'm lookin' real hard inta a recent death of one a his patients, a youngin' that had a go with Marlie back one time. Witnesses saw the Doc's truck parked a few blocks away from the barn on more than one occasion. That's where the boy an Marlie musta rolled aroun' in the hay.

"I'll tell you what son, Marlie was one fine lookin' woman, an very sophisticated too. Wouldn't a minded havin' a thrill ride with her myself, if I weren't so happily married ta my wife Ida that is," he said as he winked.

They were outside and Alvarez turned to Tip just before he got into the passenger side of the vehicle, "I'll get my man 'for you folks do. Always get my man. Never once missed. You'll see. Now enjoy some a the beauty a the *High Country* boy an do me the kind favor a passin' along any valuable information yuse folks come across there in the East, in yer Cape place there. I'd appreciate it. And keep yer tip ta yourself Tit," he burst out laughing.

Tip was so charged up that the enthusiasm spilled out of his pores. Before he drove down the mountain to Phoenix, he decided to stop by one more time at the Red Rock Daily, to see Gracie and to thank her for all her great advice. She was up against a deadline so they didn't talk for very long. They both agreed to stay in touch and to share any new details if and when they surfaced. Tip told her, "I'm a hundred percent certain that Archie got away with murder here, but he won't get away with it back home."

Gracie disagreed with him. She led him to a computer station and he composed another teaser email to the Chief and the others.

He said aloud to himself, "Can you say *Pulitzer Prize*?"

4

Tip Garland arrived at the Eatery first thing Friday morning to fill the others in on the details of his investigation. Although he felt the ill effects of the jet lag (it was five a.m. out West) the adrenaline that flashed through his veins more than compensated for any discomfort. This was his moment on the big stage and he was determined to make the most of it.

For effect, the willowy reporter stood up and addressed the group in as serious and as professional a tone as he could muster. He overacted like Nicholas Cage, it was woeful. For over a half an hour Tip relayed the most minute details of his sleuthing and concluded, with insincere modesty, that he had done a commendable job.

But what he failed to share with his audience were any of the facts that were pro Archie. He skimmed over the little deaf boy's testimony that Archie was not the person he had seen on that fateful day, because the boy wasn't credible, in Tip's mind. Nor did he think it material to tell them that Archie escaped to the Cape because of the harassments and the death threats he'd received. The way Tip left it, they were all led to believe that Archie fled Sedona because he was guilty and the townies were on to him.

Tip ended his presentation when he stated with overconfidence, "Sheriff Pedro and I are a hundred percent certain that Archie got away with murder in Sedona and that he's very capable of it again, if we don't stop him right now."

Maxwell was aroused to a frenzy, and the others agreed that they must take action before it was too late. They all looked to Chief Nickerson for guidance.

"You said that a jury acquitted him though," the Chief said.

Tip argued, "But Chief, Sheriff Pedro said it was rigged. He's like a living legend with an impeccable record and he said Archie did it and will do it again. The prosecutor was afraid that the defense would uncover his affair with Archie's wife, so he played softball, wasn't aggressive."

"I don't know about the Sedona murders and quite frankly I don't give two shits. But I can tell you that because he knows that Carrie had her bicycle with her, it seals the deal for me here. That's all that matters. Let's say he's even innocent of his wife's murder, which I doubt, that he tried to do it but botched it. I think he got the taste of blood in his mouth and wanted to satiate his appetite. So he came here and carried out his fantasy on poor little Carrie," Chief Nickerson said.

"That's exactly what Sheriff Pedro deuced Chief,"said Tip in an admiring tone.

"Scotty, the Doc and I will go over to the Hibiscus Inn and interrogate him. We'll set a trap for the bastard that he won't be able to wiggle out of this time. I'll get a confession out of him, if we have to beat him to a pulp to get it," the Chief said.

He corrected himself, "Of course that was a figure of speech. Police brutality is not in our DNA as you well know." He winked at Maxwell.

Maxwell, acted offended, and asked, "Why aren't I invited to come along for the inquisition? I'm the one who raised suspicion to his behavior in the first place. If it wasn't for me we'd all have been his victims by now."

Chief Nickerson scolded, "No Bob! Not this time. In all due respect, the man bristles at the very sight of you. This is for pros. Doc will be there to check on his health and to bear witness to our respectful manner, and Scotty and I will be there to weave our web. We don't need you to get him off track so that he can spew his venom your way. I want him to weigh every word we say and not be distracted one bit. I want to see the twit squirm and beg for mercy."

That was that..

When Martha escorted Chief Nickerson, her brother and Sgt. Scott into Archie's room, they were surprised by his warm greeting. He had a wry smile on his face when he addressed them all. "I've been expecting you gentlemen. It's nice that you've arrived. Please have a seat." They were taken off guard for the moment.

Martha went over to the large windows and threw open the drapes. The strong Fall sunlight streamed into the stuffy room and transformed it from a drab, darkened sick bay, into the pleasant, airy room she had intended it to be. She cracked open the window just a wee bit, hoping to add necessary fresh air to the stale mix.

Archie was seated in one of the high back chairs, so Doctor Nickerson chose to sit on a similar chair to his left and the Chief took the desk chair and brought it around opposite Garrett, just three feet away from him. Scotty stood to the Chief's right and leaned up against the papered wall.

Martha excused herself and told the men that in ten minutes or so, Sonia would have refreshments for them.

When she had shut the door behind her the room took on a thick air of silence. It seemed uncomfortable for Scotty, who Archie noticed couldn't stand still, his right leg pumped up and down like a nervous teenager. The Chief was bent over in his chair with his head down and eyes fixed on the floor. He rubbed his enormous calloused hands together and appeared ready to speak.

But Doc Nickerson broke the quiet, "How are you feeling? Let me check you." He reached over and felt Archie's forehead.

"Your spirits are much better than when we last met Garrett. But I'm still concerned with your fever and your paleness. I can see you're having a hard time breathing as well. Have you been taking all of your medication?"

Archie ignored him. Uncomfortable silence ensued once more.

Then Scotty stepped forward and read him his rights. When he had finished, the Chief spoke, "Garrett you said that you expected us. How's that?"

"I have an uncanny sense for the absurd, and what could be more bizarre than to have my enemies pay me a visit," Archie said with sly grin on his face.

The Chief didn't flinch at the odd statement, he played it cool and sat back in his chair, crossed his legs and placed his intertwined hands atop his knee. "Your instincts must be very sharp, for although I wouldn't consider myself your enemy, I can agree with your assessment that we're here to pay you a visit, but far from a cordial one I am sorry to say," the Chief responded.

"Oh please don't apologize, it is what it is. I'm flattered that you've chosen to bring two others with you for support. Three vs one. If you consider the players, I would suggest that all is equal. You at least are aware of your own shortcomings Chief and understand the challenges your enemy presents."

"Well I see that you haven't lost your inflated sense of self. You're quite the strutting egotist Garrett. I thought by now that with all the trouble you've caused, that at least an iota of humbleness might have crept into your psyche. But it is what it is," the Chief mocked.

The game was on.

Archie was ever so cocky and didn't filter a word from his brain to his mouth. "Einstein, I think we can all agree, was a wise man. It was he who noted, "Two things are infinite, the universe and human stupidity, and I'm not sure about the universe."

He added, "Stupidity is not discriminatory. It can be found in the damnedest places. For example, it has built itself a permanent home with those who promote fear. Your Mr. Maxwell is its leader. And it seems to flourish with those in authority who believe that they hold power over the very people they have been sworn to serve and protect."

Chief upbraided him. "Enough of your insults Garrett. Your clever quotations and sarcastic observations can masque the truth for just so long. You're practiced in the art of deception, but the time has come for you to reveal yourself. You didn't think that you could come into our peaceful village, cause insult and damage to our fine citizens, and have the arrogance to think that we'd stand by and let you mock us did you? That would be my definition of stupidity. Stupid to believe that we wouldn't use every ounce of energy to discover just what you are up to, and who you really are.

"History is written by the victors." "Churchill had it right don't you think, **Archie**" the Chief emphasized his real name.

The shock when he had heard his name wobbled Archie and didn't go unnoticed by the others in the room. He didn't anticipate they'd know anything about him. He had prepared himself for the confrontation over Carrie's death and had rehearsed how he would deflect any suspicion off of Amelia and onto himself, but this he had not foreseen. He panicked inside his head and wondered what else they knew. His palms began to sweat. He didn't want to relive the nightmare. The thought that he'd be vilified by his foes once again was too much for him.

He faked calmness and said, "Well, well, the *Keystone Cops* got their man. I can see how clever and proud you are. Are you ready to put me behind bars for withholding my first name from you? And the outrageous fact that I haven't told you what my favorite color is must be treasonous."

He extended his hands in front of himself and said to Scotty, "Slap the cuffs on me Pinkerton, I confess."

He hated that he had spoken and had acknowledged what the Chief had said. He knew he sounded even more guilty and defensive. Archie was trapped and he knew it. "Let them speak and see what they know," he told himself. "My paranoia is overblown. Shut up and don't give them anymore reasons to think that they're getting close."

Scotty stepped a few feet forward toward Archie and puffed out his chest. "We already know what you favorite color is smart ass, blood red. You want us to dredge up all of the details of your infamy, *Mr. Sedona*, and make us stupid cops remind you of all the gory details of your wife's slaughter?"

Archie's heart skipped a beat. He now had the answer to his question. He was dumbfounded, his silence betrayed him. He didn't respond to Scotty.

The Chief swooped in, "Choking on the truth Archimedes? Do we need to tell you all that we know about how lucky you were to be acquitted of murder? How, just like Houdini, you managed to escape justice? Please spare us." he mocked.

The Chief took a sip of water, and said, "I don't give a damn to know how and why you bludgeoned your poor wife and her lover and burnt them almost beyond recognition. What I want is for you to come clean on what you did to Carrie Baker. Did that first taste of blood in Sedona leave you craving for more Dracula? Did Carrie happen upon you at the pond and blow your cover? Or since you couldn't control your big girl back home, maybe if you dominated a defenseless little girl it would make you feel more like a man again? Is that it? Confess you pompous ass, your goose is cooked!"

A thousand hellish memories of Marlie crossed through his head as he tried to figure out what to do next. He did realize that they hadn't implicated Amelia in the girl's death, so was there still any need for him to take the blame upon himself?

"But wouldn't they then figure out the obvious and turn their attentions to her if they found I wasn't responsible for Carrie's death?" he asked himself.

He was surprised, as were they, to hear himself speak. "The poor girl drowned, so how's that murder?"

Scotty pounced on him. "How did you know she had ridden her bicycle? You told Annie Temple Carrie's parents were negligent because they let her go off on her own."

Archie seemed perplexed, he answered, "I must have read it in the newspaper."

Scotty said, "Sorry liar. We withheld that piece of information from the public on purpose. The only people who knew Carrie rode her bicycle to the pond were the Bakers, the Chief and me, Carrie, and of course you, her killer. So stop playing mind games with us stupid authority figures and confess that you killed her Archie. You'll feel relieved to get it off your weary mind. Be a man and own up to it. Show that ex-bitch of a wife of yours that you grew some balls after all. The Doc here says you're near death anyway, so why not, for the sake of the grief stricken Baker family, put closure to their nightmare, and make your peace with God."

"I'm confused. Someone must have told me, or I overheard it somewhere. The bicycle I mean." His face went pale and he began to sweat bullets.

The Chief stood up, his large frame blocked the sunlight and cast an ominous darkness over Archie. "Carrie drove her bicycle to the pond. You saw her, and with no one else around you approached her. She struggled to get away from you and you grabbed hold of the handlebars and wrestled it away from her. Did you try to teach her a lesson? You finally found a female you could control, was that it Archie? Did you hit her because she screamed? Or maybe you covered her mouth with your hand, to keep her quiet, and by mistake you suffocated her? Relive it man. Tell us how you did it. Did you think that when you threw Carrie and her bicycle into the pond that it would wash away your despicable sin? Confess Archie, do the right thing!" the Chief said.

Archie became odd all of a sudden. His eyes stared at the ceiling light fixture and he said to no one in particular, "Perceptions sometime reflect the truth, but the truth is always the truth. That's all that matters. When the truth is known to all there's no need for perceptions, they serve no purpose. There's no need for debate. Truth is truth. No person should be excluded from knowing the truth. But when truth is unknown, or worse is manipulated and hidden from us, that's when our perceptions take over and when conflicts arise.

"Perceptions fill the *truth void*, they are judgmental interpretations from our own individual experiences, and although they may run parallel with the truth, they can collide with it just as often.

"Does God exist? Is the earth round? Is global warming a hoax or a threat? When does life begin? There are no shortage of opinions and perceptions on these mind boggling topics. But instead of people with divergent viewpoints marshaling their resources and forming alliances to get to the truth, for the benefit of the entire world population, self-perceived *truthers*, who believe that they and their inner circle alone are the custodians of what is true, build tall fences. They separate not collaborate. They create enemies in order to validate their own beliefs. They've melded their misperceptions into their exclusive versions of untruths.

"Even more twisted are those people who manipulate us into perceiving them as someone they're not. They hide the truth and sadly, hide from the truth."

He looked at the Chief. "Ever since I've arrived here you've perceived me to be a murderer. I know my actions have brought a lot of that on me. I take responsibility for my poor choices. But you've gathered coincidental information, arranged it in a certain narrative that suits your logic, and have thirsted for it all to be true. You've convinced yourselves that I killed a precious little girl. How sick of you! It's taken hold of all of you and has blinded you into thinking that you've uncovered the truth."

Scotty shouted, "Shut the fuck up Archie! You're a certifiable madman."

"That's your perception," Archie countered.

"But it's the **truth**, isn't it Archie?" the Chief chimed in.

At that very moment Nick Temple, who had been phoned by Martha of all people, burst into the room, and his disruption caused the them all to stop.

Nick was angry. He could see that Archie was distraught, and he said, "Doc, Archie looks terrible. Does this interrogation have to happen right now? Shouldn't he be resting for heaven's sake?"

They wondered how Nick knew Archie's real name.

Doc Nickerson said to his colleagues, "Nick's right. The man's out of his head. He needs quiet. You can resume this tomorrow, he's not going anywhere."

The Chief was livid. They'd gone in for the kill and he felt that they were seconds away from a confession. But he sobered up from the euphoria and decided that he'd have to wait for the final act. The man had all but confessed.

After they left the room, Doc escorted Archie over to the bed and helped him get situated. He went over to his medical bag and removed his stethoscope and a vial of pills. He was a little put off with the Chief's and Scotty's hard line of questioning, and in particular he didn't care for Scotty's lie, that Archie was about to die. But after he had listened into the stethoscope and took Archie's vital signs, he thought that perhaps Scotty's exaggerated diagnosis wasn't too far off.

5

Whether it was due to the harassment he went through and the discovery that they knew about him, or the fact that he had relapsed, or a combination of both, Archie fell into a delirious state. Martha referred to him as being in *a coma*.

At the Eatery on Saturday, the Chief and the *Round Tablers* now felt more than ever that Archie had murdered Carrie Baker. After the Chief's careful re-enactment of the interrogation of his lone suspect, it gave them all the final piece of the puzzle. However, Doctor Nickerson warned them that there was a good chance that Archie could succumb to his illness before justice could be served.

"That would be the ultimate righteousness," Maxwell said.

But Maxwell worried that without a confession there would always be those who doubted Archie's guilt. He was adamant that a confession was mandatory and it couldn't wait. It must be recorded before Archie passed. So, gung-ho from the absolute proof presented, and without telling the others of his intentions, after their meeting broke up, Maxwell headed straight to the Hibiscus Inn, to have a final visit with the conquered infidel. He fantasized that he could get Archie to admit to Carrie's murder.

When Bob Maxwell arrived at the Inn, Martha was off premises, which he deemed to be a great sign. She wouldn't have permitted him to see the sick man.

Maxwell was greeted by Liza, and through a combination of animated hand gestures and his broken, condescending English-Russian accent, he managed to communicate his intentions to visit Garrett, Archie.

She said, "No. no. No visits. He nots to be seen. He sicks."

Maxwell gave her a flirtatious smile and ignored her plea. He hurried over to the rack and grabbed the Honeysuckle's room key. Against her protest he proceeded to Archie's room. Once he entered, he made sure he latched the bolt behind him so that they wouldn't be disturbed.

When his eyes had adjusted to the dark environment Bob was annoyed to see that Archie was in a deep sleep, he snored away in the gloomy and depressing room.

Maxwell, feeling ever so bold and righteous, went over to the large windows and threw open the drapes and shades. The shock of the uninvited brightness and the loud noise made by his exaggerated actions, had their desired effect, Archie awoke.

Bob boomed, "Well, well, Raskolnikov awakens. You didn't think you could escape into your own denial did you Rodion? Your self-inflicted pain is far more retribution than any judge or jury could ever dole out."

Archie didn't acknowledge his Dostoevsky references, and Maxwell was chagrined that Archie didn't seem to even be aware of his presence.

Maxwell stood over the bed and watched Archie as he gasped for breath. He could see the drips of sweat that glistened on Archie's forehead and the ring of perspiration that drenched through his light gray tee shirt. Archie coughed several times, but Maxwell showed no compassion, he didn't even give him a glass of water, or prop him up with pillows. To Maxwell the crimes were committed and this was their just punishment.

Archie hallucinated aloud, "Bicycles, heroes."

Maxwell almost wet his pants, excited when he heard, what he considered to be, the start of Archie's admission.

He got out his cell phone and turned on the tape recorder app. "Snap out of it man. Talk with me. I am the *Truth*. You can confide in me," Maxwell demanded.

But Archie sank back into a deep sleep and once again his thunderous snores underscored his distance from reality.

Bob became impatient and shook Archie several times, but it didn't wake him. Disappointed, Maxwell rose to leave the room, but stopped for a brief second and turned back to look at the tragic figure on the bed. He shuddered when the voice in his head commanded him to do away with Archie, put him out of his misery. Who would know? Use a pillow to smother the murderer and be done with this evil chapter in the village's history. Maxwell could later tell the Chief that Archie confessed everything to him just before he passed on.

But before he took action, if any, when Martha banged on the door and shouted, "Open up the damned door Robert!", he snapped out of his fantasy. Maxwell unlatched the door and Martha flew into the room. She scowled at him as she blew right past him.

She put her hand to Archie's forehead and was frightened by the heat that radiated from his body. She snapped over her shoulder to Sonia, who had entered the room behind her, "Please get me a cold towel and a change of clothes and call Doctor Nickerson to come at once!"

Maxwell slunk out of the room unnoticed.

6

It was nothing short of a miracle, that only three days later, after several attentive visits from Doc Nickerson, at six a.m., Archie woke from his stupor. It was Liza's caring touch with a warm hand cloth she had placed on his forehead that had broken the spell.

He was groggy and a bit queasy, as to be expected, but was aware of her presence and the state of his health. Liza read the thermometer she had placed under his tongue and his temperature was near normal, his fever gone. Her prayers had been answered.

He mumbled a question that she couldn't comprehend, so with a little more effort he said, "You are so kind to me, thanks. Could you please tell me what day it is?"

"Its bees Tuesday eight days of October today," Liza said, proud that she knew the answer. "You've been sleeps for tree days Rip van Krinkle," she laughed.

"Wow! No wonder I feel so light headed," Archie said.

"Did Caroline Cassidy get married?" he asked.

She wasn't quite sure what his question was.

Archie thought, "I've been such an asshole. As if I could ever have Caroline, what the hell had come over me. I made such a jerk out of myself and caused her a lot of embarrassment."

Then he remembered that he'd been interrogated on Friday and he became a bit confused. "Do they really know? Shit, I need to figure out how to worm out of this mess."

Just then Sonia came into the room. "Well, you looks much better. That's good. You need to eats food for strength. We makes bowl of cereal and bacon for you no?" Sonia added.

"Yes, thank you, thank you so much. I do feel weak. But my dreams have renewed my spirits. I need to change and clean up, will you leave Liza here to help me?"

"Yes of course," she answered, and turned and rattled off a quick directive to Liza.

Liza was attentive and helped him into the shower, so that he could scrub and rinse off the remnants of his fever induced sleep.

After he had showered, shaved, and cleaned off his several days' growth, he dressed. The clothing hung off of him as if he had taken them from a much larger man's wardrobe.

When he exited the bathroom he was greeted by her welcome face. Liza blushed and told him how handsome he looked. She pointed to the cereal and a plate with a few slices of bacon that sat on the table, and motioned for him to have a seat and partake. She left the room.

Archie tugged up his trousers and rolled over the belt at his waistline to keep his pants from slipping down to his knees. He felt something in his pocket and reached in and pulled out the object. He wondered how his driver's license had gotten there. Since they knew his real identity he didn't need to hide it, so he put it back into his pocket without a second thought.

He shuffled over to the small portable dining table, pulled up a chair, and devoured the cereal, but he left the bacon untouched.. he didn't like to mix starch and protein. After eating, he got up from the table and walked over to the wingback chair, sat himself down and grabbed a *Yankee* magazine from the rack. The reading tired his eyes.

At some point he nodded off and had a reoccurring dream. It was in fact an almost exact reenactment of the honeymoon trip he and Marlie had taken to Aghia Galini, an old-world Greek fishing village set into the mountainside on the island of Crete.

It was past midnight and Archie was sitting in the lone restaurant on the upper level of the village. He was reading an English newspaper when he heard an explosion. He bolted from the cafe out into the dark stone street. He thought the pipes had burst. Then he heard two Canadian girls, (the only other tourists in this remote village), scream, "Earthquake!"

He panicked and ran in the dark, down the wide stone steps to the lower level of the village toward the place where they had rented a room. The donkeys brayed, the dogs barked, and the loud protests from the other frightened animals seemed surreal in his head, as they ricocheted off of the ancient stone buildings. He turned left into a pitch-black alley and almost had a stroke when out of the shadows an hysterical old woman, all clad in black, reached out, grabbed his arm, put her toothless and wrinkled face up to his and screamed in anguish, in Greek, a language that he didn't speak. Archie's instinct was to lift his arm and strike her, until he recognized that she meant him no harm. He told her everything would be ok, shook loose from her tight grip and ran until he reached their rental. He bounded up the steep outside steps to their room, threw open the door, and there was Marlie sitting on the bed, reading a Willa Cather novel.

"Was that an earthquake?" she asked rather nonchalantly. Always cool under pressure she was.

Archie knew that the aftershocks were coming. They always did. There was no way you could prep for the quake that had come before, because it was all over by the time it registered in your mind. It was past. But the aftershocks were what mattered. He grabbed Marlie by the arm. They found an archway, cowered, didn't move a muscle. They'd wait for the aftershocks. It was scary. He hated waiting. His mind pictured disaster. The tremors never disappointed. He held his breath, held her hand and hoped that the magnitude wouldn't worsen the damage that had already been inflicted by the rupture. That's what he feared, would it get worse?

The dream's anxiety woke him up in a drenching sweat, but a few minutes later he dozed off again. This time his dreams were plentiful and more positive.

Pastor Adams had come by at Martha's request. She had made it sound so urgent that he expected Archie would be ready for his *Last Rights*. But the Pastor saw that he was resting and on the mend. The reverend stayed long enough to leave a small prayer book on the end table and placed an encouraging prayer card inside.

A few more hours had passed, and around nine thirty Annie and Nick Temple were in the area and decided to pop in on him. Her gentle tap at his door was met with, "Come in please. It's open."

Annie and Nick hadn't spoken to Archie since last week. and now, when they entered his room, they found him sitting in the chair, lamp on and magazine in his hands. They were very pleased to see him in a semi-normal state, although he was super thin and his skin so pale, that he appeared to Annie to be the paradigm of an under-nourished prisoner of war.

He lit up when he recognized his favorite visitors and urged them to take a seat.

Annie came over to him and kissed his forehead. Nick shook his hand and said, "Nice to see you have made an amazing rebound from your fever Archie."

Archie told them that he knew his pneumonia was a blessing that he had to endure in order to be whole again. He was quite sure that it was finished, although his cough still lingered a bit.

He said, "This is the longest stint in my life that I've been speechless. I must say, I'm up for a decent conversation with people whom I respect. Do you have a little time?"

"Yes. Do you remember what you told us last week?"

"I...no..well yes was that you whom I was talking with? In that case I don't want to bore you any further then. How embarrassing."

"You didn't bore us at all. Let me jog your memory. You told us about your childhood and your teen years and of your terrific practice that turned stale for you. You left off where you were in a poor state of mind and had followed Marlie and her lover to the cabin," Nick reminded him.

"It was a fine conversation," Annie added.

It took a minute before Archie decided to speak. He reached for his napkin and wiped invisible crumbs from his lips and said, "How could you two stand it? If I told you that much of my life you must have been bored rigid. We didn't talk, I did. Sorry. It may be impossible for you to believe, but less than a year ago I was considered a listener extraordinaire. And now I've become a victim, a whiner, a tortured soul. Funny, I realized that I never truly understood how my patient's anxieties and fears made them feel hopeless when they tried to comprehend themselves, until I had became one of them."

Again he wiped at his face with the napkin and spoke. "Well, if you don't mind. There's not that much more to tell you then. Let me finish the last chapter in my comic-tragedy, that I believe will end well. I can't thank you enough for your support. I have no one else on the Cape besides Amelia."

Archie told them that he had stalked Marlie and her lover with the intentions of scaring them, but when he had seen her betrayal firsthand, murdering them seemed a better option. He had become so worked up and into the heinous act, that even though he had chickened out, when he had heard that someone else had murdered them, he felt culpable nonetheless.

"Later that afternoon Sheriff Alvarez came to my home and said that Marlie and Gideon Grann had been found murdered along Oak Creek. I didn't even flinch at the announcement. I already knew, because I had done it in my mind. I was just as guilty as if I had committed the crime. I created the atmosphere and opened the door to the possibility. How sick is that Annie, Nick?

"I also viewed myself as a total failure. My psyche had sunk to its all-time low.

"It turned out that just about everyone else in town believed that I had killed Marlie, and as I just said, I felt that I had in some weird way. The community came after me with a vengeance. Just like your Maxwell and the others plan to do soon.

"This was supposed to have been my therapy, acting out their murders. But it felt so real that I could taste it, and my anger was so intense that I knew that wishing it and wanting to do it were just as real as having committed the crime. I still feel guilty today because it's hard for me to differentiate the act from the non-act."

Nick asked point blank. "You said you chickened out, are you sure Archie?"

"Fire wouldn't be my MO. I'm sure, but as I said, at the time I wanted to kill them and I was so drunk, like never before, that I don't remember anything that happened after I had bolted from the cabin," Archie said.

"Is that when you fled to the Cape ?" Annie asked.

"Oh no. Matter of fact, ten months or so later I was put on trial and the evidence was stacked against me. How could it not be? There were several witnesses who saw me there or near there and with blood on my hands. But somehow the jury saw through my craziness. They acquitted me. They believed little Cory Nigilski's eyewitness testimony (a little deaf boy) who said he had seen someone else kill Marlie and Grann. Although, most people in Sedona were outraged and thought that the verdict was a travesty. They wanted to punish me in their own way. I kept getting death threats and was assaulted in my office. That's why I take pain pills still, I'm a bit off balance with *positional vertigo* and my head hurts. Sheriff Pedro was pissed that I got off, so he harassed me a bit too. But thanks to Lupita, my wonderful friend and assistant, I managed to escape the madness and came here to rebuild my brittle psyche, while she and others work, as we speak, to find Marlie's real killer," Archie said.

Annie asked, "Why here?"

"Cape Cod holds a lot of memories as I've said before, good and bad, and it was as faraway from Sedona as I could get," Archie said.

"Who did it then, any idea? Lupita? You said she told you that you had to get rid of Marlie for good," Nick said.

"Lupita, no way...Lupita? I have no clue who killed them," he answered.

"I viewed myself as a failure. I wanted to die with Marlie gone, and that was my intention all along," Archie reiterated.

For the next several minutes he brought them up to the present. As best as he could recollect, he talked of his long journey to the Cape, but he didn't tell them if he had killed Carrie Baker, or for that matter if he knew who had.

"I'm sure you've heard that the Chief knows all about my Sedona life and he, and just about everyone else here, thinks that I got away with murdering my wife there and that I had something to do with Carrie's death as well. What a fucking mess I'm in...again!"

Nick leaned over and whispered something to his mother. She agreed with what he had said and encouraged him to tell Archie.

"We've heard a little of that. And the Chief knows that you arrived in Providence on the nineteenth. Carrie drowned on the next day the twentieth, and you checked into the Hibiscus at midnight on the twenty first, muddy and disheveled. It doesn't look good for you Archie, you'll have to admit. Can you fill in the gap?"

"I don't know? I considered ending my life, of that I'm pretty certain. I can remember walking through some woods near the bus station, and near the *Highfield Theater*, I think that's what the sign said. And much later standing on the beach and watching the waves smash on the shore. Then the next things I remember were seeing the full moon and a bright neon vacancy sign outside this Inn. I was so tired, I'm sure I had walked for days. I rang the doorbell and asked Martha to rent me a room. Not very convincing I know, but I was in a terrible way. My head was pounding and my heart ached."

All that Archie had told them in these two sessions did seem plausible. But Nick couldn't help to turn the narrative around in his mind, he tried to figure out what all this might lead to. "This unusual man had been accused of his wife's murder and is suspected of Carrie's as well. What are the odds that both accusations are false?" Nick thought.

Archie seemed spent and didn't speak for a while, so the Temples took this as their cue and stood up to leave. They assured him that they wouldn't share any of the confidential information that he had relayed.

Annie kissed him on the forehead and wished him a new lease on life.

Then Nick patted Archie on the shoulder and said, "I'm so glad you've decided to live again Archie. You were close to suicide I could see and what a tragedy that would've been. Not just for the obvious reasons, but because you've been so genuine and dedicated to others most of your life. You've so much more to give. I very much appreciate all that you've done for Amelia too. Take care. I'll come by again tomorrow."

Alone in his room, Archie became fatigued from an awful coughing fit that lasted over a minute. When it had subsided he went over to the bed and fell flat on his back. He began to snore.

Then all of a sudden he sat up erect and said to the empty room, "I'm so sorry Marlie's gone."

7

Liza brought Archie a couple of cucumber sandwiches and a pitcher of unsweetened iced tea for lunch. He was famished, and they were trying to fatten him up. He feasted on both and felt an instant and positive effect.

Archie stood up on his seldom used legs and wobbled around the room for a few seconds. His circulation worked fine, so he went over to his attaché and struggled to lift it onto the bed. He snapped open the buckle, removed the *Last Will and Testament* papers and other files and scattered them across the bedspread.

Archie tried to reread the documents because he wanted to make a few minor changes, but he couldn't concentrate. No problem, because he knew them by heart. He'd make the changes another time. But he needed to show someone else where these documents were hidden, just in case he was hit by a bus, or if that nutcase Bob Maxwell and his sycophants chose to harm him first. So Archie reached for the wooden handle on the brass call bell on the bedside table and gave it a vigorous shake.

Seconds later a panicked Liza rushed into the room. She had assumed that Archie was in trouble. She was relieved to see otherwise.

Archie smiled at her and used hand motions to beckon her attention to what he was about to show her. He pointed to the pile of paperwork and picked them up off of the bed. Then he knelt down on the Persian carpet and with great precision, in a demonstrative mode, he placed the papers and files into the secret section of his suitcase that lie there on the floor. He was precise in snapping the bottomless panel over the papers. He looked at her and nodded his head, "Understand Liza?"

Then, to be sure that she knew their whereabouts, he unsnapped the panel, removed the paperwork from its secret hideout, looked to her for acknowledgement and once again he lowered the papers back into their sanctuary and snapped the panel over them one last time. She caught a glimpse of the wads of money that were cached in the hidden compartment and she turned her head away, embarrassed that she wasn't supposed to see them. He closed the suitcase altogether, lifted it up from the floor and grabbed her by the hand. Archie marched both she and the case over to the closet where he slid it on the floor.

Liza had a bewildered look on her face so Archie said, "Liza, don't tell anyone. Yes? Don't tell Sonia. Don't tell Martha. Do not tell anyone. OK?"

Liza said, "Yes yes. I knows what you speaks. Big secrets. Not to tells peoples."

"Great! Thank you so much." He gave her a big hug and she giggled and blushed. She exited his room.

Three minutes later Liza returned and handed him a fax. He asked her to read it to him, but she told him she didn't know English.

As soon as Liza had left the room Archie squinted real hard and was able to make out the message. He could see that it was addressed to him at the Hibiscus Inn and that it was from Lupita. The news was incredible! His head became light, as light as his body.

The facsimile read: "Wonderful news. Got the real murderer's confession. Call for the details. The coast is clear. Love, Lupita."

He teared up with gratefulness that he had Lupita in his life. "I knew that I couldn't have done it. Who did then? Who killed Marlie?" Archie wondered.

Seconds later that curiosity evaporated from his mind and was replaced with complete euphoria when he realized that the news from Sedona meant that he was exonerated. He felt like he was hallucinating. He experienced an instant metamorphosis. He could feel his negative skin molting and see the new, old Archie re-emerge. Not the loathsome victim, but the man he knew he could always be. He sensed that another person had occupied his mind for so long, and that, like his fever, it had vanished. He had a brand new vision and he watched his troubles disappear in the distance.

What a great day! He was excited to get started with life again, thankful for the second chance. He was comfortable with his innocence at long last and ready to see others for who they were, rather than whom they pretended to be. Archie wanted to apologize to each and everyone he may have offended and to pledge his services for free if they'd let him. He scribbled a note of apology right then and there.

Archie now had a purpose and he wouldn't blow it, ever again. He had one major task left to accomplish before he journeyed back home to Sedona. Although he wondered how he would make the Chief and the others see that they had it all wrong about him, without getting Amelia into trouble of course.

Archie had lost over twenty pounds these past several days, but he knew that his real weight loss came when he had shed all the burdens from his mind, thanks in large part to kind Lupita, Annie and Nick.

8

Four days after he had addressed the *Round Table Group*, Tip was back in his small apartment office collating all the details of Archie's past. He was excited to begin writing his complex masterpiece. He was certain that the Boston Globe would beg him to let them publish it.

"You couldn't make this shit up!" he exclaimed. "Talk about me being in the right place at the right time."

Even though Archie hadn't been accused, yet, in the death of little Carrie, the ace reporter knew that it was just a matter of days before Archie would be behind bars. Tip figured that once a guilty verdict was rendered the media from all around the world would flock to him as the authoritative source. At the very least he'd be asked to do t.v. news spots and perhaps even be offered a book deal. Who knew, maybe a screenplay might be in his future. Like his card playing style, he was *all in* that Archie Moon's treachery would be Tip Garland's ticket to fame.

So here, on Tuesday night, seated at his desk, the pressure was on for him to get the synopsis of the article into the Globe's editors by Thursday morning. His main concern was how he wished to open the story. He couldn't decide whether to hit the readers over the head with the gruesome details of the murders, both West and East, or to do a sort of *pull on their heart strings* piece that would gradually build Carrie's sad story from her little girl innocence to her deadly encounter.

But Tip couldn't seem to get the outline on track. He was blocked. He decided that maybe a distraction was needed, to loosen up and relax his anxiety. He got up from the desk chair and went over to his dining table and poured a large glass of Sauvignon Blanc. He guzzled it down.

He turned on his iPod and plugged in his ear piece, figuring that this would help him concentrate. He lit a joint and took a couple of big drags and extinguished it in the ashtray on his desk. He was ready to create.

However, when he sat back down in front of his computer he was still fidgety and insecure. He procrastinated, he didn't want to deal with it just yet. So instead of writing, he decided to look at his emails, which he realized he hadn't checked for a couple of days. He was certain he'd gotten a few congratulatory messages for his superb investigative work.

In fact, he did get a "Way to Go! email from Stuart Holmes and a lengthy email from Bob Maxwell, who encouraged him to hold nothing back in his story. Maxwell also asked Tip to be sure to give him his props, since he was the first person to warn everyone about Archie's malicious intentions.

Tip was about to delete the rest of his emails, when his eyes glimpsed a message from Gracie Dutton. It was dated from earlier that morning, 11 o'clock. EST. In the subject header it read, "Told you so."

He felt warm and a smoke cloud of confusion filled his head. He opened up the email and it read, "Hello Tip, hope you are well. Big news. Call me for the juicy details."

They played phone tag a few times and around 9 p.m. Gracie got through to him. After their cordial hellos, Tip listened to Gracie's remarkable news.

Gracie said, "I thought you should know that today a woman came forward and told the sheriff that she had withheld a lengthy suicide recording that her twenty-eight-year-old son had made (before he had hung himself) in which he confessed to the murders of Marlie and Gideon and the unlucky neighbor, Big Bull. He'd been one of Marlie's lovers. Shocker I know. Ha!

"Lupita was the person who'd tracked down the lead. She had gone through all of Archie's files and visited almost every one of his patients. When she met with Mrs. Dexter and appealed to her for any information, it opened up the flood gates. Mrs. Dexter related more than Lupita could've ever imagined: her son Andy's taped confession.

"Sheriff Pedro sent me the recording this afternoon, it gave me chills. Andy had been dating Marlie for several months it turns out.

"Just this moment I sent you an email with the recording of his confession attached. I'll stay on the line while you listen to it, it's short."

In a complete shock Tip opened up the file on his laptop and heard Andy Dexter's voice.

"I was drivin' down 89 at the crack a dawn Sunday mornin' when I was shocked ta see this crazy guy sittin' in the middle a the goddamn road, like some sort a *Yogi Master*. I almost ran the jerk over. He gave me this bullshit story about how someone had stolen the battery from his car an that he needed a lift ta town ta buy another one. It turned out he was that radio jerk, Gideon Grann. I knew somethin' was wrong, that he was lyin' about somethin', but I told him ta hop in anyway. He said he'd left his wife all alone back at the cabin they were rentin'. I knew the one he described Daddy, you an I did some work there.

"When we got ta the Wes Sedona parkin' lot I saw Marlie's Boxter, an I wondered why she was there. So I hung around ta see what gives. Then a couple a minutes later I was blown away ta see Gideon hop inta it and start it up. I figured Marlie must be in some sort a trouble. I didn't say nothin' ta Grann, but as soon as he was out of sight I drove back ta Oak Creek ta see if I could save her.

"When I got there an looked in the window an saw that she was fine, I didn't know what ta do or think. Was she cheatin' on me with that tiny runt? Not possible.

"Anyway, I went back ta my truck but couldn't make sense of it. Then it started rainin' crazy and I decided ta sit it out.

"I wasn't thinkin' too good. I 'd been up all night an I got real mad. I musta fallen asleep for quite a while and I woke up just in time ta see Gideon drive up the path in Marlie's car. That's when I just plain went nuts. She told me I was the *one*.

"I went up ta the cabin an saw them talkin' together. I waited a while outside in the drenchin' rain, jus walkin' back an forth like some crazy animal, tryin' ta figure out what I should do. But when I found this big knife sittin' on top of a stack a wood, as if it were waitin' there jus fer me, I got my answer..

"I can't remember everythin', but I do recall lookin' in the window an seein' them makin' love, seeing Mar's body intertwined with his. I just went berserk. We were talkin' marriage for Christ's sake. So I snuck in the open door an grabbed a poker from the fireplace an went inta the bedroom an jus started swingin' the poker an the knife. It was wicked man. I could hear Marlie screamin' an I was afraid that I'd hurt her by mistake. My rage got the best a me I guess. I jus kept on stabbin' him an hittin' him. I was so scared.

"Then it all went eerie quiet. I knew I did somthin' wrong. If I had my gun with me that second I'da shot myself then and there. It was an outa body experience.

"I ran back ta my truck and hide the knife under my seat, tell Sheriff P. that's where he can find it. I started ta panic somethin' fierce. I didn't want ta be goin' ta jail fur life. So somethin' made me go back ta the cabin ta make sure they were dead.

"When I got there it was weird, I didn't recognize Marlie she was so bloody. I ran outside an found some gasoline in a can an poured it all aroun the cabin. I lit a couple a stick matches an set the damn building on fire, figurin' I'd burn the evidence.

"But this big ass dude an his little kid came by ta try ta put out the fire. I smacked the guy over the head ta try ta stop him, but I guess I killed him too, though I didn't know it at the time. Found out when I read about it in the *Daily News*, that he'd died. But the kid gotta away I'm happy ta say. But he saw me square, I knew I'd never get away with it.

"I am so very sorry that I hurt them an that Doc Moon is the suspect, but I wanted ta protect you both, so I said nothin'. An I knew I couldn't face you Momma, or Daddy, ever again after what I did. So please forgive me if you ever could an pray that I'll be a better person wherever I'm goin'. I love ya, an never knew I had this in me. Poor dear Marlie, I did love her Momma. An I never meant ta hurt you guys. I don't deserve ta be livin'. I was a good lovin' son. Please try hard, if you can, ta remember me that way. God bless. Love ya both, Andy."

Tip picked up his phone and said nothing.

"Are you still there Tip?" Tip didn't answer her.

"Dexter's mother was afraid of the repercussions and stigma that her family would face if the confession had been made public. That's why she withheld it for so long. I imagine she's in a heap of trouble with the Sheriff," Gracie said.

Gracie continued, "But when the boy's mother saw the anger and hatred the town's people had for Archie, she feared it might lead to his senseless death as well. Her husband was so distraught over his son's death that she hadn't told him about the recording, nor that their son had committed suicide. However, Mrs. Dexter knew that she had to come forward and tell the truth, before it was too late. But she procrastinated and couldn't find the courage. So it was dumb luck that Lupita's visit and her passionate appeal for Archie's wellness, were the catalysts that pushed her to fess up. The loss of her son and the humiliation were enough to bear. She didn't want anyone else's death on her conscience.

"So you see, Lupita, me and the jury got it right. Archie didn't do it, and never could have.

"Hello? Tip?"

Tip answered in a quiet voice, "Yes. But it doesn't mean that he didn't kill Carrie."

"Not a chance," she said.

"I can tell you're blown away. Well, you're not alone I can assure you. I've got to go. Let me know if you need any more details. I'd be glad to send you my article on it. Goes to press tomorrow," Gracie told him.

"Oh! Is Archie still in your village?" she asked.

"I'm not sure," Tip fibbed.

"Well please hunt him down and ask him to give Lupita a call? She'd love to be the person to tell him the great news. Bye."

Tip went numb. Tears filled his eyes as he wondered what would happen now to his career hopes and *Pulitzer* dreams?

9

Archie looked out the window and saw that it was pitch dark. It was seven forty five. His body didn't seem to be up to what his mind wanted him to do, so he went into the bathroom and from his Dopp kit took out a pain pill. He hesitated for a moment, as he wondered if he really needed to pop one. But he wanted the energy boost, even though it was bound to unbalance him a bit. He put it in his mouth, turned on the faucet, cupped the water in his hands, raised them to his lips and swallowed the pill. He figured it should have a quick effect upon him, since there was not much competition inside his bloodstream.

He went into to the bedroom and picked up the fax from Lupita and reread it, happy to see that it was real, not something he'd imagined.

Archie slipped on a navy blue sweater over his white shirt and his cashmere sports jacket over them. He went to the door, opened it a wee bit and peeked his head out to scan the immediate area. He noticed a light coming from underneath the kitchen door and heard Martha's voice. If she saw him she would demand that he get back into bed. But what he had to do couldn't wait. He wanted to share his wonderful rebirth with Amelia.

Archie made a dash for the exit and was startled when he reached the front door to see it swung open for him. When he recognized that it was the Inn's guest, Ms. Adams, he relaxed his guard and thanked her for her courteous gesture. She gave him a dirty look and scolded, "Shouldn't you be going in, not out, in your condition?"

"Just getting some fresh air," he said.

At the same time, Martha had come out from the kitchen when she had heard the front door's buzzer tripped. But when she saw that it was Gardyne Adams, she waved hello and retreated to the kitchen.

A cold wind waited for him outside the Inn and a disoriented Archie had trouble buttoning his jacket as he descended the steps. He headed in the direction of the Village Green.

When he had reached the Green he wheezed and gasped for breath, the short walk had drained his energy. He wobbled. He needed to sit down, so he shuffled over to a nearby bench.

He intended to visit with Amelia and tell her the good news, that he was healthy once again, that he was free from his past and that she wasn't a suspect in Carrie's death. He debated whether or not to tell her that he was now the lone suspect in the Chief's investigation, but he came to a quick conclusion not to. It would just be ego gratification to show her how brave and clever he was to deflect any suspicion off of her and onto himself.

The village was like a ghost town and no one had passed by the bench for the five minutes that he had been sitting there. He had no sense of time and seemed to be deep in thought.

In another moment though, on the opposite side of the Green, a car approached. The taxi driver, always on the prowl for customers, spotted Archie. Kassim drove around the Green and pulled his cab up to the curb opposite where Archie sat.

Kassim rolled down his window and shouted, "My good friend Mr. Garrett, why on earth are you in the park at this hour? It's too cold. Come hop into my warm cab and I will take you to your destination."

Archie was weak. "Hello there. If it isn't the cabdriver slash guru."

Kassim entreated him once again, "Mr. Garrett. Come into my warm car. Or shall I come fetch you?"

But when Archie stood up and Kassim saw how unstable he was, he put his cab in park, opened the door and rushed to his side. He grabbed Archie by the arm and gave his honest assessment. "You do not look well Mr. Garrett. You appear feeble and so thin. You are almost weightless in my arms. You need food and warmth. Shall I take you back to the Hibiscus Inn I presume?"

"No, no. I've just come from there. Please, take me to see Amelia at her house on Palmers Pond, it's very important that I see her."

"I shall drive you there, but first you need to eat. You are not well my friend," Kassim said.

Somewhat reluctant, Archie got into the cab and sat in the front seat. Archie spoke, "I have been under the weather for a spell, but I am happy to say I feel much better. Allah has more for me to do I guess. Please just drive me straight to the pond."

"I'm sorry to disobey your request Mr.Garrett, but if you are to have a future you must care for yourself in the present. Let me get you some food to eat," Kassim said.

Archie quoted Einstein, "I never think of the future, it comes soon enough." He then said, "Wasn't it you who told me that Allah will decide my future for me?"

Kassim was excited. "Yes! Allah will decide your future and that is precisely why he sent me to help you. It is no coincidence that I was compelled to drive in this direction. We have come together again. It is His plan. You have more to accomplish on this earth I guess. So I will take you to McDonalds."

"Thank you Kassim for caring. Does Allah recommend fast food too?" Archie said.

"No. It is I Mr. Garret who has chosen McDonalds, because it's the only restaurant open after eight o'clock", Kassim laughed.

Kassim pulled over to the drive-up window, ordered a hamburger and fries for both of them and a cup of coffee for Archie. When he received their food, Kassim parked the cab in the bright lot. He left his engine running and his heater still on high. They ate in silence. Archie didn't touch the fries.

Archie was the first to speak. "By the way Kassim, my real name is Archie not Garrett."

Archie reached into his front pocket and pulled out a one-hundred-dollar bill and handed it to Kassim. "This is for all your troubles and good deeds."

"No sir Mr. Archie. It is my honor to buy you dinner."

Archie wouldn't hear of it, and insisted that Kassim take the money. Without too much resistance, the strapped for cash cabbie obeyed.

Archie had to admit that the additional meal and the cup of coffee seemed to be just what he needed..

Around eight thirty, Kassim pulled the cab to a stop at the end of Palmers Pond Lane. He asked Archie once again if he would rather have a ride back to the Inn, but Archie refused the offer.

Archie said, "You're a kind man Kassim. I appreciate your help and guidance very much."

They bid each other goodbye. Kassim didn't tell Archie that he had no intention of leaving him unattended for the rest of the night. He decided to park at the top of Palmers Pond Lane, out of Archie's sight, just on Main Street. He would wait for Archie and give him a ride back to the Hibiscus. Unless of course, fate sent him another cab fare.

Archie was excited. The pain pill rushed high energy through his veins. He felt strong.

He stood in front of Amelia's cottage and looked up to her windows. The lights were on and her station wagon was parked in front. He yelled up to her to come down and join him for a dance in the moonlight, but his invitation was either not heard or was not accepted. He assumed the former, so he reached down on the ground and grabbed a handful of small crushed stones from her driveway. When he stood up he felt that the world had teetered off its axis. He stumbled and tried to gain his balance.

The dizziness subsided in a few seconds and Archie cupped the stones in his hands. He wound up like a baseball pitcher and hurled the small aggregates toward her windows.

Some of the stones found their mark and the sound of them beating upon the glass got her attention. Amelia switched on the outside floodlight and came to the window. She pulled back the curtains, covered her brow with her right hand and squinted to see if she could recognize who was there. A moment later she opened her front door and stepped outside, shotgun in hands.

"Don't shoot kind Ms. It's me. Come join me in the moonlight."

"Gaait? I thought yah was sick?" She leaned the gun up against the stair rail and bounded down the steps to meet him.

Archie sang Van Morrison's song, "It's a marvelous night for a Moondance".

Then he told her once she neared, "I'm cured. I feel spectacular. Come here Amelia."

When she had reached him she became concerned with his condition. He didn't look well. She had overheard in the village that the doctor had diagnosed that he was near death and that Pastor Adams had been summoned to give him his *Last Rights*. She was bewildered and wondered how he had managed to be there?

Archie rushed up to her and grabbed her in his arms. She giggled, but wouldn't let herself go along with his enthusiasm. He took no notice of her reluctance.

He'd forgotten that he wasn't going to tell her that he was the Chief's prime suspect and the words effused from his lips. "Amelia I have fantastic news for you. They know squat. Don't worry Amelia they think I've committed the heinous act, not you. I know it was an accident. You're too pure to have known what would happen."

Amelia was confused, she seemed far more concerned for his physical health and his mental well-being than to break the code of what he had just spoken.

Archie said, "They've closed in on me though. I may have distracted them too well. In all honesty, I wanted them to suspect me. How
weird is that? I didn't care for my fate. I had hoped that they'd take me
out of my misery. I felt sorry for myself and I've been pissed off at the
injustices I'd been dealt, and that I had created. Hell, I even had a Boston attorney draw up a *Will*, just in case I decided to end my misery (as
if I had the balls) or if the conspiracy assholes in this village did me in.
Oh! by the way, I named you as one of the main beneficiaries.

"However, I awoke today with a whole new purpose and outlook
on life. Major, major burdens have been lifted from my mind and
shoulders. I want to be an asset to society once again. I want to help
others and myself as well, and I want to help you too Amelia. Get you
back the dignity they've taken from you and show them that Carrie's
death was a mistake. I need to get them off of my back, but not at your
expense.

"You look concerned. Don't worry, I'll pull it off Amelia. I'd never
implicate you. By the way, my name is Archie, not Garrett.

Amelia seemed at a loss. "What the hell ah ya' talkin' about?
Archie?"

"Carrie Baker's drowning. We'll make them see that it was an honest mistake, which it was. I wish you had come forward when it had
happened though, since it was an accident, everyone would have understood and the Bakers' would have had closure. Yes you threw the bike
in the water, but that's not a crime. Carrie jumped in after it. No one
could have guessed that she would have done that. Ah well. Let's figure
out a plan to tell the Chief. You'll be free and so will I. Nothing for you
to worry about," Archie said.

"I know I have nothin' tah wahwee about, you do," she said.

Archie hadn't listened to her answer, his mind already heard what it
wanted to. "I know you would never harm an ant and that you never
meant for little Carrie to drown," he said.

Amelia had seen no need to act. She wasn't as slow witted as she
had led on. She knew that the police never suspected her, she had seen
to that. But when she just heard Archie disclose that he knew he was
the main suspect and wanted to prove he was innocent, she decided to
tell him what in fact had happened that day. So that she could get the
guilt off of her chest.

Amelia made Archie sit down on the bench and listen to her. She
relayed much more detail about the incident. She explained how, after
she had warned the child several times to stop ruining her lawn, that
Carrie became even more defiant. The little brat called her names and
spit in her direction. That's when Amelia rushed up to her and grabbed
her bicycle's handlebars and struggled with the little witch to take it
away from her. Carrie was knocked down in the mud during the scuffle,
and that made her even nastier. Amelia boiled over with anger at all the

insults and ripped the bike from the girl's grip and held it up over her head so that Carrie couldn't repossess it.

Amelia said she had planned to take the bike into her house and wait for Carrie's parents to come and retrieve it, so that she could ask them to pay for the repairs to her lawn. Instead, because the little girl had gotten under her skin so, Amelia carried the bike over to the pond and threatened to throw it in if Carrie didn't stop her tantrum. She demanded a sincere apology from the girl.

But she said that Carrie acted wild and crazy and kicked Amelia with a hurtful strike to her shin. The pain angered her so, that without a second thought, she spun the bike around her head and heaved the two-wheeler into the pond.

Amelia told Archie that she turned away from the hysterical little monster and walked back toward her cottage. But Carrie got even more belligerent and threw a heavy stick at Amelia. It struck her on the back of the head, it was painful. When she turned around to face her, the girl yelled, "You're a stupid person. Retarded whore is what Daddy calls you. Give me back my bicycle, give me back my bicycle you dirty stealer!"

Amelia said that she was so upset that she ran up to Carrie, grabbed her by the collar of her jacket and brought her to the pond's edge. "Yah little shit! Want yah bike so bad, why don't yah go in aftah it?"

"I didn't know what got in ta me? I wasn't thinkin' good." She told him that it felt like some other person was inside her mind. "I shoved Caaeee ova the edge and watched huh fall intah the pond."

She said Carrie splashed for her life, and because Amelia couldn't swim she could only spectate.

For just a brief second Archie, with all his experience, sensed that she was hiding something from him. It didn't sound sincere to his ears. Maybe it was the unusual fact that she had strung so many sensible sentences together that surprised him. She wasn't as helpless nor challenged as she always acted.

Then, like a clap of thunder, Archie burst out loud with mad and ecstatic laughter. He appeared deranged to Amelia at that very moment. His eyes seemed to roll back into his head as he continued to laugh out of control.

He blurted, "Ha ha! You are wiser than us all. I'm the accused and you're the innocent. I know I brought this upon myself. But they never have suspected you and you knew they never would. Why couldn't I have seen that and saved myself all this aggravation? They tortured me over Marlie's death and once again I'll be accused of murder here. What are the odds of that I wonder? A trillion to one? But I am innocent dammit and justice will win out, right? I've got to do something fast."

The irony was so palpable, he loved irony. He had set himself up for her defense, to protect the poor challenged woman who had a hand in Carrie's accidental death and couldn't fend for herself. But clever Amelia had already deflected suspicion from herself and was thankful that Archie had come along and had chosen to be the convenient target. She was much more clever than he, or anyone else, had realized.

Then the reality hit him. That Amelia had murdered Carrie. It wasn't an accident. Wow!

However, in denial, Archie felt that Amelia didn't fully grasp what she'd done and, therefore, he still felt sorry for her. He'd concoct a plan that would protect her, grounds of insanity or poor mental capacity. He'd figure it out.

But for now, right in this space and time, he wished to focus on the positives. Why worry, it wouldn't help any? He could deal with his troubles tomorrow. He was elated with his new attitude and wanted to celebrate his renewal. That's why he'd come here tonight. His mind was so clear, or so he thought. The past nightmares had no more significance in his life. He would live from this moment forward. Archie was back. He'd not felt this good about himself and others since that marvelous first encounter with Marlie, so long ago.

He said aloud to the darkness, "How've I gotten into such a funk for so long? Why've I been so weak and unsure? That person I was is now dead, past. The world has meaning to me again. I'll go back to my practice and help others. I'll ask dear Lupita to join me. My dependable Lupita who has loved me with all my warts. She deserves much better than me, but maybe I can be worthy of her love someday."

Wrapped up in his own euphoria, Archie hadn't noticed that Amelia didn't share in his excitement. She wondered who the hell this Lupita was.

He danced and sang the words to *Moondance* once again and rushed up to Amelia and grabbed her by the waist and twirled her around and around. She was wary of his playful madness. He had a disturbed look on his face and stared to the heavens and laughed nonstop. She was scared.

But all of a sudden his over exertions had renewed an awful coughing fit. She sensed danger and feared what might happen. She begged him to stop and sit down on the nearby bench, but he flipped off her cautions. He wiped his mouth with his coat sleeve and continued to spin them both as he sang at the top of his voice.

Disoriented from the spinning, the odd couple had inched perilously close to the land's edge. Amelia recognized the jeopardy and warned Archie to be careful. She told him this was the very spot where Carrie had gone in. She pleaded, "Please honey. I told yah I can't swim!"

"And I'm too weak to swim either, we're even," he laughed.

She took a second to calculate what he had just said, "You can't eethah?"

But Archie threw all caution to the wind, and with his back to the pond, he spun her around and then yanked her close to his side and planted a kiss upon her cheek. She let out a scream as he uncurled her from his side, and in his best rendition of a tango dancer, he pushed her away from himself. He intended to curl her back into his arms once again, but with the sheer force of his abrupt pushing action she let go her grip. Without resistance from her, Archie's opposite momentum caused him to stumble backwards toward the edge. She rushed up to him as she saw him losing his balance, but not to assist him. His right foot slipped on the muddy earth. Archie reached his right arm out to her. "Amelia!"

She didn't grab or pull the weak man out of harm's way. Instead she clutched his hand just firm enough to keep him from falling into the pond. She looked him in the eyes and stunned him when she said with a normal accent, "I can't take the chance that you'll keep quiet Garrett, Archie. You're too loose a cannon. You've made too many mistakes honey. I can't trust you.

"I know you wish the best for me, but if I let you clear your name, it would mean the end for me. You've made so many enemies here, that everyone in the village believes you're guilty. Soon you'll be charged with Carrie's murder. I can't thank you enough for that sweetie. And now that you just told me you'd made out your *Will*, you've given me the perfect opportunity. I'll say that you were so remorseful for Carrie's murder and felt so unworthy, that you wanted to give all of your possessions away before you took your life. That's why you put all the prizes you won at the *Bazaar* in my name as well. You had planned it all along.

"It was so crazy what happened with me and Carrie, that's not who I am. But there's no way that I'm going to admit to the little brat's murder. No way. I'm so sorry Archie that it has to end this way. I hope you see that I have no other choice darling. You've been so good to me and treated me with such respect that I wish there was a better option.

"But don't worry honey, I'll tell everyone that you were at peace. I'll say that you told me you felt absolved and that you said suicide was the one act that could set you free from your demons."

With that she let go of his hand, and while he teetered, she extended both of her arms and lunged at his chest to give Archie a final push to his death. But miraculously for him, he had somehow gotten a solid foothold on a sliver of earth and managed to dodge her thrust. Horrified, Amelia's attack met with no opposition. She grasped the air for resistance as her forward motion carried her past an astonished Archie and over the precipice. She screamed, "Garrett save me!"

Amelia's body careened off of a large boulder and fell into the cold abyss below, into the very spot where little Carrie Baker had drown.

Archie looked over the cliff and watched in disbelief as Amelia flailed trying to keep her head above water. Overmatched, she lost the struggle. The gravitational pull of Palmers Pond's black hole swallowed her up. The sight of Amelia's long white hair the last remnant of her being to depart to the afterlife.

Moments later, with the stillness of the Fall evening broken by their screams, Kassim rushed to the scene. It was too late, and too dangerous for him to dive in to try and save Amelia. So instead, he ran over to Archie to console him.

"I came here to celebrate my rebirth Kassim, but instead I witnessed tragedy. Why is death so attracted to me?" Archie asked.

After a long silence, Archie wondered what would become of him. He startled Kassim when he shouted, "What improbable odds! I'll be accused once again for a crime I didn't commit. Ha ha ha! It wasn't even a crime."

Kassim was frightened to see this madman in front of him. Archie's psycho eyes seemed to shoot fire balls from their sockets.

"I'm screwed! Amelia tried to murder me tonight and failed. But her death will deal me the same fate as if she had succeeded," Archie howled to the night sky.

"She was the only person who could have cleared me of the child's death. But she's gone and drowned in the same place where Carrie did, and in my presence. How sick is that Kassim? Who'll ever believe that I didn't kill them both?"

Kassim comforted him, "Please Mr. Archie do not beat yourself up my friend. You are but a human. Do not let your ego trick you into believing that you have God's powers to comprehend. Allah called for Amelia's atonement tonight."

Archie laughed, "And for my demise. Ha,ha,ha!"

Over his crazed laughter, Archie failed to hear Kassim say in a soft voice, "I witnessed Amelia's treachery. Be still. You are in safe hands. Give praise to Allah. He had me watch over you tonight."